Schooner

■ ■ ■

A Novel

Jerry S. Drake

LCCN: 2013911810

ISBN-13: 978-0-9856970-1-3

Printed in the United States of America

Other Books by Jerry S. Drake

Western Novels:
Aftermath
*Treasure Mountain

The Tom Patterson Western Series:
Breaking Trail
The Gunfighter's Apprentice
Sierra Skullduggery

Action-Adventure Novel:
Southbound

*Anticipated publication - 2013

Praise for Jerry S. Drake's Western Novels:

Breaking Trail
"The book is stylishly written and – like Thomas Harris' *Hannibal Rising* – fills in the background of a character whose past has always been something of a mystery. Fans of the Patterson novels will want to seek this one out"

–Booklist Reviews

The Gunfighter's Apprentice
". . . the author, in his first western, pulls it off with panache. Although thematically gentle, the book is written in the tough, gritty, violent style of the classic pulp western. Fans of the genre will have a good time."

–Booklist Reviews

Sierra Skullduggery
"A gripping plot, knuckle-biting adventure, and sharp delineation between good and evil distinguish this sequel to *The Gunfighter's Apprentice*. The plot adds up, and Drake puts Tom and Betty Patterson in fine form."

–Publishers Weekly Review

"Reading Drake's novel is like curling up in front of an old wood-burning pot-bellied stove on a cold winter day and having at it."

–Roundup Magazine

Aftermath

"A straightforward, lively Western written with a sure hand and a good eye for character. Drake is a newcomer to the genre, but he writes like an accomplished veteran."

–Booklist Reviews

Dedicated, as always, to Virginia

Prologue

Below the surface of the Caribbean, the sea floor slopes to the edge of the Honduran continental shelf. Where sunlight brightens the shallows, where the blue-green water is clear and illuminated, coral formations reach up, and sea grasses amidst the reefs undulate in the ocean currents. In the eerie, wondrous marine netherworld, a silver screen of small fish darts with astonishing speed, while other larger and more menacing species of oceanic life laze and drift with subsurface streams. As the seascape angles down to the lip of the shelf, the coral formations and plants are sparse on the barren sand, and the deepening gloom deprives life-giving light. Suddenly, there is a scattering of aquatic creatures, disappearing as the sound of a powerful diesel engine invades the silence of the undersea. A large ship enters the waters above, and the long hull below the surface moves swiftly. The engine slowed its muttering, the propeller idling, and the ship glides slowly out over the abyss.

An object splashes into the water; the body of a middle-aged man, securely with bound hands and feet, and with a heavily-weighted duffel bag attached to his ankles. He is still alive, struggling against his bonds, writhing against his fate as he descends, drawn by the weight into the darkness of the ocean depths.

A second body, a middle-aged woman, is dropped into the sea. Similarly trussed and weighted, her eyes are open and terrified as she screams unheard behind the tape that covers her mouth. In a moment, she is gone, gliding down into eternity.

Above, the engine revs and the propeller churns the water. The ship moves away and gathers speed. As the sounds diminish and fade away, the silence of the undersea returns. Myriad ocean species begin to reappear. Schools of fish gather and swiftly vanish at the sudden appearance of a flashing barracuda in search of prey and, another predator, a small hammerhead shark invades, relentlessly cruising.

In a different world, at a different time, a telephone begins to ring.

1

To those seated near the empty cubicle, the fluctuating trill of the incoming call was becoming an annoyance.

"That's Hathaway's phone. Where is he?" someone grumbled.

On the tenth floor of an aged Kansas City office building, telephone solicitors in a huge boiler room operation place calls, talk to prospects, hang up, and immediately dial again to harass new gullible marks. Credit card debt consolidation is the substance of their enterprise and, in this large room, many pleasant-voiced representatives are "*standing by*" to take orders. They sit upon low-cost task chairs in multiple stalls, separated by chest-high partitions; each station identically equipped with a gray metal desk, a console, a computer with a monitor, and a headset.

An attractive yet cross-looking girl in the adjacent workspace, annoyed by the persistent trilling sound, ripped off her headset, tossed it aside, and stepped around the divider. She snatched up the headphones and touched a button. "Hathaway's phone. He's not . . . oh, wait a minute. Here he comes." Then, she shouted, "Call for you, Glenn! Where the hell have you been?"

A slender young man, carrying papers and reading the topmost, looked up in surprise at the irritation in his surly co-worker's voice. He hurried to his desk and took the head set.

"This is Glenn Hathaway," he said, watching the girl return to her work with a flouncing ferocity.

"Glenn?" The telephone voice sought further affirmation.

Glenn's face became pained, and he lowered his voice. "You aren't supposed to call me at work, Mom Daly. You know that."

"Glenn, you got some mail today," the woman's voice ignored his reprimand. "You got a letter. I thought about it for a long time, and then I decided it was important enough for me to call, and so I did."

"A letter?" Glenn grumbled. "Couldn't that have waited until I got home?"

"But, it's not just a letter! It's an *important* letter!"

Out of the corner of his eye, he saw Mr. Simmons, the floor manager, walking behind a distant cubicle line of phone solicitors, pausing to observe and listen, sampling each individual's sales spiel.

"Mom Daly, I'll be home in about two hours. I'm sure that it can wait 'til then, don't you?"

"Well, *I'd* want to know what was in an important letter if I were you," the woman's voice said smugly. "By the way, don't you be late tonight. We've got hot rolls, chicken-fried steak, and corn pudding just the way you like, and—"

"Really, Mom Daly! I'm very busy. I just don't have the time to—"

"Don't you want to know what the letter says?"

Aghast, Glenn forgot for the moment that Mr. Simmons was easing along in his direction. "Don't tell me you've opened my letter?"

"It's from a foreign country, Glenn! To you! It's from . . . Glenn, where's Cure-a-cow?"

"Where's . . . what?"

"C-u-r-a-c-a-o. Cure-a-cow."

Glenn puzzled over the spelling, and then his face brightened. "I think that's Curacao. It's an island, I think, down near South America." He frowned again. "I don't know anybody down there."

"You've been named in a will," Mom Daly informed him. "Do you know a Ruth Martin?"

Glenn shook his head.

"Glenn," Mom Daly announced. "I can't just stand here and talk to you all day. I've got to get supper started. We'll talk about it tonight. Goodbye."

"Mom Daly? What? Mom Daly?" Glenn realized he was speaking into a dead phone.

"Was that a personal call?"

Glenn spun in his seat.

Mr. Simmons was leaning over him.

"Ah, I'm sorry, Mr. Simmons. It was . . . somebody died. My landlady called to tell me."

Simmons was slow to react. "Well, I'm sorry to hear that." Not willing to become embroiled in personal tragedies of his underlings, he moved off, feigning sympathy. "Nobody close, I hope."

Glenn turned back to his desk. "Close? I haven't the faintest idea."

He touched a button on his computer, glanced at the screen, and activated a sales call. "Good afternoon. May I speak to

Mr. or Mrs. Goodwin?" He listened. "You are Mrs. Goodwin? Mrs. Goodwin, we know that credit card debt is a problem for many people and, if you should happen to have such a problem, we offer a very fine debt consolidation program . . ."

■ ■ ■

Late that cool, mid-October afternoon, Glenn came out of the elevator, with eight other passengers, to join the crowd of hurrying, jostling employees of the building's firms who were as anxious as he to escape the work of the day. Glenn, a broad-shouldered young man of slightly above average height, with a nice face and an attractive smile, nonetheless seemed diffident and shy, somewhat overly apologetic as he rubbed shoulders or inadvertently bumped into other people as they rushed toward the building's exit doors. Scarcely anyone gave him notice; he wasn't a noticeable person.

Once outside, he hurried toward a bus stop a half-block away. He started to trot as he saw the bus arrive and come to a stop, jamming traffic in the lane behind it. A sizable queue of passengers was beginning to board, each person taking his or her time. At the end of the line, he made no fuss as three latecomers pushed in ahead of him. Last to board, he found no seats available.

Strap hanging, he was the only one standing. In a seat nearby, Jody, the surly girl from his work area, was studiously avoiding looking at him, looking out the side window and pretending an intense interest in the dreary surroundings of the depressed business district.

I'm twenty-seven, heading towards thirty, and what the hell's so wrong with me. Jody could be nicer to me. I've never been rude to her. I've never asked her for a date, and if I even tried, she'd turn me down flat. Not that she's any great prize.

Glenn looked away from the girl, and shifted his mind to puzzle over the mysterious letter, the so-called will, and then began to wonder about the name, Ruth Martin.

Halfway home, a vague memory kicked in.

■ ■ ■

He must have been five or maybe six at the most. A hazy image came to mind of a very pretty woman kneeling down and hugging him, a woman he remembered being called Aunt Ruth. It was the first and only time that he could recall seeing her and, seldom in his childhood, had he heard her name. On those very rare occasions, he did remember the disapproving tone in his father's voice

After his parents' auto accident, in which only he had survived with cuts, scratches and bruises, he'd once more heard the same name uttered just outside his hospital room.

"I don't know where to find this Ruth Ellison, his mother's sister," the hospital woman's voice was exasperated.

"She's his only kin?" a man brusquely asked. "Well, then, he's only eleven. We'll have to turn him over to Social Services"

"Never you mind," a woman's voice declared. "I'll take him. No one else, you hear?"

That voice, of course, was Maxine Daly, his mother's best friend. From then on, she became his surrogate Mom.

■ ■ ■

"There's room for you," a seated man nearby said, interrupting Glenn's remembrance. He gestured to the empty space next to the scowling Jody.

"Thanks, just the same," Glenn replied, frowning back at his surly co-worker. "I'm almost home."

2

A few minutes later, Glenn left the bus and walked the two blocks to a substantial, old-style Victorian house. He took the three steps up to the porch in a single bound, opened the front door and walked inside.

In the hallway, he moved past the stairway and entered the living room. Two of his fellow rooming house boarders, Pete and Ben, were seated in front of a wide-screen television set, watching the evening news.

"Hi, guys."

They nodded, absorbed in the video coverage of a Kansas City warehouse fire.

Mom Daly, short, round and sixty-two, came through the wide portal of the adjacent dining room, her face beaming at Glenn's arrival. "Oh, good, Glenn!" she enthused. "Just in time!" In spite of being only a few feet away from Pete and Ben, she bellowed, "Supper's ready!"

Both of the seated boarders rose and moved toward the dining room, their eyes still fastened upon the television. Mom Daly stood in place as they walked past her and took their regular seats at the large dining room table. The landlady smiled her satisfaction at the descent of other boarders as they came down the stairs.

"Supper's ready!" she sang again, and reached for the television remote. She turned off the TV, and then bustled back through the dining room and through a door to the kitchen.

The upstairs arrivals, three of them, nodded to Glenn as they walked into the dining room. Glenn waited as they seated themselves at the table, and then moved to his assigned chair.

Around the table, including Mom Daly, there would be seven people. Those already seated were going through what might be considered an almost ritualistic ceremony of unfolding their cloth napkins, inspecting silverware, checking the level of water in their tumblers, making sure that ice cubes had not yet melted. The ritual spoke of a very long and unswerving practice; never varied, always the same.

Glenn was seated to the left side of the empty chair at the head of the table where Mom Daly would preside during the meal. Directly opposite from him, on Mom Daly's other side, was Ben Mosser, a late middle-aged perennial bachelor. He was a heavy-set man with a male-pattern bald spot invading what gray hair he had left. Beside him, Pete Wilson was a slim, energetic widower in his late seventies who showed an uncommonly active interest in a retired school teacher, Rose Armstrong, who sat close beside him, a petite widow of similar years. On Glenn's side of the table, Betty Lundgren was a plump, plain young woman who worked in the back room of a flower shop, had few male or female friends, and seemed destined to become a stolid old maid. Next to Glenn, a social worker, Jean Hurth, was an attractive, outspoken, no-nonsense woman of middle years whose appeal was, too often, offset by her direct and confrontational manner.

The door to the kitchen opened and Mom Daly came through, bearing steaming bowls in each hand, handing the first to Ben, placing the second on the table beside him.

As she returned to the kitchen, Ben helped himself to the mashed potatoes, passed the bowl to Pete, and then spooned the green beans from the second. As before, the passing of the food seemed to be a well-practiced procedure, each person taking a heaping spoonful from the bowls as they passed. When Mom Daly brought in the corn pudding and the final platter of chicken-fried steaks, she beamed with pleasure at her boarders' keen anticipation of her food. After helping herself last, to whatever was left of each serving dish, she placed the large dishes on a sideboard and seated herself at the head of the table, nodding her permission for the meal to begin.

Across the table, Pete looked up from cutting Rose's meat. "You got a boat."

Glenn paused in the motion of raising a forkful of green beans to his mouth. "What?"

"That's what you got in the will," Pete said to him. "A boat."

Glenn put the fork of green beans back on his plate and looked around at the group. Not one returned his gaze, all were looking down at their food, and all seemed uncomfortable.

He turned to his landlady. "Did you show them my letter?" he asked, a direct accusation.

There was a long silence.

"May *I* see it?" Glenn asked.

Without a word, Mom Daly fished a folded, crumpled letter from her apron pocket and handed it to Glenn.

Glenn unfolded the letter and began to read. After a few moments of study, he raised his eyes to sweep across his dining companions. "Well, just what does everybody think?"

After another long silence, Rose spoke in a quavering voice, "We really didn't think it was wrong, Glenn. We'd let you read our mail . . . if we ever got something interesting." She sighed. "I'm afraid nothing ever is."

"Reading other peoples' mail is wrong," Glenn declared. "You all know that."

Betty raised her hand, wanting to speak. "It isn't though we are outsiders, Glenn. We're your friends."

"Probably the only friends you've got," Jean said caustically. "Lighten up, bud. Stop making a big deal out of it."

With an angry glance at Jean, Glenn brandished the letter. "And where does it say anything in here about a boat? There's not one damned thing in here about a . . ." He stopped in mid-sentence and gave a quizzical look to Pete. "A boat?"

Pete nodded. "Didn't say what kind."

It took several seconds before Glenn could ask another question. "Who said?"

No one answered.

"What the hell is going on?" Glenn demanded. "What have you people been up to?"

"There'll be no profanity at this table, in this house, Glenn," Mom Daly scolded him. "You know the rules."

Glenn let his shoulders sag, nodding to Mom Daly. "Tell me, please . . . what's going on?"

Across the table, Ben cleared his throat, deciding to speak for the rest. "Well, as you can see in the letter, there's number there to call. It's the number of that lawyer down there in Cure-a-cow."

Glenn stared at him in disbelief. "You called him?"

"Nope," Ben answered. "Pete did."

Pete nodded, showing something like excitement. "Sure did. Told him, I was you."

"If we'd waited 'til you got home, Glenn, it'd been too late to call," Mom Daly offered an explanation. "It'd be night down there." She paused, and then added, "I told Pete that it was all right, and you wouldn't mind."

Rose gave a sniff of disdain. "Most of them didn't even know how to say Curacao or where it was located. I had to show them in my World Atlas book."

"We couldn't have waited all night to find out what it was about, could we?" Mom Daly asked, still explaining.

Glenn looked around the table, a feeling of helplessness beginning to overwhelm him. "Damn it! I know you all meant well, but—"

"We didn't do anything wrong!" Mom Daly was quick to interrupt. "And you stop your swearing."

Next to him, Jean stopped eating. "It doesn't really make all that much difference, you know. Pete just asked the same questions you'd have asked." She took another bite of chicken-fried steak, mumbling through the mouthful. "Probably did a better job than you would've."

"Okay," Glenn said with a heavy sigh. "What did the lawyer say?"

"Well, he was kinda hard to understand," Pete began, obviously enjoying his narrative. "He spoke some sort of German or—"

"Dutch!" Rose corrected. "Curacao is a part of the Netherlands Antilles."

Pete was none too pleased at the interruption. "Yeah, well, that's not all that important, Rose."

Immediately, he was sorry, but Rose turned her head and scooted her chair a couple of inches away.

With a lift of his right eyebrow, Pete continued: "Anyway, this fella told me that you were named in the will of this woman named Ruth Martin—"

"Did you figure out who that might be, Glenn?" Mom Daly interrupted.

"Don't you remember, Mom Daly . . . my mother had a younger sister . . . and I think her name was Ruth." He hesitated. "They really never talked about her . . . and I never knew quite why."

Mom Daly frowned in thought, and then gave an uncertain nod.

Again, Pete was annoyed at the interruption. "Whoever she was, it seems like she named you in a will and left you some property. Fellow said it was a boat . . . of sorts."

"Of sorts?" Glenn questioned.

"Well, he was sorta off-handed about it."

"Meaning that it probably isn't worth very much," Glenn said. "What else did he say?"

"Well, he did say something about some sort of a . . . a cash offer for the property."

Glenn brightened. "How much?"

"Not a hell of . . . excuse me, Mom Daly . . . not too much."

"Exactly how much?" Glenn persisted.

"About . . . seventy-eight thousand dollars."

"How much?" Glenn exclaimed in delight.

"Seventy-eight thousand dollars," Pete, again, informed him. "U. S. dollars."

"That's more money than I've ever had in my life!" Glenn exulted. "Seventy-eight thousand!"

"A pittance, this day and age," Jean interjected. "Hardly a fortune"

Glenn ignored her and directed a question to Pete. "What do I have to do? When do they send the money?"

The boarders seemed reluctant to share in Glenn's joy.

"There's something you're not telling me," Glenn accused.

Ben cleared his throat. "Glenn, you'd never make the right decision. You'd take the money and do something like . . . well, like putting it into a savings account or something."

"Or you'd make a bad investment," Jean added. "There's lots of those around these days."

"What have you done?" Glenn said in a low, fearful voice.

"Now, don't you go getting upset with Pete," Mom Daly cautioned.

"*What* did you do?"

"It was for your own good," Betty declared. "We wanted to give you a chance. After all, you're not a kid any more. You've got not much of a job, not much of a girl, and not much of a life. What are you still doing at a rooming house, for God's sake?" She gestured around at the group. "Look at us, Glenn. You want to stay here, and end up like the rest of us?"

Mom Daly gave a small cough to draw attention. "It was the right thing to do for me to take you in here after your folks died. You had no other folks, and nowhere else to go. Your mother was my best friend, but, now, this isn't the best place for you. Betty's right, you're not a youngster anymore. You need to get out, spread your wings."

Pete nodded in agreement. "We all talked about it. We knew you wouldn't go without a push."

Glenn's confusion was mounting. "What are you talking about? Go where?"

"We turned down the money," Pete told him righteously. He held up a hand to ward off Glenn's angry response. "Now, you can still get it if you've a mind to, but we wanted you to go down there, to that island, and check out what you've got."

"You had no right—"

Betty interrupted. "Glenn, you're a nice young man, but you've got no get-up-and-go. Two years ago, we made you get a passport so you could travel, and you've never used it, never went anywhere, never moved out of this house, or even went very far out of Kansas City."

Glenn stared at her in disbelief. "Well, maybe if I had that money—"

"You'd still be a stick," Jean offered her opinion. "And I'll make a bet you'll screw up the rest of it."

"The rest of what?" Glenn asked.

By way of an answer, Mom Daly said, "You're catching the morning plane to Miami, stay the night, and then, on Friday, you'll catch another plane to—"

"Willemstad!" Rose cut in. "That's the capitol of the islands."

"We put the ticket on your MasterCard," Pete advised him, then warned, "You shouldn't leave it lying around in your room."

Glenn slumped in his chair. "But . . . what do I do about my job?"

"Land's sakes, Glenn," Mom Daly exclaimed. "There are some things you just have to take care of yourself." She looked around with a wide smile. "Would anyone like some more corn pudding?

3

"Please fasten your seatbelt, sir," the flight attendant instructed, reaching across the back of the seats to place her hand on Glenn's shoulder, rousing him from a troubled replay of his row with Mr. Simmons, the latter barely accepting a death of a relative as an excuse for a few days off. The attendant pointed to the window. "We're coming into Willemstad."

Glenn buckled his seatbelt and peered out the window as the plane banked and circled the island for its approach, giving him a bird's eye view of their destination. Still high enough to see the shape of it, Curacao appeared a long, narrow, semi-arid island. Somehow, he'd expected it to be something more verdant, perhaps with a thick covering of tropical forest. As the plane started its descent, he could see the picturesque city of Willemstad, the red-tiled roofs and pastel colors of the Dutch-style buildings. To his amazement, a large cargo vessel was actually passing right through the midst of those quaint structures. It was traversing slowly, carefully, navigating a slender waterway from the ocean that cut directly through the city, and opened up into a huge body of water inside the island. This lagoon appeared to be a sheltered, deep-water harbor with many large ships and other smaller craft at anchor.

After the airliner touched down and taxied to a position near the small terminal building, Glenn entered the stream of deplaning passengers, and descended the rollaway stairway to the tarmac. The sun was bright and hot, and Glenn could feel considerable heat rising from the tarmac. With other passengers, he entered a building and presented his scant U. S. citizen identification to the entry inspector.

"Vacation?" the inspector questioned.

"Here to look at some property I inherited," Glenn told him.

"Going to be living here?" the man asked, his manner rather severe.

"I'm just here for a quick look-see," Glenn told him. "I haven't made any real plans."

The inspector nodded, and admitted him to Curacao.

He retrieved his only article of luggage; a hard-side suitcase, an ancient, maroon-colored Samsonite loaned to him by Ben. Uncertain as to what first to do, he found a storage locker that, to his gratification took U. S. coins, and decided to place the case inside for the time being. Resolving to take care of business to begin with, he walked out of the terminal to the pickup area, searching for a taxi. To his gratification, a cab pulled up immediately. The native driver rushed out of the automobile and around the trunk to open the rear door.

"You speak English?" Glenn's question was almost timid.

The driver smiled and gave him a nod. "Yes, sir. Also, Dutch, Spanish, and Papiamento." He smiled wider at Glenn's bewilderment. "That last is our own language that we've made up." He waited for Glenn to speak, then politely asked, "You want to go somewhere, sir?"

"Yeah," Glenn acknowledged, and handed the driver a slip of paper. "I need to go to this address."

The driver glanced at it and bobbed his head. "On our way."

As Glenn seated himself on the back seat of the taxi, the driver closed the rear door, and hurried around the cab to get in behind the steering wheel. He gave the wheel a turn and accelerated away from the curb onto the paved road.

"You take U. S. money?" Glenn asked, leaning forward.

The driver made eye contact by way of the rear view mirror. "First time in these parts, sir?"

"First time anywhere," Glenn admitted. "Guess it really shows."

"That's all right, sir," the driver told him. "Yes, U. S. money is good everywhere on the island. Pay no attention to smar-tasses like me. You have a good time on your first time any-where."

"It's a really pretty city," Glenn said, leaning back into the seat, looking out the window. "One of the nicest I've ever seen." He paused. "Of course, I haven't seen too many."

Together they laughed.

As they drove into the tropical municipality, Glenn gazed out the window at the sights. Many of the Willemstad build-ings, each painted in a different pastel color, were tall and skinny with sharply peaked tile roofs. The people on the streets were of many different racial shades, most in Carib-bean casual attire. Once, he saw a pack of uniformed school children being herded by an older woman into a building beside a steepled church.

Betty and the others are_right, he mused. *First time I've ever gone any place, never been even far out of Kansas City, never did anything new or exciting. Maybe here and now is a beginning.*

The taxi pulled up in front of an older building in a drab section of the business district. Glenn paid the driver, and watched as the driver waved and drove away. He stood for a few moments in front of the building, feeling a bit uncertain about what would come next, and then entered the front door.

Inside, from a tenant directory, he found the name he was seeking and, resolutely, started up the stairway. On the second floor, he walked slowly down the hallway, checking the names and numbers on the glass-paneled doors. He stopped at a partially opened door where the wording on the frosted glass read: *Johann Gravendeel, Attorney-at Law.*

Through the doorway, a middle-aged black woman sat at a pressed-wood desk in a somewhat shabby reception room. Although there was a computer on the desk's side return, the screen was dark. The woman interrupted the reading of a magazine to glance with irritation at the ceiling fan that was, apparently, doing an inadequate job of cooling her. She noticed Glenn at the doorway just as he started to knock. "You looking for something?" she said crossly.

"Mr. Gravendeel . . . is he . . . available?"

She rolled her eyes and nodded. "Yeah, he's here." She appraised him insolently, noting the wrinkled khaki pants and the way-too-plaid, short-sleeve shirt. "You got an appointment?"

Glenn stepped inside the reception room. There were two mismatched upholstered chairs, a well-worn sofa, and a couple of fake plants. There was an open door into a private office and, from what he could see of it, it seemed only slightly nicer than the reception area. What with the grungy surroundings, and with the less-than-gracious receptionist, Glenn's earlier hopes of a valuable inheritance sagged. He crossed to the receptionist and, taking his letter from his shirt pocket, presented it to her.

"Oh, yeah," she said, unfolding it. "You're Hathaway."

"Yes, ma'am, Glenn Hathaway. I got this letter from Mr. Gravendeel and—"

"Ah, Mr. Hathaway!" boomed an accented voice.

Glenn stepped forward for a different view into the private office, and saw an older, gray-haired, very obese man in his shirtsleeves seated behind a huge desk. The man struggled to rise, heaving his massive frame up and out of the desk chair. He took a moment to take a suit coat from an old-fashioned coat rack, donned the voluminous garment, straightened his tie, and lumbered through the door with his large hand outstretched. "How good to make your acquaintance. Have you just arrived?"

Glenn lost his hand in the man's firm grip. "Yes, sir. Mr. Gravendeel?"

"In the flesh as you've undoubtedly noticed," the big man said, smiling broadly.

Glenn gestured to the letter in the receptionist's hand. "I got your letter—"

"Of course, of course," Gravendeel said, looking at Glenn with some concern. "I had you pictured . . . an impression I had . . . that you were a bit older . . . ah, something about your voice on the telephone?"

Glenn gave a self-conscious smile, but said nothing.

"Ah, well," Gravendeel said with a shrug. "Something in the transmission, I suppose."

He waited for a response and, again, didn't get one.

"Come in, come in," Gravendeel invited, waving Glenn into his private office. "I was rather surprised to hear, in that call, that you were actually coming to the island for what is a somewhat routine transaction."

"I, ah, must tell you that I'm, also, quite surprised by all this," Glenn told him as he walked into the office and, where the big man indicated, seated himself in a well-worn leather chair in front of the desk. "Are you really sure that I'm the . . . the . . ."

"Beneficiary?" Gravendeel provided the word, lowering himself carefully into the executive chair behind the desk. "Quite sure. Your aunt, Ruth Martin, apparently convinced her husband to have a new will drawn quite recently." He paused, showing a slight frown. "Although I usually handled Captain Jack's legal affairs, I must admit I had not been aware of this document." He gave a slight smile. "Did you hear from your aunt often, Mr. Hathaway?"

"No, not really," Glenn said slowly. "I'm afraid I really didn't know who she was at first."

"Then . . . you were not close?"

"Close?" Glenn shook his head. "To be honest about it, Mr. Gravendeel, I'd sorta forgotten all about her. It's been years since I'd thought about her at all."

"There's been no correspondence? No contact with others in your family?"

"I'm afraid not," Glenn told him. "My folks are both dead and, no, there's been no contact." He hesitated. "Even before, I had the feeling that she was sort of, well, the black sheep of the family."

Gravendeel considered this thoughtfully. "Yes, I would suppose that would explain why she never mentioned her relatives. Do you have brothers? Sisters?"

"Nope, just me."

Gravendeel gave a heavy sigh. "Mr. Hathaway, I mean your family no disrespect, but . . . well, Jack Martin just married your aunt a relatively short time ago."

Glenn waited.

"Your aunt," Gravendeel began. "She, ah, was a rather flamboyant woman."

Glenn waited.

"She was . . . self-employed."

Glenn cleared his throat. "I don't believe I understand, Mr. Gravendeel."

The fat man sighed. "A lady of the evening, you might say." He paused. "Retired."

"Oh."

Gravendeel busied himself by opening a side drawer of the desk. He found an inch-thick file folder and placed it on the top of the desk.

"As I mentioned, this will was drawn shortly after their marriage, apparently while they were on their honeymoon." Gravendeel opened the folder and took out a legal document. "A copy of the document came to my attention after their unfortunate accident, and you've been named the legatee."

He passed the will to Glenn.

Glenn took several minutes to leaf through the document, studying it page by page.

"Did they have other property?" Glenn asked. "A house on the island?"

Gravendeel shook his head. "He and his wife shared a rental home, nothing more. Until his marriage, Jack lived on the ship." He paused. "Meaning no disrespect, but Jack was what you would call extraordinarily frugal. The ship, and small amounts in personal checking and savings accounts, would be the size of everything."

"And I'm the sole heir of . . . this everything?" Glenn said finally.

"Yes, there were no others named. There had been a previous will, but it's of no concern now."

"I see," Glenn said. "You know, this has all come as a surprise to me. It was nice of Aunt Ruth to remember me." He sat quietly for a few moments. "No one has told me exactly what happened to her and her husband. Do you know how they died?"

"An accident at sea. Lost overboard in rough weather."

"Both at the same time?"

Gravendeel nodded. "That happens in these waters. Storms come up quickly and, well, I don't want to say these things, but Jack did like his drinks, you know." He lifted both hands in a rueful manner. "I'm told that they were both quite intoxicated." He shook his head. "Terrible to say about people, but it happens. It happens."

"On this boat . . . the boat I've inherited?"

"Yes, the *Lady Ruth*," Gravendeel answered. "Jack renamed it after the marriage." He looked at a paper in the file. "Now, have you given any more thought to selling the property?"

"For seventy-eight thousand dollars?"

"Yes, that is the amount that I was authorized to proffer."

"Who's making the offer?" Glenn wanted to know.

"The prospect wants to remain anonymous," the lawyer told him.

"Do you think it's a fair offer?"

"You must be the judge of that, sir," Gravendeel replied.

"Could I see the boat?" Glenn asked. "Is it near here?"

"You are in luck, young man," Gravendeel said solemnly. "The ship is in port this week, badly in need of repairs, I'm afraid. No charter income, this week."

Glenn frowned at the lawyer's rather glum words. "When could I go see it?"

With considerable effort, Gravendeel heaved himself out of the chair to waddle around the desk, beckoning for Glenn to rise and follow. "What about right now, Mr. Hathaway? I have my car on the street, and I'll take the time to drive you."

Without waiting for an answer, Gravendeel reached for a broad-brimmed planter's hat on the rack and moved through the door with Glenn following.

"I'll be out of the office for, at the most, two hours," he said, pausing to speak to the receptionist. "Should Mrs. Meerman arrive early, please ask her to wait." He turned to Glenn. "Shall we go?"

As they descended the stairs, Glenn was surprised at how briskly Gravendeel moved once he had momentum. The huge lawyer kept up the pace outside the building, Glenn hurrying along beside him.

"What kind of a boat is it, Mr. Gravendeel?" Glenn asked. "Pleasure boat?"

"Pleasure boat?" Gravendeel gave him a small, sad smile. "Jack Martin ran a little charter for people . . . well, those who didn't take trips on the more expensive ships."

"They do much business?"

"They made a living of sorts," Gravendeel said.

He hurried on, coming to an abrupt stop beside a gleaming silver Mercedes automobile. "Here we are!" With his

23

remote, he unlocked the doors, gestured for Glenn to get in, then trudged around to open the driver's side door.

Glenn tried not to show too much attention, but he was fascinated by the massive lawyer's careful efforts to squeeze behind the steering wheel. The seat was pushed back as far as possible and, even so, Gravendeel's lower abdomen engulfed the lower part of the wheel, giving new emphasis to a need for power steering.

Despite his girth, Gravendeel seemed at home in his auto-mobile, whipping it away from the curb and merging with other traffic skillfully. They drove for twenty minutes through the city, and then onto a paved road that followed the shoreline of the island. Resort and nautical-based commercial districts were blended into quite a number of residential communities that featured both luxury and modest homes. They passed a number of beaches and a couple of large yachting marinas before they came to a view of a beautiful ocean bay, a spar-kling blue water harbor with a marina, with a sizable variety of power and sailing craft. Many were daysailers, but there were several large luxury yachts at anchor as well.

Gravendeel pulled the Mercedes to a stop in a parking lot next to a tier of steps. At the base of the steps, a short paved path led past a guard shack and a gated entryway to the float-ing jetty that extended into the bay.

"One of those is mine?" Glenn said, excited at the sight.

Gravendeel's face showed no emotion. "Yes, I'm afraid so," he answered with a disheartening sigh. "One of those. Down there a ways, you can't miss it."

Gravendeel's somber manner caused Glenn to turn to the big man, anxiety now replacing his excitement. "Which one?" he asked apprehensively.

Instead of an answer, Gravendeel gave a nod of his head toward the marina and fixed his eyes on a distant target, giving a sigh that could only signify sadness.

Glenn followed his gaze, searching the pier.

Anchored in the midst of sleek sailing ships and powerful motor yachts, a weathered and battered motorsailer drew his eyes. It appeared out of place in this beautiful harbor; a ship with a weathered wooden hull dulled by years at sea and scant attention to maintenance. To Glenn, it more deserved the bottom of the sea rather than a place on the surface.

"That's it?" Glenn asked in dismay.

Gravendeel gave a weary shrug.

"Should I go look at it?"

"If you must," Gravendeel responded solemnly.

"Maybe it looks better . . . up close," Glenn ventured.

"As you wish," Gravendeel replied, giving his wristwatch a meaningful glance. He gestured at his considerable girth. "If you'll excuse me, I'm an old fat man and I try to avoid unnecessary exertion, you understand?"

"Of course," Glenn agreed. "You just stay right here."

"Don't be long," the lawyer said. "Remember, my other appointments."

"No, sir," Glenn assured him. "I'll just give it a quick look."

Glenn got out of the car and started down toward the pier. As he stepped onto the floating walkway, he marveled at the beauty of each vessel as he passed. Large or small, these were luxury boats and yachts, even the least of them obviously expensive.

Why couldn't one of these be mine?

When he reached the scabrous motorsailer, he walked slowly toward it, peering along each side, seeing beneath the flaking, paint on the hull, great patches of decaying wood. From what he could see of the deck and the superstructure, the entire ship appeared almost a derelict ruin, scarcely a pleasure boat.

Make a living on that? Who would charter on this?

He heard a noise behind him and turned to see an elderly man, tanned and fit, stepping nimbly from the deck of an elegant moderately-sized yacht onto the finger pier and coming toward him.

"You responsible for that thing?" the man asked, his manner accusing.

"I guess so," Glenn said in a faltering voice.

"Do us all a favor and get it out of here," the man continued, his tone just a shade away from anger.

"I'm sorry," Glenn apologized, gesturing to the ugly vessel. "I didn't know . . . well, I didn't even know I owned it 'til just a few minutes ago."

The man looked at him, mistrust in his expression. "How'd you come by it?"

"A relative left it to me."

"Well, whoever it was, sure didn't leave you much," the elderly man declared.

"May I ask you a question, sir?" Glenn asked.

"What about?"

Glenn pointed to the ship. "Would you . . . would anybody give seventy-eight thousand dollars for that thing?"

The man took a step closer, looking past Glenn at the ship. "Not likely, son," he answered, his tone of voice now softer. "Why'd you ask?"

"Because that's what I've been offered," Glenn told him.

The man turned to Glenn, now taking a keen interest in the conversation. "Hell, the Navy wouldn't even pay that to use it for target practice." He turned his gaze back to the ship. "You sure that's yours? I've seen that old scow around in these waters for a while but it doesn't seem like it rightly belongs to somebody that you'd be related to. More likely, belongs to a bunch of scalawags!" He shook his head. "Damned thing just showed up here a couple of days ago."

"Is it used as a charter?" Glenn asked, doubt forming.

"Charter!" the old man exclaimed. "Hell, no! It not used for anything." He paused, and then asked, "What's the name of this boat you've inherited?"

"The *Lady Ruth*," Glenn said in a low voice. "Some lady."

The elderly man looked at Glenn in amazement. "The *Lady Ruth*?" He gestured to the dilapidated tub. "Hell, that's not the *Lady Ruth*!" He fixed Glenn with a steady gaze. "You said somebody left it to you? You some kin to Jack Martin?"

"Not exactly," Glenn responded. "His wife, Mrs. Martin. Mrs. Ruth Martin."

The old man cackled, and did a little impromptu jig on the pier. "Well, I'll be damned," he said happily. "That was his missus' name, sure as hell, because that's what he named her."

"Her?" Glenn questioned, confused, turning to the unsightly motorsailer.

"No, no, not *her*!" the old man said with a whoop, whirling to point to the end of the pier. "*Her!*"

Glenn turned his head at the direction of his pier companion, and saw a magnificent, two-masted sailing ship moored at the end of the jetty, clearly one of the largest and finest yachts at the marina.

"There's your *Lady Ruth*," the old man exulted.

Glenn looked at the splendid ship in awe. "That can't be." He looked back at the old ship. "Maybe there's more than one *Lady Ruth*."

The old man gave a wave of his hand, dismissing the thought. "Boy, somebody's pulling your leg. Shame 'bout what happened to them . . .but if you really are kin to Ruth Martin . . . that's your *Lady Ruth*."

Glenn's confusion blossomed into jubilation. "Then . . . that one? That one is really mine?"

The old man chuckled. "How'd you ever get the idea that this old wreck was yours? Somebody actually pointed her out to you?"

"I think he was being very careful not to," Glenn replied gravely. He turned and looked back up the slope to the parking lot, just in time to see the Mercedes slowly pulling away. "He just kinda let me think so." He looked to the elderly man. "Say, mister. . . "

"Gordon," the man said, offering his hand. "Emory Gordon." He gestured to his own yacht. "I own the *Sea Mist* here. Not in the class of the *Lady Ruth*, but she's my pride and joy."

"She's a beauty, Mr. Gordon," Glenn said, shaking his benefactor's hand enthusiastically. "I'm Glenn Hathaway, and I'm *very* glad to meet you. Obliged to you, I should say."

"Well, if I've been of some help to you, I'm surely glad," Gordon said graciously. "Congratulations, son. You've got yourself a beauty there." He studied Glenn for a few moments. "You seem to be a little at loose ends. Anything else I could help you with?"

"I was kind of expecting help from my lawyer," Glenn said with another glance at the parking lot. "You're right, I'm new here on the island and a little overwhelmed."

"Gonna stay in these parts and run the charter?" Gordon asked.

Glenn didn't answer immediately. "I hadn't yet thought about that, Mr. Gordon," he admitted. "It's a possibility."

Gordon nodded and walked toward the Sea Mist, preparing to board. "I hope you do! And don't hesitate to let me know if I can be of any assistance. Be glad to." With a wave, Gordon hopped onto the deck of his yacht.

"Mr. Gordon!"

The elderly man turned.

"You suppose I could, well, maybe go aboard?"

"The *Lady Ruth*? Why not? You own her!" With another wave, he disappeared below deck.

Glenn stood for a few seconds, looking at the ship.

Impossible! Nothing wonderful like this could ever happen to me!

He turned and looked at the scaly, peeling ship.

Now something like that was much more likely.

4

Still with doubt, Glenn walked slowly toward the wondrous ship at the end of the jetty, his stride quickening as he moved and, nearly there, the fast pace became a jog.

At the end of the pier, he hesitated at the gangplank of the ship. Summoning courage, he marched resolutely up to the main deck. He looked around, expecting someone to see him, to challenge him. Seeing no one, he meandered along the perimeter walkway past the long, head-high deckhouse, and came to a halt at the back of the ship.

"May I help you?" a woman's voice asked.

Glenn whirled to face a young blond woman standing at the other side of the deck. She was dressed in wrinkled, denim shorts, and a tied-back work shirt that exposed quite a lot of her tanned midriff. Although slightly frowning, she seemed to be more questioning than unfriendly.

"You looking for work or what?" the woman asked, her tone turned just a little edgy.

"Is this . . . ah . . . the *Lady Ruth*?"

The girl regarded him for a few seconds, and then gave a practiced smile. "Yes, but I'm afraid you're a couple of days too early."

"Early?"

The young woman gave him a sympathetic nod. "I'm afraid so. We don't sail 'til Sunday." She looked past him. "Where are your things?"

"Things?"

"Luggage?"

"Not with me at the moment."

The girl studied him. "Say, you *are* here for a charter, aren't you?"

"No, not exactly."

"Then . . . what?" the girl asked suspiciously.

"This boat . . . it *did* belong to a Mr. and Mrs. Martin? Mrs. Jack Martin?"

"Why do you ask?" the girl countered.

"Because . . . I think . . . I own it," Glenn stammered.

"Own what?" she questioned. "This ship?"

Glenn nodded. "Yes, I think so."

The young woman stood for several very silent seconds, regarding him with a skeptical expression, examining him critically. Then, she turned, walked forward and shouted, "Alain! You'd better come! You'd better come right now!"

There was no immediate answer.

Then: "*Vous dites*?"

"There's a man here!" the young woman called. "Says, he owns the *Lady Ruth*!"

Again, there was a period of silence. Then, from around the long deckhouse, a handsome, strongly built, light-colored black man came into view. Aged just shy of forty or barely on the other side of it, he was clad in white shorts and a white shirt, and wore a yachting cap jauntily on his head. He paused for a moment, and then gave a wide, engaging smile as he strode toward Glenn, his hand outstretched. "You must be *M'sieur* Hathaway, is that not so? The nephew of *Madame Martin?*"

The young woman, listening, appeared confused.

Glenn took his hand. "That's right. And you are?"

"Captain Alain Tournaire. It was my pleasure to have served as second in command to . . . would you have called him, Uncle Jack?"

"I'm sorry," Glenn responded. "I'm afraid I'd never met the man . . . and I barely remember Aunt Ruth."

"Beautiful people," Tournaire said, his voice solemn. "*Qual dommage!* A terrible tragedy."

"In a bad storm, I understand," Glenn said.

Tournaire gave a meaningful glance to the perplexed young woman, then gave a nod indicating that she should explain.

"Well," she began with seeming reluctance, "the sea was very rough and . . . the decks were awash., They were in no condition to be on deck." She shrugged, as if not wanting to continue.

"I hold myself *tres responsible*," Tournaire said, taking up the story with a flashed look of irritation at the young woman. "I saw them come on deck, and I said to them, 'return to your cabin'." He shook his head. "Jack just laughed at me and said, 'I've been at sea before you were born'." He sighed. "I knew they should not have gone forward on a night like that, neither of them." He shook his head again. "I should've been . . . how you say, resolute."

"Did you actually see the accident?" Glenn asked.

"No, it was dark and I said to myself, they'll be all right," Tournaire answered. He turned his head toward the bow of the ship. "Up there, heads held high into the wind, and facing the storm. Jack was like that! He loved the sea when it was wild. He loved the challenge of it, the violence of it." He turned back to Glenn and the girl, seemingly overcome with emotion. "*C'est fait!*"

Glenn was touched. "You must've been quite close to him."

"Like a father to me," Tournaire said, his voice almost a whisper. "But it is best to move on." With a sigh, he gestured to the young woman. "*Pardon, M'sieur* Hathaway. Let me present *Mademoiselle* Jennifer Warren?"

Rather hesitantly, the young woman reached out to shake Glenn's hand. "Jenny will do."

"Pleased to meet you, I'm Glenn. Are you, ah, a member of the crew?"

"Deckhand, cook, cocktail hostess, you name it," she replied, something rather insolent in her voice.

Glenn was surprised at the young woman's manner, not understanding what appeared to be her unreceptive attitude.

"Your plans, *M'sieur*?" Tournaire asked, making a sweeping gesture at the ship. "You're planning to sell the *Lady Ruth*?"

"I'm afraid I haven't thought that out just yet; I just might keep it," Glenn answered after several moments.

"You do not wish to sell?" Tournaire asked in surprise.

Glenn shrugged. "There was an offer."

"An offer?"

"Seventy-eight thousand."

There was a long silence, Tournaire and the young woman sharing a glance.

"*Mon Dieu!*" Tournaire exclaimed. "Who would dare to make such an offer?"

"A lawyer," Glenn told him. "Johan Gravendeel."

"Gravendeel?" Tournaire repeated the name with an expression of disgust. "That thief? That greedy old man?" He rolled his eyes. "He is a sly one, never to be trusted. Your aunt and uncle should never have trusted him . . . and you must have nothing to do with him."

Glenn nodded. "I know now. I'll make other arrangements . . . by the way, are you in port for major repairs?"

"Major?" Jennifer questioned with a puzzled glance to the captain. "No, routine maintenance. Why do you ask?"

"Something else I was led to believe," Glenn replied.

The three stood quietly for a few awkward moments.

"Could I take a look around?" Glenn asked, giving an apologetic gesture. "Kinda to see what things look like?"

Tournaire gave a sidewise glance to the young woman.

"I've got a lot of work to do, Alain," she protested.

"As do I," Tournaire countered. "Show him the ship, Jenny. It will only take a few minutes." He turned his head to Glenn. "And when you're finished, Jenny will bring you to the salon. We'll have a drink and talk then." Without waiting for a response, Tournaire touched the brim of his cap in a casual salute and walked away.

With an exaggerated sigh, the young woman turned to Glenn. "Just how much do you want to see?" she asked, her voice showing some impatience.

Glenn didn't reply immediately, puzzled by her curt manner. "I'd like to see what I own, if it's not too much trouble. How about showing me the whole thing?" he responded, making it more an insistence rather than a request.

She regarded him for a few prickly moments, and then shrugged. "Whatever you wish, bow to stern, topside to the bilges. I'll give you the brand new owner's grand tour, starting right here." She swept her hand to indicate the entire vessel. "The ship is a modern version of a traditional two-mast schooner," she said, the words flowing from her, an obviously familiar narrative. "It was built in 1963 as a private yacht for a wealthy Greek owner who used it for several years, then sold it when he lost his fortune. It was then purchased and refitted as a charter yacht by a company that used it for twenty some odd years. Again, it was offered for sale, and the last owner was your aunt's husband, Jack Martin."

Glenn nodded, looking around.

"The length of the ship is approximately one hundred eighty four feet and the beam . . . that's the maximum width . . . is thirty feet." She raised her eyes to the masts. "The main mast and foremast are of hollow steel, both strengthened and stabilized by steel cables, called shrouds and stays, which are attached to the ship's hull; fore, aft, port, and starboard."

Glenn's gaze followed the young woman's hand as she indicated each set of cables slanting down from the masts to the deck at both the port and stern.

"Most of the time," she resumed, "we're under sail, although we're also well equipped with a Cummins diesel." She nodded to a deeply shadowed opening enclosed within the left corner of the deckhouse. "This is the aft hatch with steps down to the lower deck where most of our cabins are located. In stormy conditions, we can close it watertight against the elements."

She turned to point across the deck to a dining setup with a U-shaped padded bench enclosing two long tables, each with facing chairs in the middle space. "Now, in good weather, which is almost always, we serve our meals al fresco on the aft deck. It's a bit distant from the galley for us as we serve, but the guests all seem to really enjoy the on-deck ambiance."

"Many of them get seasick?" Glenn said, attempting to alleviate the tension that seemed to exist.

"A few," she replied, allowing him her first small smile. "And it's handy that it isn't far to hang over the side rails."

She walked to the stern of the ship, and led him to a console assemblage that also featured a large spoked wheel on an upright column that, at its top, contained a recessed compass.

"This is the helm," she explained. "The helmsman not only can guide the ship from this position, but he . . . or she . . . can engage and vary the engine speeds, automatically drop and raise the anchor; everything is right here at hand."

Glenn nodded his appreciation.

"Now, we'll take a quick turn around the deck, look at the deckhouse, and then head below to check out the accommodations." She paused. "Are you serious about keeping the *Lady Ruth*?"

"I might be," he answered.

"Like . . . an absentee owner?"

"Maybe not," he mused. "Folks in Kansas City might advise me to change my life."

"And move here?"

"Might be fun."

She gave him a derisive look. "None of my business, but I'd sell if I were you."

"We'll see," Glenn responded coolly.

"Let's go forward," she said, and started toward the bow.

Glenn moved quickly to join her, following a step behind.

"You notice the low rise of the deckhouse," she said as she walked, gesturing to the top of the structure. "There's plenty of headroom inside, but the whole structure is embedded into the hull a few feet. The low profile gives a cleaner look for the ship, clearance for the swing of the foremast boom, and provides some reachable in-between storage space on the roof for inflatable lifeboats and such."

A quick stroll around the foredeck gave Glenn a cursory look at its features; the nomenclature of the foremast and its sail-wrapped boom, other functionary machinery and storage bins.

"This another way down?" Glenn asked, pointing to a dark shadowed entryway in the center of a low-rise rectangular structure in front of the foremast base.

"Fore hatch," she informed him. She stepped close and reached down inside the shadowed space to unlatch and swing back the heavy top plate to reveal a short stairway down into the ship's interior. "Leads down to the fo'c's'l."

Glenn face showed incomprehension.

"That's how we pronounce forecastle, the front section of the lower deck." She explained, and swung the hatch cover closed and latched it. "Locks or opens topside or below and seals watertight when we run into a squall."

"Whatcha call battening down the hatches?" Glenn ventured.

His escort gave no response, and guided him to the left side of the deckhouse.

Weather-tight doors, on both sides of the structure, provided entry from either walkway. She opened the door and preceded him down two steps into the ship's supplementary control center.

"This is the wheelhouse or sometimes called the pilot house. Duplicate controls, same as at the aft deck helm. Handle everything from here when a tropic storm blows up," she said with a nod to the broad-view window in front of them through which the foredeck could be seen. "Doesn't happen a lot, but it's nice to stay dry while we're seeing where we're going."

Glenn tapped the front pane. "This holds up okay in heavy weather?"

"Absolutely, laminated tempered glass, expensive but worth it."

Immediately behind this control facility, within the deckhouse, she showed him the heart of the ship's navigational and communications capabilities, modern equipment in compartments on either side of the companionway.

"Radar, MF/HF radio, GPS, depth, wind, speed gauges, and all the gadgets, whatever," she said. "Latest stuff."

Glenn looked beyond the technical compartments and saw, to the left, a compact galley with a bright aluminum stove and matching refrigeration units. Across the central passageway, an open door revealed a small office. Shifting his gaze, he looked down the long corridor.

"What's down this way?" he asked.

"The splendor of the ship," she responded, a note of pride replacing her lackluster, matter-of-fact delivery. "Come."

Again, she led the way, moving along the carpeted companionway with Glenn right behind her. The first section of the passageway featured floor-to-ceiling teak paneling on the walls, and the one to their right included two matching-wood doors, widely spaced apart.

"What are these?" Glenn asked as he stopped walking at the second door.

The woman turned and walked back. "Two of our deluxe cabins," she told him. "Take a look."

Glenn opened the second of the cabin doors and stuck his head inside. The interior was the equivalent of a small bedroom of a tract home in a modest community, although with a porthole on an outer wall. A bed of the double-size category was centered under a seascape painting, with a solitary small table on one side. A locker for hanging clothes including drawers for other items occupied a corner. A doorway in a wall adjacent to the other cabin showed a small bathroom.

"That's deluxe?" Glenn remarked and closed the door.

"Wait 'til you see the standard cabins," Jenny said with a smirk as she moved on.

The paneled walls came to an end and, on either side, the floor to ceiling partitions were now of clear Plexiglas. To his right, behind the transparent divider, there was a good-sized rectangular room with beige-papered walls, and trimmed with the warm tones of teakwood. It was nicely outfitted with an extended bookcase, a computer station, some comfortable chairs and a long table in the center.

"That's what we call our library, a combination reading room, conference and business center for our guests. We also serve meals in there whenever we have a blow that drives folks inside," she told him.

To his left, the clear partition revealed an inviting and beautifully appointed salon, matched in the same woods and warm colors as the reading room.

"We'll be back to that in a minute," she said, and hurried him to the end of the corridor into a small foyer, a cross aisle that spanned the width of the deckhouse. She pointed to the doors with portholes at each end of the cross aisle. "Like up front, you can come in from either side of the ship." She turned to a central door in the wall before them. "This is the owner's cabin." She reached for the brass knob, twisted it, and opened the door to reveal a large cabin. "Alain has been using it since . . . well, temporarily."

Glenn took a step inside. The cabin was spacious and exquisitely appointed. Broad expanses of the room were wall-papered with a nautical theme; tiny sailing ships embossed in dark brown against a beige background. A queen-sized bed was centered in the cabin with brass lamps on mahogany tables on either side. There was an upholstered settee at one side of the room, lounge chairs and a small table across from it. A mahogany secretary, with a swing-down desk, was fastened to a wall.

"Nice," Glenn said. "Before the accident, where did Captain Tournaire usually stay?"

"In one of those two deluxe cabins," she said. "And he can move back if you decide to move in on us."

Glenn ignored the tart comment. He considered for a few seconds, and then shook his head. "Seems to me this would make a nice honeymoon cabin," he told her. "Or one maybe for guests who would be willing to pay extra."

The girl's face was solemn. "I guess that depends upon what you're planning to do with the ship."

"Give me time, I'm thinking about it," he responded, turning to rejoin her in the foyer. She spun around and retraced her way and entered the luxurious deckhouse salon. As he joined her, with a longer time to study it, Glenn was immediately impressed.

The tan fabric-covered walls, featuring picturesque photos of exotic Caribbean ports, were trimmed in gleaming rosewood and teak. The same woods were used in the rest of the room in the cabinetry and furnishings. A section of one wall encased a built-in entertainment center with a television screen and a recorder-player. At the forward end of the size-able area, the salon presented an L-shaped bar with gleaming barware and expensive brand liquors displayed on shelves behind it. There were soft-cushioned settees in a lounge area, each fronted by an individual coffee table.

"Meet with your approval?" Jenny asked.

"Truth is . . . this is all a bit much to take in," he responded. "Let's say, I'm overwhelmed."

She smiled briefly and, seeing it, Glenn thought he detected a softening of her attitude.

Giving him a few moments more to gaze and appreciate their surroundings, she gestured to a teakwood-banistered stairwell at one side of the companionway. "Go below?"

He nodded.

She led the way down the spiral steps. "It's a stairway, but, on a ship, stairs are called ladders," she told him.

"Ladders," Glenn repeated. "I'll try to remember."

On the lower deck, they entered another long companion-way. Jenny stopped to open a door on her right, and stepped aside so Glenn could see the narrow space. "We have twelve of these cabins, a double bed in each."

Glenn took a couple of steps just inside the open door and looked around. This stateroom was small and spare, every inch of it maximized for use. In addition to the bed, there was an undersized dressing table with a small upholstered chair, a narrow closet with a hanging drape and a settee barely wide enough for two.

"That's a double bed?" He questioned in disbelief.

"It's called an Irish double," she confessed. "They come a bit smaller."

"Ever have any fat couples?"

She ignored the quip, and closed the door as he stepped out. "Our guests don't spend too much time in their cabins anyway. Most times, they're up on deck."

She led Glenn forward through the companionway, opening a door into a lavatory. "We have three heads with showers on this deck," she said, closing the door and moving on. "Up ahead, past the guest cabins," she said as she walked, "we have the crew quarters. We'll skip that right now since it's pretty messy unless you really want to see it."

"No, that's fine. What's next?"

"Well, that's the end of the tour," she said, entering the stairwell of the forward ladder. "I suspect Alain will be waiting for you in the salon."

She went up and waited on deck until he joined her, and then extended her hand. "That's about it, Mr. Hathaway."

"Glenn, if you don't mind."

She gave him a practiced smile. "Glenn. That's fine." She gestured to the deckhouse. "Right through there."

She turned away and re-entered the hatch, going below.

Glenn opened the door to the deckhouse, entered, and walked to the salon.

Tournaire was behind the bar. "Come in, come in," he invited. "A drink?"

"A beer if you have one," Glenn said, coming to lean against the bar.

"We have domestic and imported," Tournaire told him, opening a door in a compact refrigerator.

"Imported, I guess."

Tournaire twisted the cap from the bottle and handed it to him. "Your assessment of the property, *M'sieur*?"

"It's a beautiful ship," Glenn said, taking a sip of his beer. "What would you say it's worth?"

Tournaire was slow to respond, and then shrugged. "Today's prices, it is very hard to say."

"And how is the charter business?" Glenn asked.

"It can be good at times," Tournaire answered. "A great struggle at others. There is much competition."

"How does it work?"

Again, Tournaire took his time in forming an answer and, when it came, he seemed somewhat apologetic. "How shall I say? The charters are handled through a large Miami organization, what you call a combine. They represent many yachts, large and small. We pay a percentage of what we earn to this Miami organization. For this percentage, the combine works with travel agencies; booking customers, coordinating schedules and such." He lifted his hands in a gesture of weariness. "Very complicated, very worrisome, *M'sieur*."

"Is it a worthwhile business?"

"Sometimes *oui*, sometimes *non*," Tournaire replied.

"But I *could* make a living? A good living?"

"*Je le suppose*," Tournaire answered with a sigh. "However, you could be very well off in your own country with the price that you could get for the ship. I could probably find a buyer. There are several—"

"That's all well and good," Glenn interrupted. "It's just that, maybe, I need something new in my life." He hesitated. "Some adventure."

"It is not what you'd call an adventurous life, *M'sieur*," Tournaire advised him. "It is more a hard life, filled with routine duties, maintaining the ship, dealing with sometimes difficult customers."

"You don't know what routine is until you've had *my* job," Glenn responded with a rueful smile. He looked around the salon, highly impressed. "I think I could learn to like going to sea." He paused, and then continued. "Maybe I could learn to be . . . well, I know couldn't be a . . . what would you call it? A captain? You'd have to have papers and certain training, wouldn't you?"

Tournaire gave a slight shake of his head. "*Oui, M'sieur.* But, may I be frank?"

Glenn nodded.

"You have no knowledge of the sea, no background," Tournaire said apologetically. "Perhaps you'd be wise to, shall I say, retain the ownership, and let us operate it for you."

Glenn considered, and then made up his mind. "I think that I can learn about the sea. And I don't believe in being an absentee owner." He took a long pull at his beer and placed the bottle on the bar. "I'll catch the plane back tonight, and tie things up back home." He looked around at the opulent lounge. "For a change in my life, I'd like to call *this* my new home."

"Are you sure, *M'sieur*?" There was an expression of near disbelief on Tournaire's face. "You could be taking—"

"A hell of chance, but so what?" Glenn cut in. "Look for me next week."

5

With the crew ashore, Tournaire and Gravendeel sat on the aft deck of the *Lady Ruth* in the glimmering darkness. A nighttime quietude had settled over the harbor to replace the noise and turmoil of the day's marine activities. Gentle waves lapped softly against the hull of the ship and, in the dark, the twinkling lights of the waterfront community competed with the stars of the heavens. Many of the cruisers and sailing ships in the harbor were showing lights of their own, warm glows from cabins or afterdecks of yachts where owners were enjoying the evening by themselves or with guests. Voices of merriment and contentment carried across the glittering water, sometimes loud and boisterous enough for some words to be clearly understood.

Arcing above the harbor, the blinking lights of a climbing airliner marked its path across the starlit sky.

Gravendeel jabbed a plump forefinger to the ascending plane. "Undoubtedly, our young troublemaker on his way home," he said with a sigh. "If only he would stay there."

Tournaire kept his eyes on the airliner as it gained altitude. "Why did you not know of him? You were Captain Jack's lawyer!"

Gravendeel gave a wave of annoyed dismissal. "It was the bitch's doing. His Ruthie took him to another attorney to draw up a new will. One that superseded the one I'd drawn up, the will in our favor."

"Could you not have destroyed this new one?"

"People have seen it," the huge man responded irritably. "The other attorney, witnesses in his office, the bank personnel when we opened the safe deposit box." He threw his hands up. "I had a devil of a time to regain an attorney role again."

"Even so, you are a fat, greedy oaf! What were you thinking? Trying to pass off that rusty old tub on him?"

"And pay the going price of such an expensive ship?" Gravendeel said defensively. "It almost worked and, if it had, we would have had a valuable property for a mere pittance. You would have congratulated me."

"*Quel dommage!*" Tournaire exclaimed. "Congratulate you?"

"Very well, very well, I admit I misjudged the situation," Gravendeel responded, his tone showing his growing pique. "The thickheaded man I spoke to on the phone . . . now, I believe it was someone pretending to be young Hathaway . . . said he was coming to see his property. What was I to do? I had to show him something."

"And you thought you could deceive him with that eyesore?"

"The man on the phone seemed a simpleton, someone naïve and easy to fool."

"*You* are the fool," Tournaire said with contempt. "And now, *M'sieur* Glenn knows you for the rogue that you are. Now, you must hide from sight, and you can no longer be of great help for us."

"Enough!" Gravendeel snapped. "Don't forget, for a moment, that I'm the one who has made our profitable deals with suppliers in Columbia and in the Mideast. I'm the one who arranges for distribution, launders the money, and has made you a man of means." He paused. "And I'm also the one who has set up our forthcoming deal with the Russians."

"Do we know what that is about?"

"A quarter of a million dollars for a week's work, that's all we know," Gravendeel responded. "And Kozlov made it threateningly clear that we should mind our own business and not ask any questions.

"Do they know about Hathaway?"

Gravendeel shook his head. "I don't believe it would be wise to tell them. It might call off the deal."

Tournaire shrugged; a gesture of acquiescence. "Then, what are we to do about him? Now that he intends to return and become, as he put it, one of us"

"We play along for the time being," Gravendeel mused. "We certainly cannot lose the ship at this crucial time," Gravendeel spread his hands, palms upward, "and I see him as a penniless, naïve and gullible young man." He paused. "We must find some way to keep him occupied and off the ship until we're finished with our special charter."

"We have only four weeks," Tournaire mused. "Perhaps, like his aunt and the captain, we should get rid of him."

"Another death?" Gravendeel questioned with a roll of his eyes.

Tournaire sat in brooding silence, his eyes on the airplane as it flew into the distance. Finally, he said, "Perhaps, we might find a different ship. I don't know of one available, but—"

"That is impossible!" Gravendeel cut in. "Our clients' endeavor, they told me, is based upon a ship of this size, nothing smaller." Again, Gravendeel shook his head. "And they wanted *this* ship particularly."

"Why?"

"Perhaps they chose this ship because of its charter operation. It is a ship without a set itinerary, a ship that moves through these Caribbean seas without suspicion." The big man paused and reached for his glass of beer. "For all of his faults, Jack Martin ran a reputable charter, an outfit that was never questioned. It was your actions that jeopardized that operation. Killing Jack and his lady, after all, did bring us our vexing young man."

"Well, what would you have done?" Tournaire shot back. "It was supposed to be a shakedown voyage, with only crew on the ship. They surprised us, came aboard when we docked at Bonaire. Jack wandered out on deck during the drug pickup, so we had no choice."

"You couldn't have cancelled the rendezvous?"

Tournaire shook his head. "We couldn't reach our suppliers . . . and, besides, he and his fancy lady had been at the bottle all day. We thought they were dead to the world.in their cabin."

"Instead, soon to be dead at the bottom of the ocean," Gravendeel said caustically, then drank from his glass.

"We must eliminate this young fool," Tournaire declared. "There is too much at stake to let him come down here and get in our way."

Gravendeel sat quietly, and then said, "An accident would be good, serious enough for a long hospital stay or, perhaps, even one of a fatal nature, but it must seem to be genuine, an accident seen by several who are *reliable* witnesses . . .

witnesses who will swear that it was a genuine mishap, and nothing that would arouse suspicion."

Tournaire frowned in thought. "Perhaps, we should have something ready and hurtful for him when he returns."

"On the other hand, why wait?" Gravendeel asked, laboriously heaving himself out of the chair. "Perhaps something suitable might be arranged before he leaves his home."

6

"What was it like?"

"Did you sell it?"

"What did you do?"

"What are you going to do, now?"

"Give me a chance to get in the door," Glenn said to the group gathered in the hallway. "All in good time."

"Well, we've been *waiting* to hear from you," Ben told him.

"We thought you just *might* call," Mom Daly said.

Pete and Rose nodded their agreement.

Glenn glanced at his watch, and then turned his gaze significantly to the stairway. "Look, it's almost noon. I've been on planes all night and early this morning. I need to get up to my room, take a shower and get cleaned up. I need to get downtown to turn in my resignation."

"You're going to quit?" Ben asked.

"It must have turned out well for you," Rose declared. "That's nice."

"Then, you got a good price, did you?" Pete asked.

"Nope. Not gonna sell. Gonna move to the Caribbean and become a sailor."

There was a very long period of silence.

"Well, I'll be damned," Rose said at last. She winced, embarrassed by her profanity.

"That's well said, Rose," Pete agreed cheerfully, clapping Glenn on the shoulder. "By George, I didn't know you had it in you."

"Have you thought this through, Glenn?" Mom Daly said, worry on her face. "I'm not sure—"

"Just a few days ago, you were all on me for being a wimp," Glenn cut in. "You're looking at the new me."

Mom Daly started to protest. "But there are so many things—"

"Gotta go," Glenn cut her off again with an apologetic gesture, and then started toward the stairs. "We'll talk about it tonight."

■ ■ ■

"Where've you been?" the cross girl, Jody, asked. "You weren't here for a couple of days."

"Out of town," Glenn replied. He opened the belly drawer of his desk to survey its contents. He picked up a couple of small items, reconsidered, then tossed them back in.

"Simmons wants to see you, soon as you come in," she told him, a smug smile on her face.

Glenn ignored her.

"In his office," she said, emphasizing her words. "Just as soon as you come in."

"Thank you," Glenn responded without looking up, opening a second drawer of his desk.

"Here he comes," the girl said, enjoying her malice. She turned back to her desk, making a show of efficiency.

"Hathaway!" Simmons called as he came to a stop several feet away. "My office! Now!"

Glenn opened a third drawer.

"Hathaway, I need to speak to you in private," his supervisor commanded.

"We can talk here," Glenn said pleasantly.

Jody dropped her busy pose and turned to listen.

Men and women, at nearby desks, came about as well.

Simmons took a few steps forward. "Hathaway, this isn't something—"

"We can talk here," Glenn repeated.

Simmons walked to an arm's length. "This could be embarrassing for you, Hathaway," he said in a softer voice. "Perhaps we could—"

Glenn closed the third drawer with a bang, and opened the top one on the other side. "What exactly did you want to talk about, Mr. Simmons?"

Mr. Simmons stood silent for several seconds.

"Very well," the supervisor said in almost a whisper. "We're having to downsize our operation and so we've drawn up a list of terminations—"

"Am I being terminated, Mr. Simmons?" Glenn asked loudly, turning to face his overseer.

An outer perimeter of men and women forgot their work, standing and looking to see what was going on.

"You're disrupting the whole office," Simmons whispered angrily. "I won't have this!"

"Is that effective immediately?" Glenn asked loudly.

"You're out of here!" Simmons shouted in a sudden fury. "Clear out your desk and leave!"

"Nothing in there that I want or need," Glenn responded, gesturing to the desk, and then raised a stentorian voice. "Clear it out yourself, you bureaucratic baboon!"

The entire room turned to stone.

Simmons glared, apoplectic, finding speech impossible. He glanced this way and that; suddenly appearing insignificant and vulnerable in his domain. Thoroughly cowed, he walked away, increasing his stride as he sped to and sought the sanctuary of his private office.

"What the hell did you do," Jody asked. "Inherit a million?"

"Something like that," Glenn said as he opened and closed the last drawer.

"Maybe we could get together and have a drink?" she suggested, showing a seldom seen smile.

Glenn cocked his head at her and walked away. As he headed toward the exit door to join a moving cluster of shift-leaving employees, a smattering of hand clapping began at the distant reaches of the large room, and then swelled into booming applause as the entire throng of telephone touts rose to their feet, uttering whistles and shouts of approval. Glenn paused at the door, turned with an acknowledging salute, and then went out into the tenth floor hallway.

It was quitting time for many, and the hallway was gathering with people. As the doors of a descending elevator slid open, there was barely room for Glenn to squeeze into the crowded car. As the doors slowly closed, he spied a couple of his former workmates hurrying down the hall, their faces showing disappointment at being shut out.

Wanted to know what I was all about, he surmised with self-satisfaction.

Being fired bothered him not one whit. Briefly, he pondered whether or not he would even come in later for whatever severance pay might be due him; it would be but a pittance. More than likely, he wouldn't take the trouble. Perhaps a paltry check would be mailed to his present address or to the charter address in the Caribbean.

At the bottom floor, as the elevator doors opened to disgorge the passengers, he stepped out in the lead. This day, his stride was brisk, his upbeat manner quite notable for a downsized and discharged nobody. He crossed the lobby, pushed through the entrance doors, then turned and headed toward his regular bus stop. A small crowd had already collected and Glenn, intending not to be last this time, edged through the group to be among the first to board.

All heads were turned, eyes searching the distance street for a not-yet-visible city bus. The narrow roadway, once with only single lanes heading in opposite directions, had been converted to a double-lane one-way avenue. With few traffic-light intersections along this way, each spaced far apart, this section of the street often became a rather perilous raceway, especially at the rush hour. The posted 40 miles-per-hour speed limit was blatantly exceeded, and any foolhardy pedestrian who dared to cut across was at high risk

Close buildings and narrow sidewalks in this older part of the city posed another problem: There was no room for a turn-in area at the bus stop. When the bus did arrive and stop for passenger-loading, it would bring traffic to a halt behind it, frustrating trailing drivers, and causing dangerous swerving actions. Horns would blare, and even shouts of anger would be heard as the unconcerned people at the bus stop would slowly amble aboard.

Impatient at the front of the waiting pack, Glenn leaned far forward to peer around the other leaners, close enough to the traffic to feel the whoosh of each speeding vehicle that passed. As a fast moving auto opened a wide gap between it and a slower, wide-bodied dump truck, Glenn felt a powerful thump against his back which knocked him staggering onto the street and into the path of the onrushing behemoth.

The alert driver veered the huge rig toward the adjacent lane, and Glenn lunged backward in a desperate leap for life. He twisted his torso in midair, bending away from the speed- ing steel of the truck as it hurtled by, only inches from his face and upper torso. Even so, he felt the ripping metal graze, scrape, and gouge his left shoulder and arm. Amidst screams and shouts, amongst sounds of screeching tires and crashing metal, he slammed down, half in the gutter and half across the curb at people's feet. As the truck rushed on into a sideswip- ing pileup, he rolled away; helping hands reaching down to drag him to safety. For a few more seconds, the hullabaloo of the traffic calamity and strident outcries continued.

Then, an eerie silence reigned.

"Are you hurt?" a young woman stooped down, her anx- ious face close to his.

"Who pushed me?" Glenn answered and sat up, examin- ing the bloody wounds under the torn and gory sleeve of his shirt.

"Me, in a way, I guess, I didn't mean to," she admitted. "Someone bumped into me, real hard . . . I thought I was a goner, too." She frowned at the sight of his injuries. "You need a doctor."

"Looks worse than it is." Glenn declared, his finger exploring the lacerations. "Just minor cuts and scratches." He looked up at the people crowding around him. "Who pushed her?"

"Some guy trying to get up front, I reckon," a man said, his head turning one way, and then another. "Don't see him now."

"Probably embarrassed," a different woman opined.

"Bullshit!" the crouching young woman exclaimed. "I think the bastard did it on purpose."

With the help of a pair of young men, Glenn was assisted to his feet. He nodded his thanks, assured them of his well-being, and then looked at the traffic chaos that his spill had created. The dump truck had skidded sideways and, along with a pair of crumpled cars, was blocking traffic. The entire street was at a standstill and it appeared to be a blockade which would take considerable time before it was cleared. People were out of their damaged cars, walking around them with dismay, shaking their heads at what they saw.

"Anybody hurt?" Glenn asked.

"Fender benders from what I can see," one of the young men declared, looking into the street's turmoil.

"How about you?" the young woman repeated, nodding at his torn and bloodied shirt.

"Bumps and scrapes, nothing serious," Glenn said again, reexamining the wounds.

Police cars arrived and, methodically, the uniformed officers began to assess and resolve the traffic chaos. Damaged car positions were noted and swift actions were taken to open a single lane to relieve the congestion, cars waved through one by one. One police officer came to interview the bus stop witnesses where a dozen different stories were given as to the near fatal event. Glenn and the young woman told the facts of the matter to which the officer gave a sympathetic shrug, yet voiced little hope of finding the culprit. Another officer produced a first aid kit and treated Glenn's wounded arm and shoulder.

"Have a doctor look at that," the second policeman said as he pressed a taped bandage over the raw flesh.

"I'll do that," Glenn agreed. "And thanks."

"I think I see the bus," a voice announced.

"It'll take a while before it gets here," an old man said. "Ain't gonna go nowheres 'til they get this mess cleaned up."

"I think I'll treat myself to a cab," Glenn said.

"Big spender," the old man cackled.

"Which way you going," a man asked. "Maybe we can share."

7

"Land-a-Goshen!" Mom Daly exclaimed as she opened the screen door for him. Her eyes were fixed on the bandages beneath the torn and bloody shirt, and then flicked up to watch the taxicab moving away. "What in the world happened?"

"Nothing serious," he said, limping past her on his way to the stairs.

"Looks serious enough to hafta take a taxi home," she persisted as she followed him up the steps. "You should have that looked after by a doctor,"

"I gotta change clothes," he told her, entering his room and closing the door behind him.

Mom Daly badgered him through the door. "Did someone at work do that to you?"

"Tripped and fell!" he lied loudly. "It's just a scratch, I'm just fine!"

"Young man, your age," she clucked. "Falling down's for old folks, not young 'uns who ought to be light on their feet."

"Be with you in a minute!" he bellowed. He stripped out of his torn and bloody clothes, and then selected a clean shirt and khaki trousers from the closet. He dressed quickly, approved his image in a mirror, and then reached for a glossy booklet inside his open suitcase.

"I'm just fine," Glenn insisted once again, as he opened the door and found her waiting. "And I'll watch my step, like you say.

"Whatcha got there?" she asked, nodding to the pamphlet in his hand.

"Something for you all to see," he told her as they walked down the steps.

At the bottom of the stairs, the boarding house tenants were gathered in the living room. Brushing aside their questions about his injuries, Glenn quickly passed around the profusely illustrated pamphlet extolling the virtue of a chartered sail aboard the schooner, *Lady Ruth*.

"It's absolutely gorgeous!" Rose said in wonderment, handling the color brochure of the ship as though a delicate treasure. "It's so big, so graceful, so beautiful."

"Yes, it is, Rose," Glenn acknowledged, gently taking the brochure from her possessive hands and passing it on to Betty. "And it's a new way of life for me. I have all of you to thank for getting me to get off my . . ."

He glanced at Mom Daly who gave him a broad and permissive smile.

". . . off my butt to do something exciting."

"Truth is, I never thought you had it in you," Jean said. "Sure surprised me."

"Surprised me, too, Jean," Glenn responded.

"How soon are you going to leave us?" Ben wanted to know.

"Three or four days," Glenn replied. "Settle some bills, make arrangements at my bank, change of address and all. I've taken care of my work situation."

"I don't know, Glenn," Mom Daly said wistfully. "After all, this has been your home for such a long time."

"And far past the time where I should make my mark in the world if I'm ever to do so," Glenn said soothingly. "I'll keep in touch, and come back to visit on a regular basis."

"Just see that you do," she said, dabbing the tail of her apron at her glistening eyes.

"I'm proud of you, boy," Pete exclaimed. "Everybody would love to stick it to their boss."

"Pete!" Mom Daly spoke sternly.

"I didn't swear," Pete protested.

"Coarse, vulgar language," Rose interjected her opinion. "The way common people talk."

"Sometimes, Rose . . ." Pete sighed.

"Could we . . . I don't know if I should ask?" Betty stammered, her eyes fastened on the brochure.

"Come down for a cruise?" Glenn posed the question for her. "Of course. Once I get settled in, we'll have all of you down for a week, maybe two."

"Are you sure that will be all right?" Rose asked.

"Of course it will," Glenn assured her. "I own the ship, don't I?"

"Well, I just didn't know if it would be all right." she persisted.

"About those shipboard beds," Pete said. "What with my arthritis . . ."

"We'll take care of you, Pete," Glenn responded with a large smile. "We've got just the right accommodations."

"Hadn't you better call Mary Ellen?" Mom Daly asked, changing the subject.

Glenn frowned. "I guess so."

"You've been going with her for some time," Mom Daly persisted.

"Off and on," Glenn said without enthusiasm. "It's never been steady."

"It would only be proper," she said with upright conviction. "You owe the girl a notice that you won't be around."

"She didn't give me any notice when she started going with that car salesman," Glenn responded. "We were never very involved anyway."

"Still, it wouldn't hurt to give her a call."

Glenn shrugged.

"Promise?"

"Whatever."

Mom Daly rose from her easy chair, smoothed out her dress and gestured to the dining room. "We can continue to talk during dinner. We're having a special tonight in recognition of Glenn's new career at sea."

"What's the special?" Jean asked with obvious skepticism.

"Ham hocks and *navy* beans," Mom Daly said merrily as she headed for the kitchen. "Home-made corn bread, onion and cucumber salad . . . and Key Lime pie for dessert."

"Hmph," Ben grunted. "Same old menu."

"I know," Glenn said in a low voice. "But the pie's a nice variation."

8

At mid-morning on the following Sunday, Glenn struggled down the steps to the path to the long floating pier, a suitcase in one hand, and a large soft-side bag in the other. In these, he carried most all of his life possessions; clothing unsuitable for a Caribbean climate, important documents, photographs and memorabilia of his long-gone parents, a swim suit, and the assorted odds and ends of a uneventful existence. He walked toward the schooner moored at the end of the pier, his pace quickening as he moved, excitement growing. There was a heady anticipation of something new and adventuresome just ahead.

"Need any help?" a woman's voice called.

Glenn looked up as he reached the gangplank steps and saw Jenny, with a clipboard in her hand, standing on the deck at the gangway. A moment later, a sailor walked to the rail beside her, stone-faced as he looked down.

"I can manage," Glenn said. He walked up the gangplank and placed his bags on the deck.

"Welcome aboard," Jenny said without enthusiasm.

Somewhat sobered at her tone, Glenn glanced at the sailor, a physically powerful man with a hostile manner.

"This is Bobby Ruckman," Jenny said. "Member of the crew."

"Pleased to meet you," Glenn said, stretching out a hand. The crewman ignored the hand and walked away.

"Bobby!" Jenny called out. "Take care of the man's bags."

Without looking back, Ruckman disappeared down the forward hatch.

"Bobby's like that," the girl said in an awkward apology. "Don't let it bother you." She gestured to Glenn's luggage. "Bring your gear." She waited until Glenn picked up his bags, and then turned to lead the way toward the deckhouse.

Up ahead, the deckhouse door opened and Alain Tournaire stepped out, head down and preoccupied, not noticing the approaching pair.

"Captain!" the young woman called. "Our new owner is here!"

Tournaire, with a flash of scowling surprise, recovered quickly and smiled broadly "My dear *M'sieur* Hathaway," he said with a lift of his hand. "Most happy to have you aboard. I'm sorry I wasn't the first to welcome you, but we didn't know when you were coming." He made a sweeping gesture to the ship. "We have much to do, getting ready to sail."

"Speaking of sailing," Jenny said promptly, handing the clipboard to Tournaire, "we'll be piping our guests aboard soon. Within the hour."

Tournaire gave a slight nod of apology to Glenn as he examined the papers on the clipboard; a smile of satisfaction appearing. "*Oui,* an excellent charter. Our agent in Miami says she has had most of these people before. They spend and tip well." He continued leafing through the papers, and then handed the clipboard back to Jenny as he turned to Glenn. "The owner's stateroom is booked for a well-off couple from Chicago." He hesitated. "*M'sieur,* that is rightfully your accommodation. Since you have arrived, we shall move them—"

"I've thought it over," Glenn cut in. "I'd like to get a working knowledge of how a sailing ship operates. I thought there'd be no better way to learn than to be a member of the crew."

"A member of the crew?" Jenny was taken aback.

"Absolutely," Glenn responded.

"*Vraiment!*" Tournaire exclaimed, floundering a bit. "There's no *raison* for you to do anything other than to enjoy—"

"Please!" Glenn interrupted. "I insist. I'd like to learn the ropes, if you will . . . and could you just start calling me Glenn?"

For a moment, Tournaire hesitated. "*Certainment, M'sieur* Glenn."

"No, just Glenn."

"*Oui* . . . Glenn."

Jenny gave Glenn a *what-the-hell* shrug.

"Now," Glenn said. "Where do we start?"

Again, Tournaire started to protest, but Jenny spoke first. "He can help me in the galley, Alain." She turned her full attention to Glenn. "Can you cook?"

Glenn shrugged.

"Make beds?"

"Yeah, I suppose," Glenn responded. "But that sorta sounds like a—"

"Cabin boy?" the girl said with a mocking smile. "Of course, if you feel it's beneath—"

"Oh, no, no," Glenn said quickly. "That's fine. Anything's fine."

"After all," she continued. "You *are* the owner."

"What do I do first?"

"Come with me," she commanded. "Let's get you settled in one of the deluxe—"

"No," he cut in. "I'll work as a crewman. I'll sleep where the crew sleeps."

"You are making the joke?" Tournaire questioned.

Glenn shook his head. "Not at all. Call it starting at the deckhand's level, to get the feel of how everything works. How else could I be a good owner, and not understand what's important and what is not?"

Tournaire rolled his eyes while the young woman regarded Glenn with a quizzical stare.

"You *are* a puzzle, Mr. Hathaway," she said.

"It's Glenn, remember?"

"Okay, Glenn," she said. "We've got a lot of work to do. I'll take you down to the crew's quarters . . . if that's really what you insist upon. You're the boss." She turned and headed for the forward hatch.

Glenn gave Tournaire a nod and followed the girl, moving up to walk beside her.

"What happens when the passengers arrive?" he asked.

"We need to bring aboard their luggage and get them settled in their assigned cabins. They'll want to know where things are, and we have to help them get acquainted with the ship."

"I can carry," he volunteered.

As they reached the hatch, she led the way down the ladder. At the bottom of the steps, she opened the door, and waved Glenn to follow her into the crew's quarters.

It was a rectangular, steel-walled cabin, nearly the bow-width of the ship, with double bunks, four on each side of the entryway, and a bank of lockers on either side of a central storage area door. Glenn was brought up short at the sight of Ruckman, lounging in only his briefs, on the top bunk to his left. The sailor gave him a malevolent glance, and then returned his gaze to the raw sex magazine held in his hands.

"You can sleep here," Jenny said, gesturing to an upper bunk adjacent to Ruckman's.

Glenn looked at a lower level bed. "How about that one?"

"Taken, but there's a couple of empties, take your pick," she replied. She pointed to the storage compartments. "And your gear goes in one of those lockers over there."

"How many crew people you have aboard?"

"Five," she answered. "Six, with you."

She crossed to and opened a locker and, to Glenn's complete surprise, stripped out of her wrinkled t-shirt, then her shorts. She unfastened her bra, dropped it to the bottom of the locker, and then stepped out of her bikini panties. She turned her back to Glenn as she took another pair from the locker.

"You live in here?" Glenn asked in amazement.

"Opens up a cabin for paying customers," she said over her shoulder. "You have shorts?"

"I do," he answered.

"Change into them and grab one of our shirts, and then meet me on deck," she instructed as she turned to face him, unconcerned at her nudity. "You know how to mix drinks?"

Glenn didn't answer.

"Well?"

"Yeah, I guess," Glenn said, not quite recovered from his astonishment. "I guess so. Nothing too exotic." He glanced up at Ruckman who was totally absorbed in magazine nudes rather than to observe the close-at-hand real thing.

Jenny stepped into and pulled up the bikini panties. "That's probably good enough. They're usually ready for their first cocktails about an hour or so after they come aboard."

"You live in here? With us?" Glenn repeated, unable to look away.

"Sure, this is crew's quarters."

Chuckling, she took a skimpy brassiere from her locker. She settled her breasts into the bra, reached both hands behind her back to fasten the hooks. "I generally wear this rig the first day or so. Some of the women who come aboard are quite proper at first." She gave Glenn a wide smile. "I usually have these prim ladies skinny-dipping by the end of the week."

She continued dressing, putting on a white blouse with bright blue embossed sailing ship emblem, and, then a wrap-around blue skirt that gave her an attractive and surprisingly modest appearance.

The door to the cabin opened and a wiry, energetic black man entered, immediately flashing an engaging smile to the newcomer.

"Oh, William, this is Glenn Hathaway," Jenny said. "The owner we've been expecting. Glenn, this is William Walther."

"Most pleased, sah," the man answered in English with a clipped, deliberate speech manner.

"Mr. Walther," Glenn acknowledged. "Do they call you Bill?"

"No, sah, *mon*," he responded. "They call me William. You live in masta's cabin?"

"No, I'm moving in here," Glenn told him. "I'm going to be a part of the crew."

William regarded Glenn with an uncomprehending grin. "Yes, sah, *mon*."

"You don't need to call me 'sir.'"

"Yes, sah, *mon*."

Jenny finished combing her hair and turned to leave, pausing to point her finger at Ruckman. "You! Get your nose outta the ass, and your ass outta the sack!"

Ruckman gave her a look even more threatening than his usual scowl, and slowly rolled out of the bunk. He walked toward his locker, opened it, and took out clean clothing. "I'll be up in a minute," he said to Jenny, his high-pitched voice unexpected in such an imposing physique.

"Get dressed and meet me on deck," she said to Glenn as she went through the door.

Glenn gave a look around at the austere quarters that he'd insisted upon sharing, and wondered at that decision.

■ ■ ■

Tournaire touched the button on his cell phone and listened impatiently to the ring signals

"This is Johann Gravendeel," came the obsequious voice. "How may I help you?"

"It's me!" Tournaire snapped. "He's here!"

"Who?"

"Hathaway, that's who!"

There was a long silence, then: "I'm astonished."

"You were not told?" Tournaire questioned. "That they had failed?"

"I hadn't heard at all!" Gravendeel exclaimed. "I just assumed—"

"Assumed! Assumed wrong!" Tournaire jeered. "He's here, damn it, and now he's planning to live on the ship!"

"Oh, my!"

"What do we do?"

Again, there was a long silence.

"What *do* we do?" Tournaire said again.

"Do what you must. But, be careful. It must be done before—"

"I know, I know," Tournaire interrupted angrily. "An accident."

"We will discuss it in private, not on the phone," Gravendeel said, suddenly cautious.

"There's no time for talking! We're ready to sail," Tournaire contended. "Even now, guests are coming aboard."

"Then . . . as soon as you return."

"It's foolish to wait," Tournaire argued.

For a few moments, there was no response, and then, "Perhaps you are right. Do what you must."

9

A little after noon, a small bus from the airport arrived at the parking space at the dry end of the long pier where Glenn, William and Bobby were waiting at the bottom of the steps, each with a large handcart. Jenny was the first to step out of the bus and the passengers, twenty of them to Glenn's estimate, filed out and gathered around her at the top of the steps as she re-checked each of them against her clipboard list. The driver of the bus remained behind the wheel while two muscular young blacks emerged from the bus and started unloading suitcases and soft-sided bags.

"Okay, mateys! Follow me!" Jenny shouted, beaming her bright smile at the excited, chattering, casually-clad assemblage. "Come aboard as we sail into the best times and the biggest sailing adventure of your lives!"

A moment later, steel drum Caribbean music began playing from the ship.

With a wave of her hand, Jenny stepped down to the path, moving into sort of a dance step as she moved toward the ship, the passengers surging and undulating along behind her. Glenn stood for a moment, looking after the newcomers, noting that they were, mainly, young couples, ranging in age from middle-twenties to late thirties. He did spot a few men and women of a slightly older age, likely in their fifties., As they headed toward the ship, one woman, an attractive blonde showing off her body with a cutoff tank top and brief hip-hugger shorts, turned to look back at Glenn. It was an appraising look, her eyes seeking his.

Surprised and a bit embarrassed at the woman's impudent gaze, Glenn glanced away, then back again.

The woman laughed, then hurried along with the others.

"She interested in you, *mon*," William said with a wink. He made a gesture to the two blacks handling the luggage. "Thomas and Alfred," he said. "They crew on *Lady Ruth*." He signaled for their attention and gestured to Glenn. "Mista Glenn, he owns the ship."

The two crew members bobbed their heads and gave him slight smiles.

"Glad to meet you," Glenn told them.

"Same to you, *mon*," the one named Thomas responded dutifully.

The five men transferred the considerable luggage down the steps to the carts, stacking each one high and heavy. In addition to the large bags, there were vanity cases, scuba gear bags, camera and camcorder cases, and even a couple of golf bags. As they finished loading, Glenn glanced at the ship, seeing the passengers now on deck, clustered around Tournaire and Jenny. The volume of the steel drum music had been turned down, and Tournaire was making a faintly heard welcoming speech outlining the cruise schedule and planned pleasures. Thomas, Alfred and William steered the luggage carts toward the ship while Ruckman and Glenn, carrying scuba gear, walked along with them.

They formed a relay line up the gangplank to convey the luggage to the deck where William and Alfred sorted and neatly arranged the suitcases and bags. After the carts had been brought aboard and secured, Glenn and the other members of the crew turned their attention to the welcoming ritual.

"I'm presuming that you've all tagged your luggage," Jenny was saying. "The crew will take your things to your cabins. You might want to take a few minutes to make sure that all of your belongings have arrived. We'll give you some time to follow your luggage to your assigned staterooms. After you've had a chance to settle in, say an hour from now, we invite you to the aft deck where we've prepared a welcome aboard party, with your choice of drinks and some very nice hors d'oeuvres."

"We will put out to sea this afternoon," Tournaire informed them. "The weather is fair and we have been promised a magnificent Caribbean sunset."

"And for that fair weather promise," Jenny said, "this evening, we'll be serving an al fresco dinner at seven bells, right here on deck so that you can enjoy that spectacular Caribbean sunset our captain has guaranteed." She checked her watch. "See you for cocktails in just about an hour."

The passengers resumed their chattering, some moving immediately to identify their luggage while others remained clustered around Jenny and Tournaire, the women seeking advice on appropriate dress for the evening, some of the men asking questions about the ship. With Ruckman conspicuously absent, William, Thomas, and Alfred helped various couples to identify luggage. Joining them, Glenn began to sort and place bags and other items together according to the tags.

The blonde woman from the dock stepped in front of him. Up close, she was slightly older than he'd thought, mid-thirties. Still, she was a woman worth admiring. "I think these are mine," she said, sliding a bag away from Thomas over to Glenn. "This one, that one, and that little one over there."

Glenn caught the grin from Thomas who quickly turned away to assist another couple. "Just these three?" he asked.

"No," she replied. "Two more, but we'll let Marvin bring those down."

Glenn glanced around, seeing three men in earnest conversation with Tournaire.

"That's him," the blonde told him, with an indicating nod of her head. She sighed. "The fussy one with the love handles."

Glenn noted a portly man who seemed to be in an argument with the captain.

"We'll get them all to the cabin, ma'am," Glenn told her. He looked carefully at the tags on one of the suitcases. "Mr. and Mrs. Marvin Lusk?"

"Jo Ann, darling," she said sweetly. "We're all on first name basis, now, aren't we?"

"Yes, ma'am," Glenn answered.

"And your name?"

"Glenn."

She swung her head slowly, sweeping her gaze across the expanse of the ship, then back to look him over. "I can just guess that we're gonna have a really great time."

"We hope so, ma'am," Glenn said. He tucked the smaller suitcase under his left arm, carrying the other two, one in each hand. "May I show you to your cabin?"

"Yeah, but you gotta call me Jo Ann, remember?" she said. "You just lead the way, darling."

"Is your husband coming?"

"Sooner or later," she answered.

Glenn started toward the forward hatch, the blonde following.

"My, you sure are white for being down here in all this sun," she exclaimed as they started down the hatch ladder.

"I'm new, just arrived myself," he answered, leading the woman down the companionway, bumping the luggage against the bulkheads. "Number nine," he announced, checking the cabin numbers against a luggage tag. "Here you go." He put the bags down and opened the door, stepping back to allow the woman to enter. She sauntered into the room, aghast at the undersized accommodations. "Bunk beds! You're outta your fucking mind!"

Glenn didn't comment.

"What the hell is this?" she demanded. "Do all of the rooms have bunk beds?"

"No ma'am," Glenn said lamely, "Just this one, our economy accommodation."

"Cheapest one on the boat?"

"I believe so," Glenn ventured.

"I'll kill him," she shrilled. "I'll . . . what do you call it? Deep-six him?"

"Who, ma'am?"

"My husband, the world's biggest cheapskate, who else? He booked this closet?"

"I suppose so," Glenn conceded.

"Can we upgrade?"

"I suppose not, ma'am," Glenn answered. "I think we're fully booked.

"Just put those damned bags down anywhere," she said churlishly, moving to look out the porthole. "I don't know what possessed Marvin to book this tiny rat hole on this scow."

"Well, it's a sailing ship, ma'am . . . I mean, Jo Ann," Glenn explained. "You don't spend a lot of time in the cabins."

"Well, some things you don't necessarily want to do on deck, darling," she said, giving him a brazen look. She moved to the lower bunk and sat down.

"I'll get your bags, and the other ones, too," Glenn told her and placed the luggage inside. "Anything else, ma'am?"

Jo Ann didn't answer for a moment, then laid back and stretched out on the lower bunk. "I wonder . . . should I be on top? Or, on the bottom?"

Glenn stepped out and closed the door behind him, startled to see Ruckman standing in the companionway, watching him.

"Something you need from me?" Glenn asked.

Ruckman made no answer as he shouldered past, an act that seemed more deliberate than accidental.

As Glenn came on deck, Jenny was waiting, a smirk on her face. "I see you've already made a friend," she said. "A really *good* friend."

"I think she's going to be trouble," Glenn responded.

"I can't tell you what to do, but do be careful," Jenny admonished. "We don't need any jealous husbands in a rage during our cruise."

"This happen often?"

"More likely than not. There are always some women looking for something new, somebody new," she told him. "With me, I'm usually fighting off the husbands." She allowed a small chuckle. "Usually, the swingers don't make their moves until a little later in the week."

"Lucky me," he said.

"Get 'em settled and meet me in the galley. We've got a party to set up."

Glenn assisted a very young couple with their baggage, escorting them to Cabin Five. There was no problem with the female of this union. These two were so entwined with each other that Glenn assumed them to be newlyweds, anxious to get into their cabin, and to get Glenn out of it.

He wondered if they'd be at the cocktail party.

When he brought the remaining luggage to the Lusk state-room, the man with the love handles answered his knock on the door. "Just put 'em down," the man said brusquely. "You looking for a tip?"

"No, sir," Glenn said, easing the bags past the man into the room. "Welcome aboard."

Behind him, Jo Ann was still on the lower bunk. She wiggled her right foot in sort of a wave.

"This sure ain't the Queen Mary," the man complained.

"No, sir," Glenn acknowledged. "But I think you'll find us something more than an ordinary cruise."

"I doubt it," Lusk grouched. "You got any good liquor?"

"Top brands," Glenn assured him. "See you topside." He turned and walked away.

10

The welcome aboard cocktail party on the aft deck began with a resumption of recorded music, calypso and salsa rhythms throbbing over the harbor. Within five minutes, most all of the guests were in attendance. At a small bar at the rear of the deckhouse, Jenny and William were mixing and pouring the drinks, while Glenn roamed among the passengers and served the appetizers. The mood of the passengers was vibrant; an atmosphere of keen anticipation. Guests mingled, getting acquainted, telling about themselves, discovering common interests. As time passed, the conversations became louder, with laughter erupting increasingly from group to group.

Glenn got a suggestive nod from Jo Ann, but her attention was now centered on a bare-chested young Adonis who was explaining his importance in a New York brokerage. Marvin Lusk was wandering from group to group, attempting conversation with little response, and then moving on while recurrently supping his drink.

"When do we wrap up?" Glenn asked Jenny.

"Soon," she responded, nodding at the meandering Marvin. "Watch him, he's on his fourth or fifth."

"Cut him off?"

"I'll take care of it," she told him. "I think he can be a nasty drunk."

"He wasn't particularly nice sober," Glenn said.

"Shipmates!" Jenny called out. "Last call for drinks! We're going to be getting the ship ready to sail! Now would be a good time for you to go to your cabins, to put things away, perhaps to freshen up. As always on this cruise, casual is the proper attire, but if you want to change for dinner, this might be your best opportunity. Putting out to sea and setting sail aboard the *Lady Ruth* is a spectacular experience, and I urge you to be on deck to see it all."

A couple of men came over to refill their drinks, although most began drifting toward the aft hatch. Not surprisingly, Marvin came to the bar proffering his empty glass. "Hit me again . . . scotch, no water."

"We're serving a very nice selection of wines at dinner," Jenny told him, capping liquor bottles, wiping down the surface of the bar.

"Glad to hear it," Lusk said. "The refill if you please."

"Sorry, gotta close," Jenny said. She took the glass and handed it off to Glenn, then stepped out from behind the bar and came around to tuck her arm under his, cozying up to him as she walked him to the hatch. "I've got to get to the galley and start dinner for you all." She gave him a pat on the hand as she guided him down to the first steps of the hatch. "Bye, now."

Lusk stood for a moment on the upper steps, and then descended out of sight.

"Nicely done," Glenn complimented.

"A tit against the arm will usually do the trick," she told him without so much as a smile. "It does get their minds off the booze. Come on."

In the galley, Glenn was surprised to see a dark-skinned woman working, taking packages of food from the large refrigerator unit. She was a short, heavy woman with long braided hair. Despite her considerable girth, her movements were swift and sure.

"Glenn, this is Gretchen," Jenny said. "She helps me with our first meal when we're here in port."

"Hello," Gretchen said as she stretched out her hand. "So very happy to meet you, sir."

Glenn took her hand. "Thank you, Gretchen. It's nice to meet you, too."

"I don't sail on the ship, no, sir, mister," she told him, a sly smile coming. "I'm too heavy for the ship. They think I sink it if I lean over the side."

Jenny and Gretchen laughed at what must've been a familiar joke, and Glenn joined in.

"Gretchen gets the meal started while I'm busy up on deck," Jenny explained in her matter-of-fact way. "This initial meal is very important. It's the first impression of the quality of our cuisine, and that sets the belief that we *do* offer a top notch cruise." She swept her hand toward Gretchen's food preparations. "We buy the best steaks, the best chickens, the best fish and seafood." She walked to the stove. "We cook everything, no microwave entrees." She gave Gretchen an affectionate pat on the arm. "Gretchen, bless her, could be a head chef in a high class restaurant if she wanted."

"Ha!" Gretchen gave a snort, yet she was obviously pleased at the praise. "Nice lady, but she tells big stories."

"Your aunt used to help with the meals whenever she was aboard," Jenny told Glenn. "However, I'm the cook when we're at sea, and I have Alfred help me. He's okay when we're fixing light meals and snacks. When, or if, we stop over at a couple of certain islands, I can call up some cooks I know to come aboard. They're not nearly as good as Gretchen, but they're good enough to get the job done."

Shortly after five o'clock, Gretchen stopped what she was doing, gathered her belongings, and waved goodbye.

Minutes later, Glenn felt a slight tremble in the hull.

"We're leaving port," Jenny told him, and then added, "You ought to go out and watch."

Glenn hurried from the galley, through the companionway, and out onto the deck. The ship was slowly moving, the diesel engine easing it away from the dock. Passengers were coming on deck to watch as the *Lady Ruth* gathered speed. At the on-deck helm, Tournaire's hands were on the large wheel, guiding the ship very close to the shoreline of the island. The swift passage along the island perimeter seemed reckless as they passed a beach, the sunbathers only twenty yards away. Young men and women stood up to wave, so close it was easy to see their smiles, and to clearly hear their voices as they called out good wishes for a pleasurable voyage.

"Aren't we too damned close?" a young passenger asked, worry on his face. "Won't we run aground?"

"There's deep water right below us," Glenn said, glad that he'd learned something about Curacao. "The island was formed by a volcanic eruption. It's like a giant mushroom rising up from the ocean floor."

"Do those people on the beach know that?"

"A few feet into the water, they'd better know how to swim," Glenn told him.

For a few more minutes, the ship skimmed past the shoreline of the island, then turned toward the open sea. Ruckman, William, Alfred and Thomas appeared and moved to separate stations on deck. Ruckman and Alfred unfastened the canvases for the main mast, while William and Thomas unfurled the sails at the foremast. After a few seconds, with the whine of the power winches, the sails began to unfold, rising in unison to full height. The taller main mast supported the triangular main sail that rose above the aft deck as well as a smaller foresail and the topmost fisherman's sail amidships. The shorter foremast bore the lines that carried the staysail fastened to the bow stem and the jib sail attached to the bowsprit.

As the noise of the winches ceased, the big ship slowed as the diesel was cut and the overwhelming sounds were those of the ocean waves against the hull and the slapping of the sails as the wind began to fill them. The ship turned and the sails billowed with loud snapping reports that transmitted into the steel masts creating eerie pinging sounds. The ship smoothly gained speed, a gliding motion rather than the steady thrust of the propeller.

Those on deck let out audible sighs of delight and wonder, and so did Glenn. The transformation to sail was an awesome experience and he wondered if it would ever cease to be.

He could not imagine so.

■ ■ ■

As the low sun sparkled the gentle waves of the Caribbean, Glenn and Alfred helped Jenny to prepare for the first evening meal. Navy-blue linen tablecloths were placed on the tables in the U-shaped dining area on the aft deck, tucked and secured against the wind. Next came the place settings of tableware, glassware and cloth napkins. Each passenger's name, inserted in a small rosewood holder, designated his or her seating assignment. Miniature hurricane lanterns were brought to the tables, touched to flame, and left to glow in the evening shadows.

"We arrange the guests by couples on the first night," Jenny explained to Glenn. "This is the closest to formal as we get. Informality is really the big thing on sailing cruises."

Shortly before the dinner hour, the guests began to arrive, each couple standing at the rail to look at the sunset, waiting for others to appear before taking their places at the tables. Although the proclamation for the cruise stressed casual, most of the women were dressed more for Vegas than for sailing; bare backs and deep cleavages seemed the norm. The men were much less formal. All were wearing crisply pressed shorts and tropical shirts. Mr. and Mrs. Lusk were late arrivals, Jo Ann wearing white lounging pajamas that emphasized her deep tan. She gave everyone a pleasant greeting, her glance at Glenn showing none of her previous lasciviousness. She and her mister were seated directly across from the newlyweds who came out of their entwinements to enter a conversation with them.

Glenn and Alfred moved among the guests with aperitif wines, filling small glasses with sherries and vermouths.

Marvin Lusk was the sole complainer, insisting on straight scotch.

"Is it true that we have to help sail the ship?" a worried young woman asked Glenn. "Could you tell us how?"

Before he could answer, her wiseass husband gave him a wink. "Sure, baby, that's why we're here. To learn how to sail."

"The cabins are really small," a thirty-plus, over-sized male exclaimed. "Don't folks roll off those itty-bitty beds?"

"How long have you two been married?" Jo Ann was asking the honeymooners.

"Three days," the bride answered.

"Still on the missionary position or have you discovered other pleasures?"

Glenn badly overfilled Jo Ann's glass with vermouth.

Dinner was superb. The appetizer was a fresh fruit compote accompanied by a sparkling Chilean white wine. Salad was bib lettuce, radicchio, baby spinach, and Stilton cheese topped with a champagne-and-thyme vinaigrette. A blackberry and pinot noir sorbet was served to clear the palate. Then came the entrée; fillet of sea bass encrusted with black pepper. Red and white wines accompanied the meal, and dessert was a choice between brandied peaches or a generous glass of cognac.

Marvin Lusk chose the latter.

The meal was an achievement, but the main subject of attention was the setting sun with its ever-changing display of cerulean blue's, shades of red's, and gleaming gold's; all playing upon the billowing clouds. As the banquet progressed, as darkness replaced the splendors of sunset light, the laughter and the bonhomie of the passengers became a blending of budding friendships. No longer were they strangers. They were now becoming first name acquaintances, sharing personal histories with those seated nearby, and exchanging pleasantries with others seated a little further away.

Glenn could see the camaraderie developing between certain people, and knew there would be cluster groups throughout the voyage. Glenn, Alfred, and Jenny worked quietly and efficiently, serving food and wine, clearing dishes, making their presence as unobtrusive as possible.

It was nearly ten o'clock when the dinner was finally finished. As sails were lowered and furled, and with the diesel running, some men and women strolled away to other parts of the ship, savoring the last of the splendid evening, while others retired to their individual cabins. In the galley, Alfred and Jenny loaded the last dishes in the washer, and then shooed Glenn out, the young woman indicating that he was more in their way than a help.

It was all right with him. He returned to the deck, moving to the starboard rail where he stayed for quite a while. The *Lady Ruth* was running soft and nearly silent through the gentle sea. The quietude was momentarily broken by the shuffling, burbling sounds of a very inebriated man, and an equally soused woman as they made their way to the aft hatch, the last guests to leave the deck. Even so, there was a certain charm to their intoxication, Glenn thought: a young couple much in love, having a wonderful time on their first sailing voyage. As they went below, he turned and was surprised to see Jenny standing behind him.

"Folks are having a good time," he ventured.

She nodded, leaning against the rail beside him, gazing out at the massive display of gleaming stars across the great vault of the dark blue sky. The starlight illuminated the glittering sea with caps of white foam on its gentle swells

"God!" Glenn said in a low voice. "It's beautiful, isn't it?"

Jenny gave a nod in answer.

"There are people in this world who'll never see this, who'll never know what I'm feeling, and what they're missing," he said

After a moment, Jenny spoke, "It isn't always beautiful. It can be angry . . . and dangerous."

"Right now, that's hard to imagine."

"There are a thousand things out there that can harm you, even kill you." She turned her back to the sea. "It killed your aunt."

Glenn turned. "Aunt Ruth, I barely remember her. What was she like?"

Jenny hesitated in her answer. "In some ways, she was very kind. She'd been around . . . a lot. She knew about the world, but she still had the capacity to care about people."

"I know a little about her," Glenn said. "I know some of the things that you're being very careful not to say. I know what she was or what they say she was."

"Don't think too little of her," Jenny said, her tone becoming defiant. "I do know that she was very much in love with Jack—"

"With him, or his money?" Glenn cut in.

"She was no saint, but she was honest about herself! Jack knew everything about her before he married her. Everything!"

Glenn lifted his hand, a gesture to soothe her annoyance, and then gave a shrug of apology. "I'm sorry, I shouldn't have said that. I guess I didn't really know her." He paused, and then spoke again, "I can only remember her when I was very small. She came to the house. It was Christmas, and she brought me roller skates. I remember that she was kind and very pretty. She smelled nice."

"And that was the only time?" Jenny asked. "You never saw her after that?"

Glenn shook his head. "I think there were cards, but my parents never talked about her."

"Ashamed of her?"

"I suppose."

"What do they think about her now? Now, that she's gone?"

"My parents are gone, too," Glenn told her. "Several years ago."

"You're all alone? No one else?"

"You sound like that guy, Gravendeel," Glenn said.

Jenny gave him a sharp look, then quickly turned back to look out at the sea.

"You know Gravendeel?" Glenn asked.

"Of him."

The mention of the deceitful lawyer brought an awkward pause between them. Then, Jenny took a step away, her brusque manner back in place. "I've got a few things yet to do," she said. "You'd better turn in soon."

"Anything I can help you with?"

She shook her head. "There's plenty for you to do tomorrow. Good night."

As she walked away, Glenn turned once again to gaze at the sea, his former rapture now greatly diminished. The ocean now seemed to have taken on a different appearance, grim and sinister, deep and dark, hiding menace beneath the cold, glittering canopy of stars.

He shook to rid himself of the mood, then walked to the aft hatch and went below.

11

Glenn felt a hand on his shoulder before dawn, Alfred reminding him it was time to prepare for the day. Glenn shaved and showered quickly, dressed, then hurried to the galley where Jenny was already at work. Within the hour, a breakfast buffet was laid out on the aft deck; toast and croissants, eggs, bacon, sausage, juices, Bloody Mary's, and lots of coffee.

Coffee, Bloody Mary's, and sweet rolls were also available in the library for those wanting lesser fare.

"They've had their last four-star meal aboard ship, like the one last evening," Jenny told him. "Although they'll still like what we serve."

The guests began arriving a little after six o'clock, some of them apparently early risers. Two couples remained in the library while others chose the aft deck dining area. All of the guests were now either in shorts or swimsuits, the ones on deck braving the surprising chill of the daybreak breezes.

"Leave the buffet," Jenny told him. "We'll check from time to time to make sure that the late sleepers have what they need."

"More galley duty?"

"You might see if you can give the other guys a hand."

"Learning the ropes?"

"They're called lines on a ship," she said, showing her first smile of the morning. "Don't let anybody hear you calling them ropes."

Glenn walked to the helm of the ship where Tournaire, Ruckman, and William were gathered in conversation at the wheel.

"*Bonjour*, Glenn," Tournaire greeted him. "Did you enjoy your first night at sea?"

"Immensely," Glenn responded. "Can you put me to work?"

Tournaire shrugged. "We will spend the entire day at sea. For a while, we will be cruising under sail. As the sun goes higher, we'll probably have a drop in the wind and need to run on diesel, and that will give us a chance to do some work on the rigging."

"Something wrong?" Glenn asked.

Tournaire cocked his head and shrugged. "Bobby told me there might be a problem with a sheave on the mainmast head."

Glenn widened his eyes.

"A wheel in the block at the top of the mast," Tournaire explained, pointing skyward.

Glenn looked up, noting a ladder-like series of affixed steel rungs on the mainmast leading all the way to its peak. "How do you fix it?"

"Just gotta fucking oil it," Bobby said in high-pitched disdain.

Glenn hesitated, wondering if his next question was going to draw another scornful answer. "You climb to get up there?"

"When the time comes, you can help Bobby," Tournaire told him. "He'll show you."

"And, in the meantime?"

"Come with me, sah," William said, with a wide smile and a nodding head. "I keep ship boss busy, you betcha."

"No calling me *sir*, William"

"Yes, sah, *mon*."

Glenn sighed, and fell into step with William as the sailor walked toward the ship's stern.

"Captain say show you things are, what they do," William said with solemnity. "Make you get sea legs."

"Good idea," Glenn agreed.

For the first few minutes, the native deckhand gave him a rundown of the ship's operation, including a reiteration of the wheelhouse convenience and function.

"Stay dry in the storms, sah," William told him.

"Rain a lot here?" Glenn asked.

"Caribbean rain, she come and go, soft and nice. No need stay in wheelhouse, feel good to cool off outside in rain."

For the next two hours, William and Glenn made a slow and careful examination of the stanchions, railings, and deck surface areas, looking for small patches of rust. William showed him how to grind away the spots of rust down to bare metal with a sanding power tool, then how to recoat the spots with white topside enamel.

"In sea air, wood she go rotten," William declared solemnly. "Metal, she always go rusty."

On the foredeck, Glenn moved to three adjoining white plastic bins, each five feet wide and waist-high. "What are these?"

"Watertight, open and see," William said.

Glenn unlatched the first to his left, and heard the slight sticking sound as he lifted the upper lid away from the rubber-strip seal. Inside, there were several coiled lines and a number of docking fenders, a couple of mops, and a pair of buckets.

He lowered the lid, latched it, and opened the middle storage bin which was imprinted with a large marker, *EMERGENCY*. The contents of this bin included several fire extinguishers, a bullhorn, a pile of life jackets and life preserver rings as well as a sizeable molded plastic container case labeled *FLARES*. He released both catches to open the deep case, and laid back the lid to reveal a pair of flare pistols, cartridges and hand-held flare sticks as well as a half-dozen jug-sized canisters.

"What this?" Glenn asked, picking up one of them.

"Careful, *mon*," William cautioned. "Float flare. Pull cord, maybe give you burn on hand, not careful . . . send pretty smoke up, jiffy quick, to bring help if ship in trouble."

"Speaking of the ship in trouble, where's our lifeboats if we need them?" Glenn asked as he replaced the canister with the others, closed the box, and latched the bin.

William pointed to the deckhouse. "Blow 'em ups on top. In roof boxes."

Glenn studied the compact storage containers atop a forward section of the deckhouse, and it took a few moments for Glenn to comprehend before he nodded. "Inflatables?"

William nodded. "Another blow 'em up down in locker 'low deck."

By mid-morning, everywhere on deck, the guests were in various stages of semi-nudity; women in bikinis, men bare-chested in slightly more modest swimming trunks. There was an occasional aroma of coconut oil wafting across the deck, everybody slathering on tanning lotions to prepare skins for frying.

As the tropical sun rose higher, Glenn looked up as the *Lady Ruth* turned into the light wind preparing to lower sails. William excused himself and hurried to assist Thomas with the forward sails while Ruckman and Alfred brought down the main. Glenn walked to the aft deck as the latter pair furled the sails in accordion-fashion, rolling the folds onto the booms and binding them securely. Glenn stood behind them, watching in fascination as the sailors worked in swift, synchronized motions. He rather yearned to take part in the effort, sure that he would screw it up if he tried.

A few minutes later, Ruckman was attaching a canvas bosun's chair to a line that fed up and over a pulley near the top of the main mast.

"Beats climbing the thing, I guess," Glenn said, nodding to the mast's ascension rungs. "You going up?"

Ruckman gave him a withering look, and shook his head. "You say you want to be one of us crew?" He held out an oil-can. "Give a squirt or two to everything that rolls up there." He paused, then added with obvious scorn, "Unless, of course, you'd want to be boss, and just as soon I do it."

Glenn looked to the top of the main mast, wondering how high it was.

Sixty feet? More?

"Just as soon I do it?" Ruckman asked again.

"No, that's okay," Glenn responded quickly. He looked at the skimpy sling. "What do I do?"

"Just stick your butt in there, and I'll give you a ride," Ruckman told him.

Several of the passengers gathered around them, aware that there was something different about to happen. Conscious of their attention, Glenn pulled the bosun's chair down, and then sat on the wide canvas strip that served as a seat. Ruckman touched a button on a small winch at the base of the mast and it began to whine. Using a variable speed control knob, he eased the canvas rig up, and lifted Glenn from the deck, the electric motor changing pitch as his full weight increased the load.

Despite Glenn's initial qualms, they quickly disappeared and a feeling of exhilaration came as he rose slowly, the winch-up giving him an escalating lofty view of the ship and the white-capped waves surrounding it. Below him, the passengers were diminishing in size as his distance from them increased. Halfway up the mast, he could swivel his bosun's chair fore and aft, looking down at the ship with his now omniscient view; creating a lift of spirit as well as that of his body. Above him, two tubular steel spreaders, one appreciably higher than the other, jutted out from each side of the mast to separate the cables that helped to support and balance it.

Finally, he was at the very top, and he turned his attention to the masthead. He examined the attached blocks at and near the top of the masthead; stainless steel shells with plastic wheels over which ran the lines that raised and lowered the sails. Glenn could see neither signs of damage nor rust in the axles of the sheaves and, with lines taut over them, there was no way he could rotate them.

He was leaning forward to oil the top sail block when the sling seat suddenly ripped free. He fell, flailing wildly, reaching for something and finding nothing. He fell almost fifteen feet before he caught the last spreader with both hands, the force of his fall sending a tremendous shock to his arms and shoulders. Pain surged through his upper body and, for a panicky moment, he thought he couldn't hold on. His right hand, wet with sweat from the tropical heat, slipped from the rounded steel shaft and he could barely cling with his left.

Below, there was an outcry in unison as the passengers reacted; a collective roar of alarm; screams and shouts.

Glenn felt his left hand fingers slipping. He tightened his tenuous hold and lunged upward, his right hand reaching for and missing the steel shaft. He lunged again and, this time, grasped the spreader. Daring to switch one hand to the opposite side, he gripped the shaft as tight as he could. Then, he turned his body toward the mast and inched his way to it, wrapping his legs around it. He scooted up close against the mast, and then reached one hand to the nearest ladder rung, then the other, shifting his body across, his left foot firm on a lower tread.

As a clamor of cheers and exhalations of relief soared up, Glenn looked down

Ruckman had moved out from under him, standing well away from the winch control, callously watching. Moments passed and then, casually, he strolled to the base of the mast and started the line down. When the ripped and useless canvas seat came down level with Glenn, the line suddenly stopped.

With a glance at the descending rungs on the mast, and another look down at a taunting Ruckman at the winch controls far below, Glenn reached for the line above the dangling yoke. He pulled it to him and, grasping it with both hands, swung his body onto the line and waited for the surly sailor to bring him down.

It was only a couple of minutes, but it seemed much longer before his feet touched the deck and the spectator applause erupted.

"Man, that was close," said one of the male passengers.

"That was fantastic," enthused a sunburned woman. "I thought you were a goner."

"So did I," Glenn admitted. He turned to Ruckman who was examining the broken bosun's chair. With a quick motion, the sailor cut the dangling canvas seat loose with his knife.

"I kinda wanted to look at that," Glenn said. "How the hell did that happen?"

Ruckman stepped to the rail and tossed the canvas strip over the side. "Rotten canvas. Just ripped loose at the side," he said. "No big deal."

Jenny had come from the galley at the sound of the commotion, and she pushed through the crowd. "What happened?"

"Nobody hurt," Ruckman said. "Little accident with our landlubber. He's okay."

"Are you?" she asked, turning to Glenn.

"I guess so," he said, then added, "Gave a bit of a show for our guests."

"You should have seen him," Jo Ann said in great admiration. "Caught one of those things up there or he'd been splattered all over the deck. Regular Tarzan, he was!"

"I was lucky," Glenn said, now examining his hands, seeing shreds of torn flesh in his palms.

Jenny looked at his hands, and then turned to the surrounding passengers. "Show's over, folks. Let me take Glenn down for a little doctoring and everything's just fine."

She waited until the passengers moved away, and then took Glenn's hands in hers. "We ought to put something on those."

"In a minute," Glenn said, taking his hands away. "There's something I need to do."

He turned abruptly and walked toward Ruckman at the rail, stepping in front of him to prevent him from leaving. "Something we need to settle, Bobby," he said. "Ever since I came aboard, you've been a pain in the ass. I may not be a sailor yet, but I've had enough of your comments. Remember I own this fucking ship and, if you want to stay on, learn how to treat me and everybody else with a hell of a lot more respect." He paused, and then added, "If you have a problem with that, we'll find you a way back to home port."

Ruckman bristled, balled his fists, and shrugged his shoulders as if preparing for to attack.

Jenny quickly stepped forward. "Bobby, get the hell out of here!"

The sailor's face showed no change of expression, but the eyes held menace, shifting from Glenn to Jenny, then back again. Without another word, he brushed past Glenn and strode away.

"What the hell happened?" Jenny wanted to know.

Glenn gestured to the top of the mast. "I was up there and the hoist broke."

"What were you doing up there anyway?" she asked, directing her anger at him.

"Hey, I was trying to be of help," Glenn responded, showing some anger himself. "And, why in the hell are you always bitching at me?"

Jenny didn't answer immediately, biting her lower lip. "I'm sorry," she said finally. "I guess this was quite a scare." She gave him a very small smile. "Glenn, it's just that a ship can be dangerous if you're not really familiar with this kind of life." She paused again. "Don't you really think you'd be better off just owning the ship and not trying to be a sailor?"

"And stay on land where it's safe?"

"Yeah, why not?"

"And that's another thing," Glenn told her. "You're not only unfriendly most of the time, you always act like you're trying to get me off the ship. Do I annoy you that badly?"

Jenny took her time in answering. "I think you're a nice guy, Glenn, but I'm concerned about you. You think you know what you're doing but . . ." She shook her head, not finishing.

"What exactly am I doing wrong?"

"Just watch your step," she told him, starting to walk away. "Be careful. Be very careful."

"Careful? Of what?" Glenn asked, but she was already moving toward the deckhouse and didn't look back.

12

Glenn shifted the tool kit to his left hand and rapped on the door of Cabin Nine with his right.

It opened immediately.

"You called and, ah, need something fixed?" Glenn asked.

"Well, aren't you Johnny-on-the-spot," Jo Ann purred. "I thought maybe they'd have you lying down somewhere, getting over your narrow escape and all." She stepped back and gestured for Glenn to enter.

Glenn moved into the cabin, looking around for her husband, really not surprised to find him absent. Jo Ann wore a brief swim outfit, a thong not quite hiding pubic hair, a narrow bra barely containing her ample breasts. She was still glistening from suntan oil with spots of new sunburn redness overlying her well-tanned body.

"What's the problem?" Glenn asked.

Jo Ann made a dismissive gesture at a panel door, partially open, on a hanging locker. "That thing, it won't stay shut."

Glenn moved to the locker, inspected the door, and reached for a screwdriver. "Catch needs tightening, that's all," he said, performing the task as he spoke. Finished, he turned to leave. "Looks like a screw kinda worked itself a little loose."

"Thank you, darling," Jo Ann said, stepping close, touching the hanger door, opening and closing it. "It just kept swinging back and forth, back and forth. You can't imagine how annoying that became." Her hand touched Glenn's bare shoulder. "I'll bet you have a lot of fun, don't you?"

"Fun?"

"You know, cruising around, meeting new people all the time . . . people that you can enjoy . . . and not having to worry about getting involved with them."

Glenn edged toward the door, but Jo Ann didn't move out of the way. Instead, she moved up against him. "Do you like me, Glenn?"

"Like you?" Glenn replied, stepping back against the locker. "Sure, Missus Lusk. Why, ah, I like you just fine. We're, ah, happy to have you and your husband . . . what the hell are you doing?"

With two swift motions, Jo Ann was out of her bra and thong. A third motion was her hand unzipping his shorts.

"Missus Lusk!" Glenn exclaimed.

"Ah, there you are," she said, looking down. "Rising to the occasion."

"Missus Lusk, please!"

"What's the matter with you, darling?" she said, looking up. "You gay or something?"

"No, ma'am," Glenn protested in a strangled voice. "It's just that—"

"What?" Jo Ann asked peevishly. "You don't like me? You don't find me attractive?"

"It's just that . . . I'd like it to be my idea."

She didn't answer for a moment. Then: "Okay, we can stop now if you want."

She moved against him.

"Oh, shit," Glenn groaned.

Suddenly, three hard raps on the door sounded, followed by Jenny's strident voice. "Glenn? If you're in there, we need help on deck. Now!"

Startled, Jo Ann stepped back. Glenn moved immediately to the door, opened it, and went out into the passageway. To his relief, Jenny was already striding down the corridor, in no position to see the naked woman.

"Hope that works fine for you, Mrs. Lusk," Glenn said loudly.

"I still believe there's a screw missing," the woman countered with a lascivious smile. "Maybe you could come back when you're not so busy." She closed the door.

Glenn hurried along the passageway to catch up with Jenny as she started up the hatch ladder. "Hey, Jen, I wasn't—"

"Of course you were," she interrupted, pausing on the third step to look down at him. "You're just the right shape and age for the horny ladies you're going to meet on every charter, bar none." She motioned for him to follow as she went up on deck, and then continued as he walked alongside her. "Go back if you want, I'm not the morality matron on board."

Glenn continued to walk with her.

"Look, Glenn," she resumed speaking. "Sex on the *Lady Ruth* is a given. Most of our passengers are couples in their twenties and thirties, a few older. Maybe it's their hormones, maybe it's the warm tropical seas, or maybe it's just a week-long break from the every day routine of ordinary living." She stopped walking to face Glenn. "But, ever so often, we get a wife or a husband who makes it with somebody else's husband or wife. And ever so often, we have a donnybrook on board that can really be dangerous out on the open sea. Or, at the very least, those little extracurricular adulteries create bad feelings that screw up the vacation not only for those involved, but for everyone else as well." Again she paused. "When they play those games, and they often do, we try to hold them off 'til we're only a day or so out of home port, and not enough time for things to get ugly. And that goes for the crew as well." She looked back toward the hatch. "If you must, see if she'll have you next Friday night or Saturday morning when we're on the way in." She started to move on, but turned as Glenn remained where he stood. "Something wrong?"

"My tool kit," he told her. "I left it back in her cabin."

She stared at him for a few seconds, and then laughed. "You go on, I'll fetch it."

◼ ◼ ◼

Late in the afternoon, the *Lady Ruth* anchored in a cove of a small, uninhabited island. Making several trips on a pair of inflatable boats, the crew transported the guests to the sandy shore. Glenn, Jenny, and Alfred made the supply trip, bearing cookout food and a variety of beverages, while Ruckman and William gathered wood and lit a bonfire on the beach. The guests were ready to party. As the evening sky darkened into a clear azure night; they swam, sang, told jokes and stories, ate and drank, danced and flirted. Some couples crept away from the light of the fire and later returned, flushed and loving.

Later, when all were aboard once more, Tournaire drew Glenn aside. "We'll be underway soon. You've been assigned the midnight watch, *mon ami*. Is that agreeable?"

Glenn fought the temptation to protest the captain's ingratiating style of request. "Sure, that's fine. Give me duty, just like the others."

"I know it has been a trying day," Tournaire went on, seemingly considerate. "After all, your unfortunate accident."

"No, that's okay," Glenn told him.

Tournaire shrugged and started away. "You will be relieved after four hours. *Bonne nuit*."

"Good night," Glenn responded.

A few straggling passengers remained on deck past midnight, but soon went to their cabins and the night was quiet. Glenn walked the deck, suddenly glad of his solitude, enjoying the slight breeze that rippled the surface of the cove and stirred the leaves on the island palms. The only sounds were of the soft wind, and the lapping of gentle waves against the hull.

Shiver me timbers, I'm a changed man. A high-rigging acrobat putting on a show for the folks, and, next, damned near a seagoing lecher. Whatever happened to the old Glenn Hathaway, the milquetoast from Kansas City?

He shook his head and massaged his right shoulder, the one most affected by his desperate high grab for life. In his mind, images of his near fall vied with other graphic memories of his aborted sexual session with Jo Ann. The latter proved to be the more preferable remembrance. He thought, then, of Mary Ellen, his erstwhile girlfriend in Kansas City, and of the few other girls he'd been with in his earlier life. Sex had been infrequently granted, usually a grudging act allowing little innovation, and had often been accompanied by hints of marriage. By comparison, Jo Ann had been a new event in his life, a sexual predator that could've been interesting. With a slight sense of guilt, he rather regretted the lost opportunity, and pondered Jenny's suggested late-in-the-week return to Cabin Nine. Then, he thought of his rooming house friends, and wondered what they might think of the new and randy Glenn Hathaway.

New and improved? Or, maybe, just newly depraved?

■　■　■

The sky was still dark when William came to relieve him. "Have a good night, sah?"

"A thoughtful one," Glenn responded.

"That's good," William enthused, gesturing out at the ocean. "So big, we so little."

"Much smaller than we can imagine," Glenn said.

The tone of his voice caused William to cock his head and lose his smile. He looked up to the top of the mainmast. "You think about you almost die?"

"Some of that," Glenn agreed as he followed William's gaze.

"You live, you die, no big deal," William philosophized. "Your people die, you get ship. You die and, maybe, somebody else get something. That okay. Way life is."

"Maybe so," Glenn said, starting to walk away. "Trouble is, dying probably hurts."

13

Dawn arrived stormy and uncomfortably cool on Friday morning, and threatened to turn worse during the day. Glenn, wearing shorts and a short-sleeved *Lady Ruth* polo shirt, was surprised as he came onto the aft deck, to feel the sharp wind whipping gusts of cold spray at his bare arms and legs. The same hard wind was making the sea choppy although the *Lady Ruth* seemed steady and smooth as the big ship cut through the rolling whitecaps.

Shrugging away a shiver, he hurried to the deckhouse door, entered, and followed the companionway past the salon and library to the galley. Jenny had apparently been up long before, and she was in mid-preparation for the breakfast victuals. The large coffee urns were ready with regular and decaffeinated blends, and the skillets on the stove were sizzling with bacon and sausage.

"What happened to the sunny Caribbean?" he asked.

"Sometimes, it changes its mind," she said over her shoulder.

."Well, that's a hell of a thing," Glenn observed. "I wonder how our guests will like it?"

"We'll soon find out," she responded brusquely. "You're late. I've already fed the crew. Grab something for yourself while we've still got a little time."

Glenn ate his breakfast standing up, drank two cups of coffee, and then hurried to the library where the long table had been draped with overlapping table clothes, and dishes, glasses, and tableware had been set in place. In addition, two card tables had also been unfolded and positioned at each end of the central dining surface to accommodate, if required, a need for greater seating

Soon, the passengers arrived, coming in pairs, four-somes, and a few coming separately. Most every person was swaddled in whatever warm clothing he or she had found in their mainly tropical wardrobe. As Glenn, Jenny, and Alfred moved among them, replenishing food and beverages for the buffet, they could hear their comments about the weather. The general attitude of the guests seemed a bit somber, but the conversations tended to blame the flukes of nature rather than the ship's course or its crew.

Marvin Lusk, the last to appear, brought an early inebria-tion and a surly attitude to the breakfast buffet.

"Thish ain't what the brochure showed . . . damned weather! Thish ain't fair!" he slurred as he placed his overbur-dened plate of food at an empty space at a card table. "Outta refund our damned money!"

"You want all of it?" a nearby diner asked sarcastically.

"At leesh fer today," Lusk persisted.

In the middle of the long table, Jo Ann rolled her eyes and shrugged her exasperation for her mate's inanities. Seated between two other women's husbands, she had not given in to the intemperate weather. Clad only in the barest of bikini swimsuits, she had the full attention of the men on either side, and the glares of their wives.

Lusk turned to Alfred who was adding freshly cooked scrambled eggs to a chafing dish. "You, there! Schoss on rocks here!"

Alfred pointed to a pitcher of tomato juice with gin and vodka bottles nearby.

"None of that bloody swill," Lusk groused. "Gimme a real drink!"

"Eat some food, bozo, and sober up!" Jo Ann bellowed. "Stop playing the fool!"

Alternative plans for the inclement day occupied the conversations at the table and, as breakfast ended, most of the guests retired either across to the salon or to their cabins. Glenn, Alfred, and Jenny cleared the left-overs, collected the dishes and tableware, stripped the soiled tablecloths, and vacuumed the library. After preparing the library for a noontime meal, they returned to the galley to wash the dishes and launder the tablecloths.

"We're done here for now," Jenny told Glenn after Alfred left the galley. "Take it easy for a while."

"Maybe I should go see if I can be of help somewhere else," he countered.

She shrugged and turned away.

He followed the companionway forward to the wheelhouse where Tournaire was standing behind Ruckman who was at the helm, guiding the ship. The wind-driven rain was drenching the forward glass, and the large windshield wipers were sweeping back and forth across the large, thick panes to afford brief moments of smarmy clarity. Under the intensified power of its diesel, the ship was now bucking a heavier sea, and an occasional jolt could be felt whenever it plunged into an oversized wave.

"Morning," Glenn said with a nod to them.

"*Oui, M'sieur.* However, it seems to be a most dreary one," Tournaire said in return. "Our guests are upset?"

"Most seem okay about it," Glenn told him. "Think it'll let up?"

"Squalls gonna last all day," Ruckman declared, an unusually even-tempered comment in his squeaky voice.

"Any outside chores we need?" Glenn asked.

Tournaire shook his head. "William and Thomas stood watch during the night. They secured everything after seeing weather clouds." He cocked his head to the ship's interior. "You might tell the guests to expect a rough sea."

Glenn smiled. "We carry any barf bags?"

Tournaire smiled in return, then sobered. "A word of caution, *M'sieur.* It would be wise that none of our guests should venture onto the deck. It is wet and slippery—"

"Speaking of," Glenn interrupted, nodding their attention ahead.

As each pass of the wiper blades, misty clarity revealed a bundled figure lurching along the port side of the foredeck, one hand on the rail and other gripping a flask

"The lush Mr. Lusk," Glenn declared. "Somebody's got to go after him before he falls overboard."

No one moved.

"I'll get him,' Glenn volunteered, and moved up to the port-side door.

"Be careful, *M'sieur*," Tournaire said.

Glenn nodded and stepped outside.

The onslaught of hard wind and driving rain did not quite stagger him, but the force of it was enough to cause him to pause momentarily before he bent his head and walked toward the deck rail. Lusk was a few yards ahead, swaying more from consumed liquor than from the pitching of the ship. The man was apparently working his unsteady way toward the bow of the *Lady Ruth*, for whatever ill-conceived reason, Glenn couldn't fathom.

"Marvin Lusk!" Glenn shouted. "Come back!"

Either the man didn't hear, couldn't comprehend, or had no intent to respond. With a swig from his flask, he kept reeling along toward the point of the bow.

"Marvin! Where the hell are you going?" Glenn shouted at the top of his lungs as he hurried forward.

Lusk, befuddled, slowly turned to the shout, removing his steadying left hand from the rail as he sought to recapture the flask falling from his right.

Just as Glenn reached for Lusk, the ship hit a heavy swell and heeled, surprisingly hard, to the left, the deck slanting steeply. Immediately, both of them were hurled from their feet, the elevated angle and their impetus sure to carry them high against the now lowered port rail, and even over it.

Glenn's buttock slammed against the upper railing, and then he was airborne with his arms flailing, about to cartwheel over and into the turbulent ocean. Suddenly, he felt a jab at his midsection and a catch at his belt;

Marvin Lusk, flat on the deck had his fingers hooked into Glenn's belt and was straining to hold on. The ship's bow plunged into another sizable wave and, this time, righted the yacht and bounced Glenn forward to fall beside Lusk.

Face to face on the deck, they lay still.

"Lucky fer you, I wass out here taking the air," Lusk muttered.

A wry smile came to Glenn's face. "You could say that. Thank you."

"You been boffing my wife?" Lusk asked.

The question surprised Glenn. "I . . . ah . . . no, sir."

"You don't havta deny it," Lusk continued. "She's always on the prowl."

Glenn sat up. "No, absolutely not! Get that straight!"

Lusk didn't immediately respond. Finally, he nodded as he attempted to sit up. "I wass thinkin' 'bout that after I grabbed ya . . . and if'n I shoulda helt on.".

Glenn rose to his feet and, with one hand on the rail to steady himself, helped Lusk to rise. "We'd better get inside."

"You shay sho, good idea," Lusk compliantly agreed.

Positioning Lusk with his hands gripping the rail, Glenn moved protectively beside and behind him. Buffeted by the gale-driven rain, they sidestepped slowly their way aft along the arc of the railing.

As they came abreast of the deckhouse, Glenn pondered the now stable cruising of the *Lady Ruth*. The bow was still cutting into and through each oncoming wave, but the ship's rise and fall seemed moderate, the motions probably little worrisome for the crew and passengers within.

"Must've been a hell of a wave we hit," he muttered to himself.

"We wass almoss goners," Lusk responded, believing the comment was directed to him. He cocked his head to peer at Glenn. "Ain't you the fella who damned near fell off the mast?"

Glenn nodded. "That was me."

"Fella, you gotta learn be more careful."

Glenn glanced up at the top of the main mast, and then at the tempestuous sea. "I couldn't have said it better myself."

He took Lusk by the arm, walked him across the open deck space to the deckhouse door, and escorted him inside.

14

On Saturday morning, the *Lady Ruth* returned to her home port and discharged her passengers. Luggage had been collected and taken to the waiting bus, and the assembled crew stood on deck at the gangway to bid each guest a hearty farewell. Jo Ann gave Glenn a quick peck on the cheek, and then moved on to pat William's rump as she stepped away on the gangplank.

After the bus departed for the airport and the crew scattered, Jenny motioned for Glenn to follow her into the deckhouse.

"Unfortunately, we've got an open week," she told him as she preceded him along the passageway. "Last minute cancellation."

"How often does that happen?"

"Not often, but it's a bit of a bitch when it does," she replied. "However, there's forfeiture money which is considerable, so it's not a complete loss to us. In fact, it's kind of a good thing to give us a break."

"So, what do we do? Maintenance on the ship?"

Over her shoulder, she said, "You seem to be accident prone. Maybe now's the time for you to find a place to live on the island, and reconsider being a dryland owner."

"We've had this discussion before," Glenn said stoically. "I'm staying aboard."

She glanced back with a disdainful look.,

"There *is* something I'd like to do this week," Glenn said. "I saw some diving gear in one of the storage room . . . and I'd like to learn how."

"To dive?" she asked, as she stopped walking and turned toward him.

"Can someone on board teach me?"

"I don't think you're ready for diving."

"Well, I won't be if I don't get started. What do you say?"

She shrugged and started walking forward again, waving him to follow. When she reached the small office, she entered it and moved to a file cabinet. She opened it, and rummaged through assorted papers and stationary items. She found a small card and handed it to Glenn. "This is a divers' outfitting company. See Billy there, and tell him to fix you up with diving gear. You also tell him to get you certified this week."

Glenn examined the card and nodded.

"We run an account there. Tell him to bill everything to us. If you're set on doing this, Billy's the right guy. And while you're taking lessons, we'll shape up the ship."

Glenn waited, expecting to hear more.

"Well?" she questioned with impatience in her voice. "I've got work to do."

Glenn regarded her for a moment, then turned and walked away. On the deck, he headed for the aft hatch, thinking about the last of the conversation.

What the hell's going on with her?

Is it her?

Or is it me?

The Shaw Dive Equipment store was a weather-beaten, clapboard structure over water on the end of a short pier. A sign over the door was barely readable, the lettering bleached by assaults of sea spray, and the constant rays of the tropical sun. Glenn walked through the open door into a large room that displayed a chaotic shamble of underwater gear. Off a center aisle, random narrow paths wound through a jumble of opened boxes containing regulators, fins, masks, gloves, and snorkels. As he walked slowly down the center pathway, he looked at bordering racks of neoprene rubber and spandex underwater suits. At end of the aisle, beneath a large sun-filled window, a makeshift counter had been fashioned from a solid-core door supported by sawhorses, the gap between the legs crammed with even more cardboard boxes.

"Hello!" Glenn called.

"Be right with you," a man's voice answered from behind a huge pile of used diving equipment.

"Looking for someone named Billy!" Glenn declared loudly.

"That's me." An elderly man, clad only in shorts, emerged from the clutter. Billy Shaw was short and lean, almost skinny. A man in his late sixties or early seventies, his face, bare legs, and upper torso showed the crust of long exposure to punishing sunlight; brown and leathery skin stretched over ropy muscles. He stuck out his right hand. "You got my name, boy. What's yours?"

"Hathaway," Glenn responded as he shook hands, feeling the horny calluses. "Glenn Hathaway. I'm on—"

"The *Lady Ruth*," Shaw finished for him. "Heard you was taking over the ship."

Glenn hesitated, then shook his head. "I don't quite look at it that way . . . at least not for a while." He glanced around. "Jennifer told me to see you about setting me up with diving equipment. And I need to learn how to use it."

"Never dived before?"

"Nope, never," Glenn admitted. "She also said that you could get me certified."

Shaw nodded. "I run classes. Regular class takes some time. You in a hurry?"

"We don't have a charter this week," Glenn told him. "I need to be ready for our next trip."

The old man looked Glenn up and down, and then bobbed his head. "Shouldn't be a problem. I don't have a class scheduled. Want individual training? Cost ya some extra."

"Whatever it takes."

"Want to start tomorrow?"

"Sunday?"

"Rather go to church?"

Glenn laughed. "What time tomorrow?"

"Ten o'clock. Right off the pier." He gestured out the window, then turned and headed back into the labyrinth of underwater odds and ends. "Be on time."

"What about my equipment?" Glenn called.

"Make it nine!" Shaw called back. "Take care of that in the morning."

■ ■ ■

Tournaire opened the door and entered the outer office. Gravendeel's receptionist didn't come to work on Saturdays, so he strode past the empty desk and into Gravendeel's private office. The obese lawyer sat behind his desk, and another man was pacing restlessly back and forth.

"Good day," Tournaire said as he settled into a chair. "So sorry, to be late."

"*Dobry den,*" the other man gruffly returned the greeting. "Is everything still satisfactory?" He spoke understandable English with a strong trace of an eastern European accent. Yuri Kozlov was in his early fifties. His face was large and round, with blunt features, under a head of coal-black hair with white streaks at each temple. His barrel-shaped body was more muscle than fat; a man who moved with surprising agility for his bulk. "Two weeks from now?"

Gravendeel lifted a reassuring hand, glancing to Tournaire expecting agreement.

"*Oui, M'sieur,*" Tournaire said. "We are ready."

"Is it possible for you, now, to tell us more about the charter?" Gravendeel asked.

Kozlov came to a stop, and shook his head. "You are being exceptionally well paid. When we are aboard, we will tell you more, but only what you need to know." He paused and took a chair beside Tournaire. "You *will* not ask that question again."

Gravendeel fluttered his hands in apology. "Whatever you wish. As you say, we are well paid to do whatever you ask of us."

"Something concerns me," Kozlov suddenly declared. "The death of the old captain and his woman. Why did that happen?"

"Unavoidable," Tournaire said. "They decided to sail with us at a most unfortunate time. Wrong for us, and very wrong for them"

"It was important for everything to be as normal as usual for our charter," Kozlov persisted. "Perhaps, along with the rest of you, they could have been paid very well for their cooperation."

"They wouldn't have cooperated," Gravendeel disagreed, with a shake of his head. "They really didn't have a part in . . . in our other enterprise."

"Still, it must have drawn unwanted attention," Kozlov countered. "Did you not consider that?" He waited for an answer. "We *have* considered going elsewhere for a different ship."

"We do understand," Gravendeel said with a sigh. "It was an unavoidable circumstance. However, no one has questioned the incident. We are under no suspicion at all. To everyone in authority, we are still of good reputation."

"The *Lady Ruth*, myself and the crew; we have always been well regarded," Tournaire interjected. "No one knows of our other business."

Kozlov sat in silence for a few moments. "Even if what you claim is so, you should have told me sooner for our deliberation. As it is, now there is no time for a change." He paused. "Are there any other problems that you have failed to mention?"

Gravendeel spoke quickly. "There are no such problems."

"Is that true?" Kozlov turned to Tournaire.

"*Certainement, M'sieur*," Tournaire said. "We await your arrival. All will be exactly as you wish."

"It had better be. If all goes well, you two will be much richer men," Kozlov said. He rose and walked toward the door to the outer office. "However, you will be dead men if anything else goes wrong. *Do svidaniya*." He crossed the space to the outer door, opened it, and closed it behind him as he left.

"Russian mafia, they are called?" Tournaire asked, after making sure that Kozlov had left the building. "I still wonder, why did they come to us?"

Gravendeel shrugged. "Maybe our drug operation isn't as secret as we thought." He smiled. "Just be happy that he did."

"And what is he after? What are *we* after?"

"To pay the sum he has offered, it must be something quite special," Gravendeel said. "Perhaps, it must be something very valuable and very hush-hush."

"I ask again, why *exactly* do they need the *Lady Ruth*?"

Gravendeel shrugged. "Perhaps, they wish merely to move about the Caribbean without creating suspicion. What better than a ship known for its random itinerary pleasure cruises?"

"And, why so much interest in the *size* of our ship?" Tournaire questioned. "Why is that a matter of such importance to them?"

Again, Gravendeel shrugged. "Very, very soon, we may have your answers." He paused. "Whatever Kozlov so highly values, perhaps it may be of even greater value to us."

Tournaire smiled.

15

The following Friday, Shaw gave Glenn his PADI Open Water Diver Certification card.

"You ain't exactly a scuba vet, mind you," Billy warned him. "Make damned sure you dive with people who know how to take care of you."

Shaw helped Glenn pack up his gear. "I don't rightly know most of your crew nowadays," he said. "I know Tournaire, and the young lady, of course." He shook his head. "Different bunch now than when Captain Jack was running things."

"How do you mean different?"

The old man shrugged. "Oh, I'm talking a while back I knew most of Jack's deckhands. Ain't unusual for crews to come and go, but Jack's former guys were pretty steady. Tournaire's been with him for a while, but it seems to me that some of the other regulars started drifting away about a year or so ago."

"How long has Miss Warren been with them?"

"Jenny?" Shaw gave a smile. "Less than a year, I'd say. Don't know much about her, but she's okay. She's in here, pays her bills, takes care of whatever is needed on the ship. Nice, friendly girl, I like her."

Friendly? Glenn thought. *Must've missed that trait.*

"And the rest?" Glenn asked.

Again, Shaw shrugged. "I wouldn't know 'em if I saw 'em." He finished packing the diving equipment in a canvas carry bag. "When you're underwater, you do just exactly what Jenny tells you to do, and you won't get yourself in trouble."

"I appreciate all your effort," Glenn said, taking the bag from him. "I'm sure I'll see much more of you from now on."

"Take care of yourself, son," Shaw said. "You'll be fine but . . ."

Glenn, turning away, turned back.

"I've loved the sea all my life," the old man said in a soft, deferential voice. "Lived near it, worked in it, worshiped at the beauty of it, but I've always been skeered of it just the same." He paused. "You be skeered of it, too."

He waved goodbye and walked away.

■ ■ ■

"How'd it go?" Jenny asked as Glenn came aboard.

"Good, very good," he replied, hoisting the equipment bag to show her. "Wet suit, all the gear. Billy made sure I got what I needed."

"Probably sold you the highest-priced stuff in his shop," she said brusquely.

"Not at all," Glenn's response was edgy. "Matter of fact, he steered me away from the overpriced gear."

"Probably because we're keeping him in business," she told him. She pointed to the bag. "Stow your gear down in the aft locker, and then meet me back up top."

"And what will we be doing?"

She gave him a wide smile. "The honey wagon will be coming. I'll be showing you how to empty the holding tanks from the heads."

Glenn grimaced, and Jenny laughed.

"I know," she chuckled. "But shit happens."

■ ■ ■

The week's layoff had been advantageous in some respects, allowing the crew to spruce up the *Lady Ruth*. The Cummins engine was examined, tested, and given routine maintenance by diesel mechanics from the island. Mattresses and blankets were brought up on deck for airing under the heat of the tropical sun. The heads were scoured and mopped. Lines were examined and replaced where necessary. Cabins were thoroughly vacuumed and cleaned. The galley got special attention, refrigerators and stoves were scrubbed, and counters sponged. Woodwork in the library and salon was polished and brought to a high luster.

By sail day morning, the *Lady Ruth* gleamed from bow to stern, above and below deck.

"New day, new charter," Jenny said as she finished inspecting the newly mopped deck. "Nice job."

Glenn squeezed water from the mop into a bucket, and nodded his thanks. "What's next?"

"Stow everything, then grab a little lunch, and take it easy 'til our next group arrives." She checked her watch. "Three or four hours."

"Going to be like the last group?"

She gave him an unexpected smile, almost a sly one. "Every charter is different."

"What's this one like?"

"Wait and see."

Glenn caught something in her voice. He had come to expect a certain degree of antagonism from her, but at this moment, there was a hint of impish behavior. Now, she seemed less aloof, almost playful. He neither understood her continuously cool attitude towards him, nor could he understand this unexpected out-of-the-blue merriment.

"What's up?" he asked, suspicious.

"Wait and see," she repeated as she turned and walked away. "Every charter's different."

Glenn watched as she walked to the deckhouse and entered. Then, he squeezed water from the mop into the bucket, leaned the mop against a rail, and emptied the bucket over the side.

"I hate it when she's in a good mood," he muttered, then picked up his mop and pail and headed astern. "Whatever she's up to, I'm sure it's nothing good for me."

▨ ▨ ▨

Glenn and others of the crew were waiting as the bus from the airport arrived. As Jenny stepped out and opened the vehicle's sliding door, the new passengers filed out, one by one.

And Glenn understood Jenny's scarcely concealed amusement.

The men stood in pairs, some hand-in-hand, others with arms around their companions' waists. Most were young although a few older men were present and coupled with like-aged mates. As a group, they were excited as they pointed at the ship and exclaimed their gleeful expectations.

"Happy fellows," William said in a low voice to Glenn.

Glenn surveyed the group and noticed three young men standing apart from the others, each regarding each other. Then, one by one, they looked directly at Glenn.

William broke a smile. "I think they like you, *mon.*"

■ ■ ■

"Come in!"

Glenn stepped inside and brought both soft-side bags with him. "Mr. Harmon?"

"Just put them anywhere," the young man said. "Hi, my name's Sonny. What's yours?"

"Ah, I'm Glenn."

"Glenn, nice to know you," Sonny said, giving him an appraising once-over. "We're going to have a good sail?"

"We should," Glenn replied. "It's a fine time of the year." He turned to leave. "Anything I can do for you?"

Sonny gave him a sly look. "I can think of a couple of things."

Glenn stepped quickly into the companionway and closed the door behind him. As he turned to walk forward, other doors opened as a few more slender young men stepped out.

Acutely aware of their appraising stares, Glenn fixed his eyes on the deck and walked swiftly through the gazing gauntlet.

■ ■ ■

"How often does this go on?"

Jenny gave him a smirk. "Often enough. On this charter, they can be whatever they want to be, and do whatever they want to do." She laughed. "I love it! Nobody's patting my ass for a change."

"What about my ass?" Glenn rejoined with a wry smile.

"Up for grabs," she chuckled.

"Not if I can help it," Glenn said, becoming serious. "Really, how do I deal with this?"

"Look," she said, sobering to the subject. "They are our guests, and they've paid for the cruise. If one or two of them hit on you, just be pleasant and say 'no'."

"What if they persist?"

"Keep saying 'no'."

Glenn and Jenny continued setting out the hors d'oeuvres for the welcoming cocktail party. Many passengers were on deck, making new acquaintances, renewing old friendships; all reveling in the exhilaration of the upcoming sail. Much like their heterosexual counterparts, the couples shared loving embraces, sharing their excited anticipation for their week ahead.

"Can you make a tolerable *Presidente*, my dear fellow?" came a soft voice, its slender owner coming to the bar. Beside him, a sturdy companion rolled his eyes in apology. "For God's sake, Terry, this isn't the Top of the Mark."

Terry flashed a prim smile.

"White Label rum, dry Vermouth, a couple of dashes of Curacao," Jenny murmured. "Dash of grenadine, stirred with ice, and strained." She shook her head. "Know the making's, but, sorry, no can do on this ship. How about a rum punch?"

"I suppose," Terry responded with a sigh.

"Any Irish whiskey?" the other man asked.

"Bushmills or Jamison?"

"I'll settle for Jamison," he answered. He turned to Glenn. "Nice vessel. We've been on a couple of other sailing ships, but this one's in a lot better shape."

Glenn nodded. "So I've been told."

"I'm Mike," he said, and gestured to his companion. "This is Terry." He extended his hand.

Glenn took his hand. "I'm Glenn,"

"You gay?" Mike asked with a smile, not releasing his grip.

Glenn was taken aback, and then shook his head.

"Maybe AC-DC?"

"Only girls," Glenn managed to say.

"Not ever tempted?"

"No, 'fraid not."

Mike released his hand. "Never hurts to ask." He caught the look of dismay on Terry's face. "Now, don't go getting all upset. I'm true to you . . . most of the time."

"Do you hate gays?" Terry asked, now sipping the rum punch and making a face.

"No," Glenn replied. "It's not an issue with me."

"And not an issue with any of our crew," Jenny put in. "You're here to have a good time, and we intend to see that you do."

"Pity about you, Glenn," Mike said jokingly, accepting his drink and taking Terry's arm as they moved away.

"May I ask a favor?" Glenn called.

Mike and Terry stopped and turned around.

"You mind passing the word?" Glenn asked. "Save me having to say it a half-dozen times."

Mike thought for a moment, and then gave a gracious nod. "Be my pleasure, my young friend. Consider it done." They turned, linked arms again, and strolled toward the bow.

"Then . . . you're not gay," Jenny said with a smile.

"Good Lord!" Glenn exclaimed. "Why would you think that?"

Jenny shrugged. "I don't know. You're young, but not too young. No wife. Haven't heard you talk about a girlfriend." She shrugged again. "Maybe you're one of those undersexed guys."

"I'm not gay, undersexed, or bisexual!" Glenn declared.

"Keep it down," she cautioned, gesturing to the passengers, some turning toward them.

"I'm . . . just between things," Glenn told her.

"Most guys like you would be trying to get me into the sack," she said, merriment shining in her eyes. "You haven't shown much interest."

"Haven't I?" Glenn exclaimed in a low voice. "I've thought about you, but you've made it pretty clear that I wouldn't have any kind of a chance."

Jenny pursed her lips in a moment of reflection. "I haven't been very nice, have I?"

Glenn didn't respond.

"Glenn, I don't mean to be ugly to you," Jenny said. "But there are things that you don't know. There are reasons—"

"That's something else I just don't understand," Glenn cut in. "Ever since I've come aboard, I've felt some sort of a strain between us. Even now, you seem to be trying to say something to me." He paused. "What is it?"

A wary look came to her face. "If I had something to say, I'd say it straight away."

Glenn waited.

"All right, you asked," she said, "I think you're a nice, but naïve young man who doesn't understand the sea and the dangers of it. Truth is, you shouldn't really be here. You shouldn't have anything to do with me, or anyone else on this ship. In fact, if you were smart, as soon as we return to port, I think you should pack your bags, make arrangements to sell the ship, and go where you ought to be . . . safe at home."

Glenn regarded her in silence, wondering where the pleasantly contrite young woman of only moments ago had gone. "I guess that's saying it straight away."

Jenny, her manner dismissive, turned to smile at a trio of men approaching the bar.

"Safe at home?" Glenn repeated under his breath. "Hell, lady, with you I'm not even making it to first base."

16

Glenn's next voyage on the *Lady Ruth* explored a different course over the Caribbean waters. One of the benefits of such a chartered ship, Glenn discovered, was the liberty to go to wherever the passengers wished to go. These gay guests had no collective wish to visit crowded ports; they preferred days and nights at sea, or the privacy of the beaches of small, uninhabited islands.

It was apparent that Mike had spread the word of Glenn's sexual preferences, and no one put him to any kind of a test. On the contrary, Glenn found himself quite at ease with various individuals.

"I envy you," said Maurice, a librarian from Dallas. It was the second evening after supper, Glenn sitting in with one of the small conversation clusters watching the brilliant sunset. "Chuck your job, and come down to live the life of a vagabond sailor." He gave a wide smile to his companion, Max, an electrician.

"More guts than I've got," Max voiced his opinion.

"I'm not as daring as all that," Glenn countered, wondering if he should mention that he owned the ship.

"It's what we'd all like to do," Maurice said. "Get out of the rat race, head for the tropics and live the good life."

Both were lean, strong, athletic men who were casually affectionate, well versed in many subjects, and articulate in speaking their opinions.

"I'm finding out that it isn't quite as glamorous as it might appear," Glenn told them, relating a few of the demanding chores he was encountering.

"Sure," Maurice chided in good humor. "I can see you're dying to go back to . . . where? Kansas City?"

In his second week of actual sea duties, he found he was busier, better able to perform such chores and, consequently, given more to do. Although he continued to puzzle over Jenny's unpredictable manner, she'd voiced no further derisive opinions concerning him, and she'd resumed her standoffish behavior, even more brusque and uncommunicative.

On the third morning of the cruise, the guests and crew got set for diving. The helmsman had anchored the ship in shallows over the underwater slope of a small island.

"You should stay aboard," Jenny said crossly to Glenn. "I don't want you out there quite yet."

"Billy said I was okay," he countered.

They argued about it for several minutes; Jenny objecting, Glenn persisting. Finally, she gave an exasperated sigh and agreed.

"I know you believe you're qualified, but I want you to stick close," Jenny told him, severity in her directive. "We take two groups of six at a time, each diver with a buddy. You're paired with William." She gave a troubled frown. "You ought be with me, but I've got a couple of other inexperienced divers to watch out for. You two stay close with the rest of us and don't stray away."

Glenn nodded, dividing his attention between she and William; the latter who was helping him adjust the buoyancy control device backpack.

"Okay, *mon*,' William said, tapping him on his head. "Tank full, regulator okay. You set, we ready to go, *mon*."

On Jenny's signal, Glenn and the others joined her at the amidships ladder, all walking and looking like strange amphibians in their wet suits and carrying their webfoot fins. One by one, they descended to the inflatable raft that served as a dive platform floating at the waterline. Maurice and Max were among Jenny's diving group, each giving Glenn a thumbs-up signal.

The divers attached their fins, rubbed the glass panes of their masks with antifogging compound, and dipped them for a rinse into the seawater. Pair by pair, the divers made final equipment inspection for one another, adjusted airflow and BCD pressures, then rolled into the sea.

With four heads bobbing above the water, William and Glenn rolled off the platform. At Jenny's signal, each diver deflated his BCD and followed her into the depths of the ocean. Jenny led the way, legs fluttering, down to the ocean floor. As instructed, Glenn did his best to keep up with the group, impressed with Jenny's swift swimming strength. A number of times, she turned her head, signaling impatiently for him to keep up with William who was showing no signs of being a buddy. Glenn, new at regulating buoyancy pressures, had a tendency to flounder.

The sea bed displayed a beautiful, mystic topography. There were exquisite coral reef formations, stretches of sand, clusters of seaweed, and flowing fields of seagrass. Myriad species of small to large fish moved lazily near, undisturbed by the intrusion of wet-suited creatures into their habitat.

As the divers glided over the ocean bottom, they came to a long substantial rock wall that was pocked with niches, dark caves, and multiple deep fissures. It was apparent that two of the divers in this group were experienced. That pair moved into a crevice passage and disappeared from sight, bent on exploring. With a backward glance at Glenn, Jenny inflated her BCD to gain a height advantage, treading in position, trying to keep track of her charges.

Glenn moved down to closely examine a small creature as it emerged from sand, and then scuttled over the sea floor to bury itself once again to hide from this unfamiliar predator. Glenn smiled at the thought of him being a danger. He glanced around, suddenly thinking of predators that might be stalking him.

Nothing big or dangerous in sight.

He swam slowly, entranced with the wonders of marine life. A huge grouper floated near, then moved on. A small bright-colored fish appeared, seemed to be regarding him, and then darted away.

He checked his depth gauge

Nearly sixty feet.

He looked back, seeking sight of his group. He had drifted further than he'd thought, and there was no one in view, not even his diving buddy, William. Although the water around him was clear and sunlit, his undersea vision was limited. At a certain distance, the clarity became opaque, then obscure.

A trace of panic invaded him. He shook the feeling away, and began swimming to where, he hoped, Jenny and the others were still there. He wasn't particularly concerned since it had only been a few minutes, and he hadn't gone that far. He swam steadily, his head up and watching for William, Jenny, or any of his dive companions. He came to the rock wall and paused, floating, looking around. He swam one way, and then another, hunting for Jenny, hoping that she'd appear at any moment, mad as hell at him for wandering away.

He inhaled.

No air!

Panic came in a bolt, and he twisted the face of the pressure gauge toward him.

Empty!

Glenn started clawing toward the faraway surface.

Suffocating!

Desperate, he began to thrash his way upward.

Never make it, no air!

Two hands grabbed him by the shoulders and turned him; he was facing Maurice. In a swift move, Maurice passed him the mouthpiece of his alternative unit and helped him adjust it. As Glenn gasped precious air into his lungs, Maurice's arms embraced him and, as a clustered unit, the pair began to slowly rise toward the surface.

■ ■ ■

Jenny, once realizing a pair of her charges were missing, had aborted the dive, much to the dismay of the others. With everyone back on deck, Glenn tried to ignore the accusing looks of the frustrated divers, and knelt to examine his gear. It was the new equipment that he had used, without malfunction, during his training and qualification dives.

"Find anything?" Jenny asked, bending down to join him.

Glenn shook his head.

Jenny knelt beside him, her eyes searching the equipment. She touched the regulator. "You checked this yourself?"

"William."

She continued to inspect, then hesitated. "Where did you get this tank?"

"William."

She examined the valve, and shook her head. "I know this tank . . . it's one of our old ones. The valve's been damaged. It was supposed to have been deep-sixed long ago. Didn't you check your pressure gauge? Didn't you see a steady stream of air bubbles?"

"I guess not," Glenn admitted.

"Well, that's a hell of a thing," she snapped. "I've got enough to keep my eyes on without babysitting you. Watch your ass!" She rose swiftly and lifted the tank. "You test your own gear from now on. Better still, don't go down at all." She walked away, carrying the tank, anger in her stride.

Glenn collected his diving equipment and carried it to a nearby hatch, descended, and made his way to a storage room where he stowed it. He returned to the crew's room, stripped and showered in the adjacent head. Dressed in fresh white shorts and a navy blue shirt, he returned to the deck only to meet Jenny at the top of the hatch.

"You okay?" she asked, her earlier anger spent.

"I'm fine," he hastened to assure her. "I'm sorry to be such a bother."

She started to speak, but, at this moment Captain Tournaire strolled into view, and her manner became gruff again as she stepped down into the hatch. "Just watch yourself."

Once again, confounded at her bewildering temperament changes, Glenn took a tentative step after her, then stopped, spun about and strode away, nodding to Tournaire as he passed.

■ ■ ■

Tournaire turned his gaze to the hatch where Jenny had descended. He pursed his lips in thought, and then walked aft to the stern where William stood behind the wheel.

"Yes, sah," William was speaking into ship-to-shore handset. "Coming, just now." He handed the unit to Tournaire. "Mista Gravendeel, sah." He turned back to the wheel and guided the ship through the gentle swells of the sea.

"Tournaire," the captain spoke gruffly.

"Just a reminder," Gravendeel's voice intoned. "Our important guests will be arriving within a very few days."

"This is your reason for a call?" Tournaire vented his irritation. "To tell me what I already know?"

"Just to make sure that our problem has been resolved."

"We are working on it."

"Still a problem? I'm disappointed that it has not yet been . . . repaired."

"There is no need for your concern, *mon ami*," the captain sighed. "A couple of efforts to repair have been unsuccessful. We *will* find a way."

"You're expecting, shall we say, smooth sailing?"

"We *do* expect a fair wind."

"Good to hear," Gravendeel said. "I will look forward to your success. Goodbye."

Tournaire returned the handset to William, and fixed the sailor with a somber stare. "You failed, William. You had him deep in the ocean, and let him live."

"Not my fault, *mon*," William protested. "Make look like accident, that what you said."

"We're running out of time," Tournaire barked. "We must get him off this ship some way. Cripple him, kill him . . . I don't care how."

William sighed. "As you say, sah. Will find way."

17

The diving incident was not discussed during the evening buffet. Maurice gave a smile and another thumbs-up signal, but made no further reference to the hazardous event – for which Glenn was grateful. Jenny remained in her gruff, no-nonsense mood. She issued curt orders and direct complaints about the job he was doing in helping her with the buffet. On this next to last day, the guests were in a mellow mood, given to long conversations and serious topics, a somber atmosphere, most likely due to the realization that the merry cruise was ending.

As soon as the leftover food was sacked, the dishes and glasses cleared, Jenny motioned for Glenn to follow her to the galley.

"We make port tomorrow," she said as she loaded the dishwasher. "If you won't take my advice about going home, then why don't you, at least, take the next two or three weeks off?"

"This again?" Glenn sighed. "Off the ship? Why?"

She nodded. "You could use more work with Billy on your diving and—"

"That was equipment failure," Glenn cut in.

"And maybe it would've been obvious for you to make sure it was working if you had more experience," she reminded him.

Glenn shrugged.

"It would do you good. Explore the ABC islands, maybe some others in the Caribbean. Hang around Willemstad . . . get acquainted with the town, and maybe look for an apartment."

"An apartment? Why so?"

"Look, living on the ship is okay for a while, but you need some land living, too. Get to know the island people, learn about their lives and their customs."

Glenn wrinkled his brow, considering. "Maybe later. Right now, I'm concentrating on getting my sea legs." He hesitated, than asked. "You have such a place on shore?"

"Sort of," she replied. "I sometimes share an apartment, off season, times when business is slow, or we're in for maintenance."

"Oh?"

"There are three of us. One is on another charter and the other is full time at a shop in town."

"Two, ah . . ."

"Women, if that's what you're getting at." She gestured at the collected refuse. "I'll put this in the compactor if you'll pick up topside."

He nodded. "On my way.

He took a bag from a locker, left the galley and walked through the companionway to the wheelhouse, and out onto the foredeck. A couple at the bow rail turned and walked aft, hand in hand, as they bid Glenn a goodnight. Glenn picked up a few plastic drink glasses, napkins and a couple of paper plates. The ship was moving swiftly through the moonlight night, the white sails still full with the steady wind, leeward to the port side. He scanned the deck for any other refuse, found a few discarded items, then stepped to the rail. For a moment, he considered dropping the bag over the side, then reconsidered with a self-chastising environmental guilt. He walked along the port side of the ship, inspecting the deck and found nothing to add to his litterbag.

When he reached the stern, he collected the trash, scanned the deck for any litter he might have missed. Satisfied, he put down the trash sack and walked to lean on the stern guardrail and looked down at the roiling white wake, glittering in the moonlight. He raised his gaze and spotted a small dark shape on the ocean some distance away. He watched it for a few minutes and wondered what kind of a vessel it might be.

Another sailing ship like the Lady Ruth? Perhaps a commercial craft, a fishing boat, certainly not large enough for a freighter.

At the sound of footsteps, he turned, somewhat surprised to see William and Ruckman approaching, their walk purposeful.

"Evening, guys," Glenn said cheerfully.

Neither spoke, but they continued their deliberate advance.

Glenn turned away from them and, with his left hand, gestured to the open sea behind them. "Guess you saw it, too," he said. "We've got company, coming up pretty fast."

The two sailors stopped still, their attention abruptly arrested, each gazing at the craft that was rapidly closing the distance.

"Fishing boat," Ruckman said irritably. "Riding our rump, goddamn it!" He cast an angry glance at William who, by contrast, broke into a wide smile.

"Yes, sah," William said with a slow nod. "They's plumb curious, them fisher folks. Gonna shinny up and see what's happening here on the *Lady*."

Glenn walked over to retrieve the trash sack from the deck, and then wheeled about to his shipmates. "I'm calling it a day, one that I'm glad is over and done," he told them. "Good night." With a wave, he strode toward the deckhouse.

■ ■ ■

A few moments later, Tournaire walked from the deckhouse to join the two sailors as they watched the fishing boat motoring by. "You disappoint me."

"How lucky can that son of a bitch be?" Ruckman complained defensively. "We was just getting ready to chuck him over. He'd been food for the fishes 'cept for that nosey trawler comes crawling up our wake."

"He cannot be aboard this coming week," Tournaire said with intensity.

"He like pussy cat," William added unexpectedly, a wry smile on his face. "Him got nine lives?"

"That cat used up three already," Ruckman said fiercely. "That's all he gets."

18

The *Lady Ruth* slipped into her berth at the Curacao dock and, at mid-morning, discharged her passengers. The gay men walked down the gangplank with genial expressions of farewell, vowing to return, schedule permitting, at the same time next year. Tournaire, Jenny, and Glenn were the only members of the crew to shake their hands, while the rest of the sailors, standing back from the gangway, merely bobbed their heads to each departing guest.

"Glenn, you haven't been off this ship since you arrived," Jenny said to Glenn. "Most of us are taking overnight shore leave. Why don't you?"

"Splendid idea," Tournaire added. "Willemstad is, now, your home port, and you should get to know it better."

"And don't forget what I told you," Jenny said.

Tournaire gave her a questioning glance.

"That he should find himself a dryland berth, some place where he could spread out rather than spend all his time on the ship," she explained.

"Matter of fact, I do need some time ashore," Glenn agreed. "I need to touch base with my lawyer—"

"Gravendeel?" Tournaire cut in.

Glenn smiled and shook his head. "No, not that fat crook. I have another attorney thanks to our *Sea Mist* neighbor, Emory Gordon."

"Good man, that Gordon," Tournaire said, with a nod to the smaller yacht berthed a short distance away. "I'm sure he sent you to the right man."

"He did, and I'm meeting with my new guy this afternoon. He agreed to see me on a Saturday after we got in. I also want to hurry to our bank and get some spending money," Glenn told them. "I'd like to have some in my pocket when we're in some of our other ports of call."

"I think *Mademoiselle* Jenny has a good idea about securing living accommodations here on the island," Tournaire said in a serious mien.

"Thanks, but for the time being, I'd just as soon continue my shipboard education," Glenn countered. "Maybe later, when the season slacks off."

"Well, at least, go out tonight and have a good time," Tournaire said, and then gave him a meaningful smile. "You're a nice looking fellow and . . ." He didn't finish the statement.

Jenny flashed a smile that could have been in agreement. "I'm sure you've seen the motorbike we carry in the aft storage locker. Help yourself and save cab fare."

■ ■ ■

Glenn sped to the bank just a few minutes before it closed at noon for the weekend, parked the motorbike at the curb, and went inside. He withdrew a sizable amount of money from his recent established checking account, pleased and exceedingly cognizant that this cash in his billfold was more than he had carried ever before in his life. Even so, the frugal practices of his past took him to a fast food restaurant for lunch rather than one of the pricey ones.

Afterwards, he wheeled around the city for over an hour, sightseeing, and enjoying the cool breeze of the ride while he killed time, waiting for his scheduled appointment. Arriving at a downtown law office building, he attended a thirty-minute consultation with his native-born lawyer, a dusky, white-haired gentleman named Charles Drejou. A cheerful, learned man in his sixties, Drejou's heritage included Dutch, African, Spanish, English, and even Arawak Indian ancestors.

"Of course, I knew of Jack Martin although not personally," the attorney said, near the end of their conference. "Frankly, I never quite understood why he had any dealings with Johan Gravendeel."

"Gravendeel has a bad reputation?"

The lawyer took a few moments before answering. "A questionable one, I would say. Rumors here and there, although nothing that could be stated as fact."

"How does he stay in business?" Glenn asked.

"Precisely because of what I just said," Drejou said with a gentle smile. "There were stories told, but nothing that could be proved."

"I count myself lucky to be rid of him," Glenn said. "And, I'm grateful to Emory for recommending you."

Drejou gave a disarming shrug, then tapped a sheaf of papers on his desk. "Well, I've checked everything as far as your ownership of the vessel is concerned, and I've found no problems. And now, you've had a short while to evaluate the operation, how do you find it?"

"Shipshape, I suppose would be the seagoing way to say it," Glenn responded with a grin. "Seems like the crew knows how to handle the *Lady Ruth* on the seas . . . and the captain and Miss Warren apparently know the charter business quite well."

"I've looked over the financial records," Drejou said with an affirming nod. "No discrepancies that I can see." He leaned back in his desk chair. "Not an extraordinary profitability, but a fairly substantial return. It should provide you a very comfortable living." He paused. "One thing more . . . I've heard a story or two about members of the crew."

Glenn raised his eyebrows.

"They seem to be big spenders for charter operation sailors," the attorney said. "Perhaps even your Captain Tournaire."

"Something out of line?"

"I might be wrong," Drejou said, tenting his fingers and looking down at them. "On this island, there are no signs of extravagance by Tournaire, but I've heard that, during the off season, he spends freely on another."

"Aruba or Bonaire?"

The attorney shook his head. "Not in our ABC islands, I believe, but somewhere in a different locality. I know not where." He shrugged once more. "Perhaps there is nothing to it."

"What about Miss Warren?" Glenn asked.

"Nothing here on this island, but there seems there are some questions about the young woman's past in other areas of the Caribbean." He lifted his hands in a gesture of apology. "You must understand that, up until you becoming my client, none of this it has been of my concern." He glanced at his wristwatch. "Keep in touch, young man."

Glenn acknowledged his cue to leave, and rose from his chair. "I'll do that, sir. Thanks for your help."

As he left the office and walked out of the building, he pondered the lawyer's inferences about the crew of the *Lady Ruth*.

What do I really know about them? Any of them? Jenny had made some sort of a caution about herself and other members of the crew.

Once more on the motorbike, Glenn cruised aimlessly for a while, wondering what he should do with his emphatically advocated shore leave. With money in his pocket, a goodly sum in his bank account, and with assurance from his lawyer that the charter business was holding steady, he had options.

Perhaps I really should find myself a place on the island.

His brief stint as an ordinary seaman on the ship had been helpful, but living aboard was confining and, eventually, might become a bit of a bore.

Fair to say, maybe I am a born drylander.

With a work permit to allow him to live in the Caribbean for the time being, he was more and more thinking about the future. He intended to always retain his United States citizenship even though he had no intention of returning to Kansas City other than for visits. Perhaps he could move the home-port of the *Lady Ruth* to the U. S. Virgins or to Puerto Rico.

That would mean a change in the crew. William, Thomas and Alfred would need to be replaced and, certainly, the disagreeable Bobby Ruckman. What about Tournaire? He might move although Drejou indicated he might have invested interests on a different island.

Glenn slowed the motorbike, guided it to the curb where he parked out of the traffic.

And Jenny?

He was attracted to the young woman; she was an attrac-tive yet mercurial-mood woman; warm and desirable one minute, cold and demanding the next.

Probably she'd go elsewhere, but not necessarily with his ship. Pretty girl, but there are lots of pretty girls in this part of the world. Maybe now is the time to find out.

He revved the engine and sped into the flow of traffic.

19

Glenn stayed clear of the seediest Willemstad bars and gin joints that festered near the waterfront and turned, instead, through the doors of a saloon that seemed neither too rowdy nor too tame. There was a salsa band playing, and a dance floor where many young men and women were having what appeared to be very good and sensuous times. There were lots of young women who seemed to be without male companions, and an even greater group of young men who hoped to pair up for, at least, the night.

Clothing was colorful, touristy, and, on any number of bodies, downright skimpy. An abundance of skin was shown in shades of white, black, brown, bronze and, often, the blistering reds of today's sunburns. What with his recent days of observing partial and complete nudity unashamedly displayed aboard the *Lady Ruth*, Glenn had lost his Kansas City sense of modesty. With his full shirt and mid-thigh shorts, he almost felt overdressed.

An hour earlier, he had checked in at an upscale hotel located on the waterfront. As a former lodger of an old-fashioned rooming house, it was hard for him to choose this expensive hotel for a single night ashore, although the lawyer, Drejou, had assured him that his charter ship operation could well afford such occasional luxuries.

Following the check-in, he had inspected the room on the sixth floor and, even though he found it clean and comfortable, he was a bit disappointed in the décor and furnishings. The air conditioning worked well, and a window showed a nice panorama of the sea. Even so, he mused, a high price to pay for a view that didn't measure up to those he'd seen again and again from the ship.

What's more, the staff of this supposedly high-class facility had been less than cordial. His arrival on a skinny motorbike, registering for only one night without luggage, and dressed only in inexpensive clothing; it surely caused the parking attendants, bellboys, and desk clerks to eye him with evident disdain.

Next time, I'll try to look more stylish.

Now, in the nightclub, he wove his way through the bustling bodies toward the bar in the center of the large crowded room. Its elliptical counter surrounded a many-shelved core that displayed an impressive array of liquors and spirits. In the oval work space, behind the encircling counter, five bartenders were working with practiced precision to fill the orders of clamoring customers, although giving preference to the needs of the room-circulating waitresses.

With apologies, Glenn stepped between two obliging young men at the counter and waited until a harried middle-aged bartender made eye contact.

"Whatcha have, *mon*?"

"Rum and coke," Glenn responded quickly.

"You got it," the bartender said and, with astonishing speed, the iced drink was placed on the counter before him. Glenn overpaid and, carefully protecting the filled glass, moved away from the counter and worked his way to a some-what less crowded corner of the barroom.

There were booths lined along all four walls, but each one was jammed with merrymakers, so Glenn was relegated to standing space with a group of young men and women. He sipped his drink and watched the dancers over the heads and shoulders of those who stood between him and the dance floor.

Just as he was about to drain the rum and coke, a young Latin woman stepped into the standing cluster and, as she turned to face the dance floor, she gently bumped his elbow. She whirled to him, concern on her very pretty face. "Oh, I'm so sorry," she said. "Did I—"

"Helped me finish my drink?" Glenn responded and lifted his empty glass. "No spill, no harm."

"I really apologize—"

"There's no need," Glenn rushed to assure her, surprised at how easily his words came out. "Perhaps it gives me a chance to make your acquaintance."

The young woman's eyes narrowed as she regarded him knowingly, and then reached out her hand. "All right, I'm Vicky."

Glenn took her hand in his and held it for a few moments. "And I'm Glenn."

"Vacationing?" she asked, withdrawing her hand.

Glenn shook his head. "Shore leave."

"Shore leave? You're what? You're some sort of a sailor?

He was hesitant before he nodded. "I'm sort of a landlub-ber learning the ropes." He immediately corrected himself. "They tell me ropes are called lines on a ship."

She laughed. "Where in the States do you lub from?"

"Heart of the landlocked country. Kansas City. Missouri."

"What's a Kansas City rube doing on a ship?" she asked, her smile belaying any slight. "And what sort of a ship might that be?"

"Sailing ship, a two-masted schooner," he told her. "Charter yacht."

"That sounds like fun," she said. "Expensive?"

Again, Glenn shook his head. "We get just plain ordinary folks."

"Plain ordinary folks . . . like me?"

Glenn looked her up and down. She was a head shorter than he, with an attractive face framed in luxuriant black hair. Her attire, like others in the tavern, showed a bare tan midriff between her half-blouse and the high-cut shorts that revealed almost all of her shapely legs. "I'd say you're anything, but ordinary."

She smiled at the compliment, than asked, "You with anybody?"

"No, you?"

With a slight shake of her head, she asked another question. "You looking to hook up?"

"I could tell you some interesting things about Kansas City," Glenn said.

"I'd rather hear about how a landlubber becomes a sailor," she responded and moved closer to him.

■ ■ ■

"You live here?" Glenn asked, as the young woman led him up the steps toward the second floor of the apartment building.

"I share a place with a girl friend,"

"Will she be home?"

She paused for a moment, and then smiled down at him. "Too bad for you if she is."

At the top of the central stairway, a wide corridor with apartment doors on each side ran the building's length, right and left. It was an older structure, but one that had been well maintained. The carpet runner in the hallway showed no signs of long time wear, and the light beige paint on the walls appeared of recent application with no marks or damage.

Turning right, he followed Vicky as she walked to the last door on her left where she fished a key from a tiny pocket in her shorts, and then unlocked the door. She opened it and disappeared into the dark interior of the unlit apartment.

"She's not here," Vicky's voice came out of the gloom. "Come on in."

He took a few steps into a shadowy apartment and closed the door behind him. He could see the girl's silhouette with the faint light of a shaded window behind her.

"Where's the light switch?" he asked.

Strong arms grasped him from behind, two assailants coming from a dark corner of the room. One clamped his powerful right arm around his neck, the bulging bicep hard against his throat while the second aggressor pinned his arms against his side. Glenn struggled to no avail, the advantage of the surprise assault and the strength of his attackers too much to overcome.

"Hold him tight," the young woman said as she took something from her purse. What she carried in her hand as she approached, he could not tell until she raised it into the dim light.

A hypodermic syringe!

"Hold him tight," she said again and, a moment later, he felt the sting of a needle in his left arm. For a few moments, he experienced no reaction, and he wondered with what he had been injected. Then, the shadowy room began to blur, and the woman's shadowy figure lost shape. In his last few seconds of consciousness, he felt the arms release him and, with unreasoned anger, he blamed the hooligans for letting him fall.

20

A return to consciousness was very slow and very confusing. Dim light came to his rapidly blinking eyes, but focus took its time. He could finally see the patchy nap of the worn gray carpeting, but it took even longer for Glenn to realize that the sore place on his cheek was the result of having lain on it for a long time. The only sounds that came to him were the ins and outs of his own breathing.

When, at last, he sat up, he realized he was not in the apartment of his last consciousness. Instead, he was in a small, bare room with a high slit of a window that gave muted daylight to the space. The room was entirely empty, the dingy sheetrock walls covered with stains and blemishes. He sensed that he might be in a basement or in an empty room of an older building which, from the vacant and deteriorated appearance of his surrounds, might even be an abandoned one. The size of this space indicated that it might have been a storeroom at one time although, now, there were no shelves, boxes or scattered items in it

I've been moved, God knows where!

He sat for a while, waiting for the haze to clear from his mind, and for recollections to appear. He remembered fragments of small talk with the girl in the barroom, the intimacies that she had allowed, the touch of his hands on her bare skin, and the closeness of her face to his as she had clung to him. He recalled his excitement and eagerness to accompany her to her apartment – he, Glenn Hathaway, the wannabe seadog was about to get laid!

Stupid! A prostitute's easy mark!

He touched the bare skin of his left arm, rubbing the slight irritation of the needle puncture.

But, why the hypodermic? And, why all the trouble to lure me to an apartment? Why not simply knock me on the head, rob me, and dump me in an alley instead of in this room? All this for a measly three hundred dollars? A kidnapping, maybe? For what? It doesn't make sense.

He crawled to a wall and used it to lever himself up from the floor, feeling the weakness in his legs and wondering when strength would return. His watch was missing, his pockets were empty, the keys to the motorbike gone, and not even any change was left. He reached for his hip pocket and was not surprised to find his billfold had vanished as well. His sum of money, split by Vicky and her goon buddies, wouldn't have seemed quite worth all this trouble. He had some concerns about his driver's license, work permit, and his single credit card, but the card could be cancelled, and the other wallet items could be replaced once he was out of this confinement.

However, getting out might be a problem.

He kept his hands on the wall as he moved along to the door and, cautiously, tried the knob. "Shit!" he exclaimed under his breath. "Locked in a fucking drywall cell."

He leaned forward and placed his left ear against a door seam to listen for sounds of activity on the other side. After a long period in which he heard nothing, he leaned away.

"What the hell!" he said aloud, and began to pound on the door. "Hey!" he shouted. "Anybody out there? Open the goddamned door!"

Once more, he leaned his ear against the seam to listen and, after some time without a response, he decided to risk some effort of escape. Calling upon what little strength he could muster, he gripped the doorknob with both hands, and strained to lift the lock bolt out of the notch. He could feel the heavy door move a fraction of an inch, but he couldn't budge it any further. He held it on the verge of success for a few moments more, but then he could hold it no longer.

After repeated tries, strength waning, he gave up and leaned exhausted against a wall, frustrated and dejected. "All that shouting and rattling around, must not be anybody out there," he grumbled aloud. He looked at the door once more. "Maybe if I had some sort of a tool."

He slowly walked the perimeter of room, his eyes searching everywhere although he knew that there was no such implement in it. His assailants had evidently removed anything that might have been of use for his escape.

He hooked his thumbs in his belt as he considered his dilemma. He presumed it was Sunday although he couldn't tell for sure, nor could he estimate the time of day. He considered that it might even be a Monday before anyone entered this area of the building to discover and rescue him. Or, if this happened to be an abandoned building, even weeks might go by before a homeless person found his starved, dehydrated and withered corpse.

Suddenly aware of where his thumbs rested, he looked down at the leather belt threaded through the loops in his shorts. The spider lady and her cohorts had left his clothing intact, no doubt figuring his shirt, shorts, sock and deck shoes would be of no robbing value. Swiftly, he drew the belt out of his shorts and slid the buckle the length of the leather to form a small loop. He slipped the loop over the doorknob, and then pulled it tight. He turned his back to the door, stooped down and, with the length of the belt over his right shoulder, grasped it with both hands. Although the drug of the previous night had rendered him woozy and weak in his upper body and arm strength, Glenn reasoned that the muscle power of his legs might do the job.

Clutching the end of the belt tightly, he drove his body upward, thrilled to feel a significant move in the door behind him. Straining not to lose his leverage, he looked over his opposite shoulder and could see a minute separation in the seam between the door and the frame. With a deep breath, he heaved up with all of his might and fell forward to the floor as the heavy door came free and slammed open behind him.

His energy spent, he rested a few seconds, and then rolled over to look through the now open doorway. His guess about the vacant building had been correct; he saw a large empty room and another one beyond it. It appeared to be an abandoned structure, likely a narrow retail shop of bygone better shopping days. It seemed to still be in good structural shape although there were broken windows along one side and a large front window that had been boarded up.

He rose and walked out of the storeroom, re-threading his belt about his waist as he surveyed this dilapidated facility. To his left, in this intermediate room, a crazed-glass side door was partially ajar, probably where Vicky and her companions had carried his unconscious body inside. Still a little unsteady on his feet, he moved toward it and gave it a push so he could walk through.

Outside, he gained a quick understanding of why this place had been selected for a victim dump. It was the third of a trio of narrow, abandoned shop buildings on a desolate side street. He had no idea of the homeless population of Willemstad, but he thought this blighted set of buildings, in the States, would have been prime units of make-do shelters for derelicts.

He also had no idea of where in Willemstad he could be. A glance up at the sun made it mid-morning.

Sunday?

He hurried along the side street, catching a glimpse of a busy thoroughfare two blocks away. Without a dime in his pockets, there was no way to pay for a cab or even to ride a city bus. When he reached the avenue, he saw a bus stop at the curb on his side of the street. Two men, dark- skinned natives, were standing in the shade of a nearby tree, one talking on his cell phone. Glenn took a glance down, acutely aware of his disheveled appearance; wrinkled floral shirt, and grimy white shorts. He ran both hands through his hair in an effort to fin-ger-comb it into some semblance of neatness. With a shrug, he threw his shoulders back and strode toward the two men, who regarded his approach with solemn expressions.

"Excuse me," Glenn began in an apologetic manner. "Do either of you speak English?"

The man with the phone turned his back and continued his conversation while the other man slowly shook his head.

"You, sir," Glenn said, raising his voice to the man who had turned away. "You with the phone . . . I've been assaulted and robbed. If you understand, would you call the police?"

The man turned his head to regard Glenn, spoke softly into the phone, and then snapped it shut. "You say you've been robbed?"

"Last night," Glenn said and pointed down the street. "Locked me in an old abandoned building down there. I just got myself out."

"What do you want me to do?" the man asked.

"Call the police," Glenn replied. "Tell them I've been attacked, robbed, mayb even been kidnapped."

The man gave him a questioning look. "What else do you want me to say to them?"

"Tell them where we are . . . and ask them if they'd please come and get me. Tell them I don't know where in the hell I am."

21

"Welcome aboard, Mr. Kozlov," Gravendeel said unctuously, struggling up from the settee as Tournaire escorted the burly, bearded man into the ship's main salon. "We've given you the best cabin—"

"*Bezrazlichno*," the Russian mobster interrupted impatiently. He strode across the salon to the lounge grouping, seated himself across from the lawyer and, imperiously, waved Tournaire to Gravendeel's settee. "Sit! Both of you!" he commanded, a scowl on his face. "Why do we not yet sail?"

Gravendeel sank back down onto one of the white leather divans.

Deliberately defiant, Tournaire remained standing, and then answered, "You and your people have arrived quite early ths morning, *M'sieur*. We cannot raise anchor until we are ready this afternoon, not before." He paused. "However, now would be a good time to give me your course."

"*Niet!*" Kozlov said in a clipped, toneless manner. "At sea, no sooner."

"Do we sail north . . . south?" Tournaire persisted. "At least, give me a general direction!"

"I'll tell you when I'm ready, Frenchy," the burly newcomer snapped.

The threesome fell silent for a long awkward period, until the corpulent lawyer cleared his throat and posed a question. "Yuri, now that we are all aboard, could you, at least, tell us the nature and purpose of our voyage?"

"*Niet!*" Kozlov said again, making a slashing gesture of this right hand. "Last meeting, I told you not to ask."

"But, now is a different time," the lawyer said in a soft-spoken complaint. "We don't know what we are getting into, and what risks are involved. Don't you think we have a right to know?"

"You're in a risky business, that of smuggling drugs," Kozlov countered. "For this voyage, you are being overly well paid for whatever risks might come."

"An exorbitant fee?" Gravendeel questioned. "I beg to differ, sir. In fact, with such a mysterious voyage, perhaps a reassessment—"

The Russian angrily interrupted, "No need to discuss. Two hundred fifty thousand American dollars, as agreed for only a few days. You will ask for nothing more."

"All right, all right, you've made your point, but may we, at least, have our advance?" the lawyer questioned.

"No advance. We pay when the job is done," Kozlov said. "No sooner."

With a concerned glance to Gravendeel, Tournaire spoke, "*M'sieur*, it was our understanding—"

"Subject is closed!" the mobster cut him off.

"The ship does not sail without it," Tournaire said brusquely. "We can demand as well."

Kozlove glared and sat in silence for a long time. Finally, he bobbed his head. "Very well, you shall have it. However, in the future, you should be very careful in the manner you ask."

Again, there was silence.

At last, Tournaire lifted his eyes to the ceiling and walked to the bar. "May I fix you a drink, *M'sieur*?" he asked, his tone bordering on disdain. "Or was I careful enough in how I asked?"

"Nothing now," the Russian said, ignoring the gibe. "What about your crew? What do they know about this business?"

"We've told them nothing," Tournaire responded. "They do what they are told."

"All can be trusted?" the mobster asked. "Any one of them that would . . . what do you call it? Do the double-cross?"

"I think you'll find them jolly good cutthroats, each and every one," Gravendeel said sarcastically, now plainly irked at the newcomer's blunt manner. "They can be trusted as much as you trust your own crew.'

"Trust my crew?" Kozlov said with a glimpse of a smile, his first flash of humor. He sobered immediately, and switched his gaze to Tournaire. "What about the woman?"

For a moment, the captain hesitated. "She's all right."

"Something causes you doubt?" Kozlov questioned.

"Perhaps a trifle squeamish when the owners had to be dealt with," Tournaire explained. "Nothing more."

"Squeamish? A quality I would not expect in your crew. What did she do?" Kozlov asked.

"She did not like what happened, but she did not object," Tournaire told him.

"Get rid of her," the mobster demanded.

"She has many duties on the ship which, by the way, will include preparing your food," Gravendeel countered. "If she is not aboard, I hope you like microwave."

Kozlov took several moments to consider, and then shrugged. "You are sure she will not be a problem?"

"She will not!" Tournaire exclaimed. "She is one of us."

The mobster shook his head. "I still do not like . . . someone squeamish."

There came a knock at the salon entrance and Jenny stepped in. "The cabins are all ready, Mr. Kozlov," she said. "Shall I have the boys stow the luggage?"

The Russian rose from his chair and turned toward the young woman. "I come," he told her. He looked back at Gravendeel. "Will you be sailing with us, fat man?"

"Indeed I will," Gravendeel assured him. "And . . . the advance?"

The burly man's stare was icy in intensity, but he lifted his shoulders in a compliant shrug. "When I return, I will wire one hundred thousand to wherever you say."

"Meet us in the radio cabin," Gravendeel told him. "One hundred thousand will be most welcome."

As the Russian followed Jenny into the companionway, Gravendeel struggled to his feet, stepped close to Tournaire, and spoke in a low voice. "Did you take care of Hathaway?"

Tournaire shrugged. "Bobby and William have not yet returned. They assured me that, this time, they will not fail."

Gravendeel bobbed his head to indicate the now departed mobster. "I don't think our Cossack friend intends to pay us in full, and I think a few of his men might even be sailors."

"I'm sure they intend to kill us once we've served their purpose," Tournaire mused. "When we reach their destination, *we* will do the killing before they have the chance."

22

Glenn sprinted to the end of the pier just in time to see the *Lady Ruth* motoring slowly around the promontory rise to his left, and then disappear from sight.

"Damn!" Glenn exclaimed.

Earlier at the police station, Detective Classen, to whom he had related his story of assault and abduction, had seemed more amused than concerned, but had promised to investigate and search diligently for the young seductress who Glenn had so thoroughly described.

"We will do what we can," Classen had assured him. "But you should be much more careful in the future. Ladies of the evening will—"

"I'm going to be late," Glenn cut in, his eyes on the hands of a nearby wall clock.

"Jan will take you to your ship, I'm sure there's plenty of time," the detective said. "Jan is a very safe and careful driver."

Indeed, the Willemstad policeman, Jan, had been an unduly safe driver: a stickler for staying well below the city's speed limits.

Now, at the dock, after the police cruiser had slowly moved away, Glenn turned at the sound of footsteps coming up behind him. "Just missed her," Emory Gordon said as he came to Glenn's side. "How come you're late?"

"Long story, Emory," Glenn replied. "I just didn't think they'd shove off without me."

"How come they did?" Gordon asked. "You being the owner and all."

"If I was on board, I'd damned well ask them," Glenn said peevishly.

"Well, maybe they're not so far ahead . . . you want to catch 'em?" Gordon asked.

Glenn turned and cocked his head toward Gordon's yacht. "Your *Sea Mist*?"

"Naw, takes too long to get her set to go," Gordon said. "But, I got a thought. Come with me."

With a wave of his hand, he beckoned for Glenn to follow as he strode halfway back along the pier. He stepped to a side of the wharf's edge as Glenn joined him. On the deck of a sleek and well-maintained fishing boat, two young men were at work, preparing the craft for an afternoon charter.

"Hey, Jamie!" Gordon called. "Ahoy, there!"

One young man's head came up sharply, a grin on his tanned face. "Hi, Emory! What's up?"

"Care to do me, and this fellow here a favor?"

"I 'spect I would. What do you need?" the young man responded.

"James Brenner, this is Glenn Hathaway," Gordon said with a hand gesture to Glenn. "Just missed his ship, the *Lady Ruth,* and he'd like to catch 'er. Heard you had an afternoon charter?"

"I 'spect I could put him aboard, soon as my clients arrive," Jamie told him. "They're due any minute, now." He turned his attention to Glenn. "You one of the *Lady Ruth* guests?"

"Part of the crew," Glenn responded.

"Glenn, here, is more than that," Gordon put in. "Matter of fact, he *owns* the ship."

"Well, I'd be glad to take him even if he didn't," Jamie said cheerfully. "Come aboard, Glenn, we'll cast off soon as our folks arrive." He waved and turned away, heading to the bow of the fishing vessel.

"You got a few minutes," Gordon said, facing Glenn. "Got time for that long story?"

Glenn gave him a sheepish look. "Tell a part of it. I expect it isn't anything new. Met a girl at a bar, thought things were going pretty good and—"

"You got rolled," Gordon cut in with a knowing smile.

"Rolled, doped, and even kidnapped," Glenn told him. "I woke up this morning, found myself locked up in an old building, money, watch, everything gone." He shook his head. "Got myself out okay, but that's about the size of it."

Gordon's smile had turned to a serious frown. "Boy, that's pretty goddamned serious. I'd say you're lucky to still be walking around. You go to the police?"

Glenn nodded. "They'll do what they can."

"You got a place to stay if Jamie don't catch your ship?"

Glenn shook his head. "Not tonight. I'm broke 'til the bank opens tomorrow."

"You can bunk in on the *Sea Mist* if that's okay, I got an extra stateroom," Gordon offered. Then, he nodded to the fishing craft. "I expect Jamie won't have any trouble. He'll catch your ship easy." He looked away. "Here come the fishermen. Best get aboard."

The skipper sounded his ship horn again as they closed the distance between his vessel and the *Lady Ruth*. As the schooner slowed, and the smaller craft came abreast of it, their arrival brought a string of curious men to the port side rail. To Glenn, they appeared to be an uncommon group of guests; burly, hard looking, and unsmiling.

"There's a cheerful crowd," Jamie Brenner said. "Sure you don't want to let 'em sail on without you?"

"I haven't acted much like an owner up to now, but that's just about to change," Glenn said meaningfully.

Standing on the deck of the smaller craft, he looked up to see Tournaire and Jenny watching him; Tournaire's face stern, Jenny's as well. Glenn waited until both vessels came close together and, as Alfred placed the utility ladder down the ship's side, he reached for a rung and climbed up onto the *Lady Ruth's* deck.

"Thanks for the ride, Captain Brenner," he called back to the skipper of the fishing charter. "Surely appreciate it."

"Any time, my friend," the young man replied. He gunned the engine, and veered his vessel away as the fishermen waved their farewells.

Glenn turned to survey the cluster that surrounded him, a ring of crew members and the tough-looking guests he had seen at the rail. Up close, these passengers, young as well as middle-aged, appeared an unlikely vacationing group, with a couple of heavily tattooed men who looked like thugs.

Glenn returned his gaze to the captain of his ship and the young woman beside him. Both were regarding him with serious, nearly resentful expressions.

"You sailed without me," Glenn said to Tournaire, his tone strong and accusing. "You might tell me why."

Tournaire forced a smile, although his eyes were focused on the departing fishing craft. He returned his gaze to Glenn, and he affected an apologetic mien. "We did not know where you were, *M'sieur* Glenn. And our sailing schedule—"

"Alain, I've been robbed and kidnapped, locked up in an abandoned building overnight," Glenn cut in heatedly. "I've spent the morning at the police station and, from what I learned there, not one single question came from this ship as to my whereabouts or my well-being."

"We did not know, *M'sieur*," Tournaire said in awkward apology. "We had talked about you spending some time ashore. We just assumed you were enjoying—"

"That doesn't wash with me," Glenn interrupted again. "Any one of our crew that went missing, I'd be trying to find out what happened to him!" He glanced at Jenny. "Or her! I damned well wouldn't be sailing off without getting some answers."

"Alain was right," Jenny said in a sharp tone. "You missed the ship's sailing, and that's pretty much what we'd expect from such a klutz. No reason to find fault with us." Her eyes shifted to the fishing craft only a short distance away. "Maybe we should call back your friends and you could take time off away from us. You're pissed and, frankly, we are a good bit ourselves."

Glenn was taken aback by the unexpected reprimand, and he took a few seconds to reach a calm. "Well, *Miss*, I *will* be staying aboard. This klutz is about to make some changes."

The young woman regarded him with an icy stare and, without another word, turned and walked away.

Glenn watched until she entered the deckhouse, and then shifted his attention back to Tournaire. "When I first arrived, you made a big deal of saying that I should assume the own-er's privileges. I didn't agree with you then, but I do now." He paused and looked at the gathering of crewmen and male guests standing around them. "After this charter is completed, you will still be the captain, but, from now on, you will report to me, and not the other way around."

Tournaire did not respond.

"I'm going down, collect my gear, and take one of the smaller cabins for myself," Glenn said. "In the future, I'll take an upgrade cabin, but we'll still leave the master suite for who-ever pays well for it." His eyes swept the surrounding cluster of swarthy men. "And who in the hell booked these people?" Without waiting for a reply, he strode away, heading for the fore ladder.

■ ■ ■

Tournaire stepped quickly to a pair of his crewmen, Ruckman and William, speaking in a low angry voice. "I thought the two of you had taken care of him? What's this about a kidnapping?"

"The man, he is a devil," William declared solemnly.

"We were going to tell you," Ruckman said defensively. "We couldn't find him. We looked ever'where's." He shook his head. "He just gone and disappeared. We was going to cut his throat or bash his head, but we couldn't come across him. I don't know nothing 'bout no kidnapping.

"Failing to take him out was something you neglected to tell me," Tournaire accused.

"When he didn't show, we just figured maybe he'd run into trouble on his own," Ruckman admitted grudgingly. "If not, we'd have laid for him, and took care of him when he come back."

"Well, he's aboard now, and we must deal with him," Tournaire said in anger.

The door of the pilot house opened and Gravendeel, along with the Russian leader, stepped out onto the starboard side of the deck. The heavyset lawyer led the way, lumbering to join the cluster of men surrounding Tournaire.

"What's going on, Alain?" Gravendeel asked. "Why is the ship stopped?"

With a furtive glance at Kozlov, Tournaire said, "Our missing crewman has rejoined the ship"

"Hathaway?" Gravendeel asked, his eyes widening. "Where is he?"

"Gone below," Tournaire replied. "He's going to be a problem."

"Damn it, Alain! You said we were done with him!" Gravendeel complained.

Kozlov, mystified and left uninformed, was beginning to fume. "*Ti menya zlish*! What is happening? Tell me!"

"A man has come aboard who we must deal with," Gravendeel hastily replied. "Not a matter for your concern."

"What is this that you're not telling me?" Kozlov demanded, looking back and forth between Tournaire and Gravendeel. "Who is this man, and what is he?"

There were a few moments of awkward silence.

"A regrettable loose end, I must admit," Gravendeel said with a sigh. "He is the new owner of the *Lady Ruth*, and he has unexpectedly boarded the ship. We truly thought he would be out of the way, and not be of concern for us while we are on this voyage."

"A new owner? And you never told me about him?" Kozlov asked acidly.

"Unfortunately, we did not," Gravendeel acknowledged. "We did not know of him ourselves until only a short time ago, well after we had made our arrangements with you. Even though he's been a bit of a bother, we were sure we had him out of the way and under control—"

"Under control?" Kozlov cut him off, his voice full of scorn "I have hired incompetents."

"We'll take care of it!" Tournaire said tersely.

"Why wait?" the burly Russian wanted to know. "Get rid of him now!"

Tournaire bristled. "When we are further away from ocean traffic, the sea will soon claim him. We will teach this meddle-some pest a lesson. We'll drop him into the deep, just as we did with his aunt and uncle—"

"More of this buccaneer nonsense? You intend to make him walk the plank?" Gravendeel interposed sarcastically. "The time comes, why not merely a simple shot to the head?"

"It pleasures the crew," Tournaire said dispassionately. Then, a disturbingly virulent smirk came to his face as he added, "And, perhaps, it amuses me as well."

"But, Alain . . . such a horrible way for the young man to die," Gravendeel protested.

Kozlov chuckled, his aggravation abating "The fat man is also squeamish . . . like the woman." He turned to Tournaire. "Do you actually mean . . . to drown this bothersome person alive?"

Tournaire nodded. "Unless, of course, you would prefer a gunshot execution."

"*Niet!*" Kozlov objected, broadly smiling as he turned to Gravendeel. "'Walk the plank' did you say? Something out of those old pirate stories that happened right here in these Spanish Main waters, did they not?" He paused, gave a slight nod, and then continued, "That could be quite an amusement for me and my men as well." He turned to Tournaire. "I, too, would be pleasured. Do it."

No one spoke.

"Yuri," Gravendeel said after a few moments. "I'm afraid we don't have a plank."

The Russian laughed.

23

Glenn's anger continued to simmer as he collected his few belongings from the crew's quarters, and moved to one of remaining unoccupied lower deck cabins. He had considered taking one of the deluxe units near the salon, but he had no idea of how many guests were aboard and where they might be assigned.

It had been a matter of opening a few cabin doors until he found one without personal belongings inside. He had not encountered anyone on the lower deck, and he presumed that most of the passengers, if not all, were topside. If so, it meant that this charter was underbooked and not particularly profitable.

The narrow confines of this cabin contained the standard bed and the minimal furnishings; a wardrobe locker, a small desk against one wall with a straight-back chair and a compact easy chair. Even though cramped, Glenn was pleased to have privacy for the first time aboard the schooner.

He seated himself on the bed, and decided that this move was a significant one. Perhaps, he considered, it marked his transition from naivety to whatever in the future he was now determined to be.

His recent ponderings about the future of the *Lady Ruth* and its present crew came to his mind again. Today's disregard and disparaging treatment of him had sparked resentment and a latent resolve

I'm a klutz all right, a naïve nerd who inherited property I probably didn't deserve, and certainly didn't know how to manage. Well, that's just about to change!

When the ship returned to Willemstad, he decided, he would contact the attorney, Drejou, to start making arrangements to transfer the ship's homeport and charter operations to a United States island. A dock in the Virgins or in Puerto Rico would do quite nicely. While arrangements for the change were in progress, he decided to take Jenny's earlier advice; to find a rental unit on Curacao where he could live for a short time, and stay in touch with his lawyer as needed. There would be no more pretense of living aboard, and continuing the charade as an ordinary seaman.

The charters would continue during the period prior to the transition, he decided. Then, with adequate notification, each and every one of the crew would have to go. The surly deckhands would be the first off the ship, and even the suave Captain Tournaire should probably be replaced. Undoubtedly, there were many other capable skippers available in the Caribbean.

And Jenny? Despite her hard edge, he had become rather attracted to her, but her words just spoken continued to sting and saddened him. In recent days, she had seemed friendlier and, occasionally, had dropped a bit of that disdain when she was with him. At times, he thought he had detected even a smidgen of affection. Today, however, it seemed there was neither affection nor even affability between them. She and Tournaire had made quite an embarrassing show of their disrespect in front of that curious bunch of passengers.

The passengers? Who and what are they?

He shook his head. Something about this charter seemed way out of kilter. Heavyset and hulking, these voyagers had more a look of workmen rather than vacationers and, he thought, maybe that is the answer. Perhaps this is not a charter at all; perhaps, a transport of laborers on their way to perform some sort of heavy work.

He looked aside to the nearby pillow, and a surge of fatigue coursed through him.

"I'll check it out later" he said aloud as he stretched out on the bed, his eyelids heavy. "And, maybe, raise a little hell with all of them."

■ ■ ■

Glenn came awake in the dark cabin, the sudden cessation of sound from the diesel arousing him. He stood and turned on the bedside lamp. He glanced at his bare wrist where his stolen watch was missing, then gauged the time to be long past the hour in which he had fallen asleep. He wondered if the ship was under sail, but there was no indication of forward motion, only the slight rocking of the *Lady Ruth* on a gentle sea.

The length of his slumber concerned him; he presumed his lassitude to be the residual effect of the knockout drug still affecting his body. He looked down at his rumpled clothing, the same shirt, shorts and underwear he'd been wearing for the entire weekend. He considered a shower and a change, but curiosity about the heave-to of the ship took his immediate interest. He wondered if something had gone wrong.

An urgent rap on the door heightened his concern.

"Mista Glenn, sah!" William's voice was of high concern. "Captain need you on aft deck, jiffy quick!"

"Something wrong?" Glenn shouted.

"Yes, sah, mon! Come now!"

"Tell 'em I'm coming," Glenn called.

Glenn took a few seconds to rub his hands over his face, and tried to shake the cobwebs from his sluggish thought process. Considering a myriad of possible problems, he opened the door and stepped out into the empty passageway, walked swiftly to the aft ladder and went up the steps to the deck. The vault of the dark sky was strewn with glittering stars, a magnificent sight at sea, far from land and the lights of civilization. There was a light wind that touched his face, bare legs and arms; a cooling zephyr that brought relief from the below-deck stale heat.

For some reason, the ship was unmoving in the water, no running lights showing, the sails furled, and the engine idling. On the port side of the aft deck, near the gangway threshold, there was a curious gathering of the burly male passengers and the entire crew. At first, Glenn wondered if there must be something in the sea that had caught their attention, but they were not at the rail and looking down. Instead, they were standing motionless and silent, and their eyes appeared to be looking straight at him.

Puzzled, Glenn walked toward them, while Ruckman separated himself from the others and strode toward him. The husky sailor's manner of surly intent had always raised a sense of menace and, this time, a foreboding of danger came with alarming intensity. Ruckman's right hand was at his side, some sort of an object in it that Glenn could not identify.

"Hey," Ruckman said. "We been waiting for you." He swung his arm up and, immediately, threads of numbing electricity shot from his hand-held stun gun. Glenn cried out and fell to his knees, bending his head nearly to the deck in an effort to assuage the searing hurt. Then, as it began to wane, Ruckman aimed and triggered a second charge that brought the torment back again in full force.

Face down, doubled in pain and striving to catch his breath, Glenn was only vaguely aware that others had rushed to surround him, lashing his legs together with ropes. Then, his hands were being pulled sharply behind his back, and he felt them being tied, the stout cords biting cruelly into his wrists and rendering him helpless. As the stun-gun pain slightly lessened, he twisted his head, trying to see his attackers. One was William, but he had no chance to identify any others as men in front of him placed their hands under his shoulders and dragged him across the deck into the center of the large gathering of ominous observers.

Glenn raised his head again and looked up to see Tournaire and a foreign-looking man gazing down at him. The latter, a person he had never seen before, crouched down to place his face a few inches away.

In a husky voice, Glenn demanded, "Who the hell are—"

"A new and very brief acquaintance," the foreigner interrupted in his accented voice. "Hello and goodbye, young man." With a smirk on his blunt featured face, he rose to his feet.

Before Glenn had a chance to speak again, William pulled his head back while Ruckman roughly pressed first one, and then a second strip of duct tape over his mouth. Unable to do anything except make a muffled wail of protest, he struggled futilely against his bonds. In desperate fear, he looked up again and his eyes widened as he saw the corpulent figure of Johan Gravendeel step forward to join Tournaire and the taunting foreigner.

Surprise and dismay joined fear as he saw, at the back of the gathering, Jenny regarding him with a cold, unrelenting stare. Their eyes locked for a few seconds, and then she moved out of sight behind other smirking onlookers.

Abruptly, he was pulled past the rear of the deckhouse onto the port walkway, close to the open gangway space, the onlookers lining up at the rail to watch. Again, he felt someone doing something with the ropes that bound his legs together. He twisted his head to look and saw that Ruckman was tying another line to his ankle bindings. Horror replaced fright as he saw, at the end of that short rope, a large canvas duffle bag had been securely attached. As Ruckman finished the knot, William hefted the bag toward the open space between the rails and, from his strain to lift it, Glenn knew something inside was very heavy. Tournaire raised his hand, a restraining gesture to William who, in response, placed the bag at the very edge of the deck. The captain stepped close and knelt over Glenn, then ripped both duct tape strips from his mouth and held them in one hand. *"J'en suis au regret, M'sieur.* You have left us no choice. Last words?"

"For God's sake, why?" Glenn muttered. "What have I done?"

"You got in the way," Tournaire said and brought the tapes towards Glenn's face, ready to replace them.

"This is murder!" Glenn shouted.

Tournaire nodded. "A necessary tool when needed." He pressed the tape over Glenn's mouth, and rose to his feet.

Looking down, he touched the fingers of his right hand to the bill of his cap in a mock salute, and then nodded to Ruckman and William.

The two deckhands smiled and returned the salute as they grasped the top of the duffle bag and swung it toward the sea.

Glenn was jerked across the deck, and then his body soared out in an arc toward the dark water. In three seconds, the bag splashed into the ocean and Glenn had only a moment to take a breath before he plunged in after it.

24

As the sea enveloped him, Glenn's terror suddenly turned to calm; he knew death was upon him. His flat-on-his-back splash into the sea had momentarily slowed the downward drag, but then the weighted bag drew him feet first into the darkening depths. He was continuing to hold his breath, a reflex instinct of the body beyond his control. A curious lucidity came, and he realized that this would last for only seconds until the rigors of drowning would begin. It flashed through his mind that it was a terrible way to die.

Pray?

Too late?

Oblivion?

Behind him, a creature of size in the murky sea was coming toward him.

Shark!

Surprise and elation surged through him as, barely seen, Jenny swam into his vision. Naked, and with a knife in one hand, she grasped the rope that tethered him to the duffle bag and, with two sawing strokes, severed it and the bag disappeared into the blackness below.

Glenn's descent slowed, his lungs in torment, as the young woman hooked her arm across his chest. Swimming with powerful strokes, she pulled him up toward the dark hull of the ship at the far away surface. It was all he could do to keep from inhaling, and he despaired at the distance they had yet to rise.

Agony!

Suddenly, his head broke above the surface, and there was air! Life-saving air!

Jenny's head was close to his and he could feel her arm still across his chest, keeping him from sinking. They were under the bow curve of the hull at the starboard side of the ship, the out-of-sight deck high above them. He could hear the pulsing of the idling diesel, and a new fear arrived; that it would rev up and drive the vessel away.

Jenny moved her face inches from his and whispered, "Don't make a sound or you'll kill us both." Before he could nod, she ripped the tape from his mouth. "Don't say a word."

She ducked beneath the surface, and he felt his legs come apart as she cut the ropes that bound his ankles. Seconds later, she cut the cords at his wrist and reappeared at the surface.

"Now, listen to me," she whispered. He saw her hand reach for a rope that dangled from the deck above; a lifeline he hadn't noticed before. "I'm going up. If it's clear, can you climb?"

He nodded.

"If I run into anyone, our goose is cooked," she said, her voice barely audible. Without another word, she put the knife blade between her teeth and began to climb, hand-over-hand, up the rope.

Glenn was amazed at the strength of the young woman. Her progress up the rope was steady and sure. Just below the edge of the foredeck, she hung motionless, and then eased her head slowly up. A half-minute later, she hoisted herself up to and over the rail and disappeared from view.

Glenn waited with his hands on the dangling rope, dreading a shout of discovery, more concerned now for Jenny than for himself.

Jenny appeared above, a dark profile in the night, and her hand waved him up.

Unsure that he could match the strength of his rescuer, he tightened his grips and began to work his way up the water-slimed rope. He was awkward and clumsy in his struggling ascent, his handholds slipping three times. Near the top, he could go no higher. Drug-debilitated, Tasered, and nearly drowned, he hung exhausted, his strength almost gone.

Jenny, outlined against the glittering sky, reached over the rail to grasp one of his hands to prevent his fall.

With a surge of manly resolve, Glenn heaved himself up to a knee stand on the outer side of the rail. He looked right and left, searching the deck for any one of the crew or the hoodlums. There was no one other than Jenny in the surrounding area; no one in sight. He swung over the rail and lay flat on the deck next to her. The murderous ship's crew and the foreign conspirators were apparently still gathered astern where they, with voices raised in loud laughs and boisterous conversations, were in a macabre jubilation over his watery demise.

Loathing for one and all invaded Glenn's psyche. Alien to his good nature, hatred took hold of his mind and ebbed deep into his subconscious, there to remain.

Although the malicious men were perilously near; the deckhouse, the base of the foremast and the storage bins on the foredeck hid Glenn and Jenny from direct view. However, a stroll forward by any one of the hoodlums could likely notice them lying flat on the deck.

"We've got to make it below," Jenny whispered. She cut through the knot tied at a stanchion and dropped the climb line into the ocean. "Hide in the aft locker."

"Where'll you be?"

"In the shower, if I make it," she answered. "Someone will want to know why my hair's wet." Turning and crouching low, she moved toward and past the foremast understructure, her naked body gleaming even in the deep shadows of the night. She hunkered down for a few seconds, and then made a dash to the hatch's entry. She stepped down and dropped down out of sight. Moments later, he saw her hand waving him to follow.

Glenn moved on his hands and knees, practically crawling, he scuttled across the starlit deck to the hatch. With a sigh of relief, he came down slowly where Jenny was waiting near the bottom of the steps. Cautiously, she peered around a corner of the adjacent bulkhead.

"Go!" she whispered urgently. "All clear."

He turned past her, moving toward the large storeroom door located on the left side of the aisle at the aft end of the ship. Not yet there, he stopped and turned to look back.

Jenny had not yet entered the head, her head turned and her eyes searching the nearby stairwell, perhaps hearing a sound that had caused her, unknowingly, to strike an exquisite pose; a still frame moment of beauty in flesh and form.

Damn, she's a desirable woman, Glenn thought. *But what else is she? A part of this hellacious evil, maybe just a little less inclined to murder? Who and what in hell is she?*

Unaware of his gaze, she opened the door, entered and closed it behind her. Then, he heard the sound of the shower.

Suddenly, Glenn heard voices becoming louder, two or more men descending the aft hatch. Cursing himself at this dangerous time for lingering in the passageway with his carnal thoughts, he had no time to get to the locker. Frantic, he opened the door of the nearest cabin and slipped inside.

No one here! Thank God!

He leaned close to the door to listen, and heard a casual conversation between two men speaking in a tongue he could not understand. To his relief, the sound of their voices diminished as they walked on past along the passageway. He heard a door open and close, and then another opening and closing. He inched open this cabin's door, and gave the companionway a close scrutiny before he ventured out.

Walking quickly, he moved to the door of the aft storage compartment, turned the handle and slipped inside. He closed the door behind him and flipped on the overhead light. It was a relatively large storage space. There were shelves of smaller supplies against three of the bulkheads and, scattered about, a jumble of different items of equipment, supplies and accessories. The space contained diving gear, air tanks and compressors, bedding supplies, cleaning materials, scrub buckets, mops, brooms, and a variety of many miscellaneous objects. At the very back of the space, he saw a pile of life jackets and, to his elation, the deflated dive raft.

He pictured an appropriate path though the jumble of the ship's gadgets, tools and devices, large and small - and then turned out the overhead light. In total darkness, he slowly and carefully felt his way past and over each and every obstacle until he reached his destination at the end of the lightless room. He sat down and tucked himself behind the limp plastic raft, making sure that no part of him, hands, arms or legs, would be visible. As he settled back, exhaling his relief, he heard the ship's engine rev, and then felt the *Lady Ruth* begin to move.

A place to be safe . . . at least for a while!

25

Jenny and William were busy clearing the breakfast dishes from the aft deck dining area, while Gravendeel and Kozlov lingered over their coffee. The ship was reaching in a constant wind abeam, the breeze-filled main and foresails moving it on a course at a good clip. A short distance behind them, at the helm, Tournaire was in earnest conversation with Ruckman who was at the wheel.

The sun was high at mid-morning and the heat was intensifying, uncomfortable for the Dutch attorney in his voluminous, long-sleeved shirt and heavy, capacious trousers. Under his broad-brimmed planter's hat, sweat continued to bead on his forehead, and he often wiped at it with a soggy handkerchief. By contrast, Kozlov was shirtless with a thick mat of black, curly hair on his barrel chest. Wearing a baseball cap, cargo shorts, and sandals on his feet, he appeared quite comfortable.

After Jenny and her helper had finished and disappeared into the ship, Gravendeel cleared his throat as a prelude to speaking, "We thank you, at last, for providing the course."

.Kozlov made no response.

After a few moments of awkward silence, Gravendeel continued, "The captain tells me that there is very little habitable land in this part of the ocean, merely a scattering of small barren islands . . . is it one of those?"

"When we arrive, you will know."

"Alain said we should arrive at the general destination area late this evening or perhaps early tomorrow," Gravendeel said, mopping is brow once again. "Would you like to move inside out of the heat?"

"The ship is moving, and the wind is cool," Kozlov countered. "Go, if you wish."

Unsure how to respond, Gravendeel was gratified to see Tournaire breaking away from Ruckman and walking toward them.

"Ah, Captain!" Gravendeel hailed. "Will you join us?"

"I have work to do," Tournaire replied as he came to stand over them. "A few minutes, however."

"I was telling Yuri that we should arrive—"

"We get there faster on the engine?" Kozlov cut in.

"It is a sailing ship, *M'sieur*," Tournaire said. "Under sail or power, the speed is very much the same." He paused. "With a fair wind, why waste our fuel?"

"Sooner we're finished, the better I like it," the mobster boss said.

"I must get back to work," Tournaire said again, turning away. "Perhaps we can meet for lunch in a couple—"

"What about the girl?" Kozlov interrupted.

Tournaire turned back. "Well, what about her?"

"She was there last night?" Kozlov asked.

"She was standing near me," Gravendeel said.

"All the time?" the Russian wanted to know.

"I don't remember," Gravendeel admitted with a shrug. "She might have gone below."

"No stomach for it?" Kozlov persisted.

"Why does it matter?" Tournaire spoke sharply, plainly irritated. "Hathaway is at the bottom of the ocean, and that is the end of it."

"I do not like an emotional woman on board," Kozlov said.

"You dislike this woman or all women?" Tournaire said caustically.

The Russian gave him a wide smile and a wink. "Only on sheets, not in business." He wrinkled his face into a scowl. "How long has this Jennifer woman been with you?"

"A year or so," Tournaire answered.

"Just a year?" Kozlov questioned. "About the time you began your contraband enterprise?"

"What are you getting at?" Tournaire asked, irritation strong in his voice.

"Come, come, Alain," Gravendeel interposed as he turned to face the Russian. "To answer your concern, Yuri, we did a thorough check on her before we brought her into the operation. As you probably know, we replaced Captain Martin's crew with people of our own and—"

"The girl!" Kozlov interrupted. "Get back to her."

"She has a record," Gravendeel said. "Teen-aged prostitution . . . although she will not admit to that. Worked in the Caribbean to mule drugs, and then arrested for distributing for a Columbian cartel. She did two years in a Florida prison."

"Who vouched for her?"

"The Columbians," Tournaire said.

"She sought you out?" Kozlov asked.

Gravendeel shook his head. "For a long time, Jack Martin had only an all-male crew for his cruises. His new wife thought it would be better for the charter operation to have a woman aboard as a sort of hostess rather than having all men. She, herself, served in that capacity some of the time, but she felt it would be better to have someone younger and prettier to be the hostess." He shrugged. "She would not have it any other way, so we looked for someone to fit her needs and ours. Miss Jennifer has been an asset to our legitimate business, and has no objections to the other."

Kozlov looked up at Tournaire, a smirk appearing on his blunt-featured face. "You have soft spot for her? Perhaps she and you—"

"None of your concern," Tournaire cut him off.

"Our business will soon be concluded," Gravendeel counseled. "Forget the girl, she's no problem."

"On the other hand, perhaps we should drop her over the side like the young man," Kozlov suggested.

Tournaire's face twisted in irritation, and even Gravendeel seemed shocked.

"Making joke," Kozlov said. "You people have no sense of humor."

■ ■ ■

The locker door opened and closed, and the overhead light came on.

Under his covering raft, Glenn stiffened and took very shallow breaths, careful not to make any movement or sounds that would betray his presence.

"Glenn, it's me." Jenny's voice was a whisper.

Glenn leaned his head out from under the deflated raft.

"I brought you something to eat, peanut butter. Sorry it isn't anything better," she said. She moved through the obstacle course of ship's stores to hand him a paper-wrapped sandwich.

"I owe you my life . . . and, honestly, I don't know why you took such a chance," he said. "Why is everybody trying to kill me?" He took a small bite as he awaited her answer.

"You got in their way."

"That's what Tournaire said . . . in the way of what?"

"I can't tell you right now. I can't stay but a minute or I'll be missed," she told him. "You should be safe in here, at least for a while, but you mustn't make a sound."

"Tell me now! I've got to know," Glenn persisted although he kept his voice low.

She sighed, exasperated. "Okay, this much I can tell you. We're trafficking drugs," she said hurriedly, her eyes shifting toward the door. "Big time, and we're getting bigger."

Glenn took a few seconds to consider her statement and then asked, "Drugs? My aunt and her husband, they were in on it?"

She shook her head.

"Gravendeel, and Tournaire?"

"That's right, the entire crew."

"What about this new bunch of cutthroats on board?"

Again, she shook her head. "This is something quite different. I'll tell you when I come back."

"Before you go, I have to know," he hurried to say. "What really happened to Captain Jack and Aunt Ruth?"

She didn't answer immediately, and then: "The same as what they tried to do to you."

Glenn was stunned. "Were you aboard? And let them die?"

"I didn't know Tournaire's intent for them. I was below deck and came topside just as it was over. There was nothing I could do," she replied. "When you walked onto this ship, you blundered into the biggest mistake of your life." She turned to leave.

"You still haven't told me . . . are you a part of these thugs?. Why did you save me?"

"If I'd been smart, I'd have let you drown," she said in exasperation.

"So tell me!"

"I haven't got time. Staying in here puts my life in danger," she said angrily.

"You're already in trouble," he countered. "They find me, they're going to know I didn't get here by myself. They'll have questions about you . . . what do you call them? Your partners in crime?"

"All right, I guess you'll have to know," she acknowledged. "I'm DEA."

Glenn fell silent, then sputtered, "I don't quite—"

"Drug enforcement, damn it," she cut in. "Rescuing you has probably screwed up our entire operation and, God knows, we've had our hands full keeping you alive."

It took a few seconds for Glenn to comprehend. "All these things that have happened to me, they were—"

"They didn't want you on the ship at any time, but especially not when these Balkan bastards were due to come aboard. Tournaire's idea was to either put you in the hospital or, if that failed, in a grave."

A thought came to Glenn. "Kidnapping their idea?"

She smiled. "Well, that was Vicky. If we get out of this alive, remind me to have a talk with her about letting you get away."

Glenn considered this with a wry face. "She's DEA, too?"

"Different agency, but a part of the overall," she told him. "Look, we could've arrested Gravendeel and Tournaire, the whole bunch, some time ago. Over a year ago, we got wind of something pretty damned illegal going on with this charter ship operation. We built a criminal background for me, and made me available. Once I got in, my job, originally, was to get leads on their suppliers and, then, the stateside distributors. We were just about to drop the hammer on the trafficking when these new hooligans came into the picture."

"And who, exactly, are they?"

"Eastern Europeans, Balkans, Russians; whoever and whatever they're after, that's what we want to know. Their leader is a man named Kozlov."

"He's the foreign-tongued bastard who wished me goodbye?"

She nodded. "We think they're up to something rather special. We intend to find out exactly what."

"Any ideas?"

"Some," she acknowledged. "We have a hunch."

"What's the hunch?

"That's why I'm still aboard," she answered. "To see if we're right."

"What can I do to help?"

She laughed. "You do two things pretty well. You get into trouble and, Lord knows how, you manage to find some way out of it."

"Maybe only one thing well," he told her. "I didn't get out of drowning without your help."

"I've got to go," she said. She stepped through the scattered equipment and supplies as she made her way to the door. "Tonight, we'd better hide you in a safer place."

"Where?"

"A place where they're not likely to look."

"What if somebody comes in here before you find a place and finds me?"

"Pray that they don't," she said as she turned out the overhead light. "Or we're history."

26

Glenn's eyes opened as the light flooded the locker and fright mingled with self-recrimination for sleeping. He held his breath.

"It's me, again," Jenny whispered.

Glenn breathed out a sigh and peeked out from under his hiding place. "I thought I was caught," he whispered. "What's happening?"

"Everyone's up on deck, having supper," she replied. "This may be the best time to move you."

"Where?"

"Under this deck, into the bilges," she told him.

"Into the what? The bilges?"

"It's the space at the bottom of the hull."

"Some place wet and nasty, full of rats?"

She laughed softly. "May be a little damp, but the bilge pumps should keep your fairly dry. It's the last place anyone is liable to look." She beckoned him with a wave. "Let's go."

With a cautious glance into the passageway, Jenny stepped out and led the way forward to a carpeted square in the flooring at the end of the aisle. She quickly unfastened the recessed twist locks at each corner, lifted it, and set it aside to reveal a dark space under the deck. She motioned for Glenn to climb in, whispering,. "This isn't the lowest section."

"No light?" he muttered.

"Get in," she hissed, her gaze darting from the nearby ladder to the empty passageway. "Hurry!"

"No more room than a coffin," he complained.

"Get in, damn it!"

Glenn slipped into the opening and wriggled down into the black hole, and then looked up. "Am I going to be able to breathe?"

"It's not airtight, you'll be fine," she assured him. "Again, don't make any noise."

"How about a flashlight and a book?"

"How about shutting the hell up?" she said and replaced the cover plate, closing him into darkness. He heard her twisting the locks, and then heard her footsteps as she walked away.

In the pitch-black partition, he reached out his hands to touch and explore the dimensions of his confinement. Although the area around him was larger than he had originally thought, it was anything but spacious. For the first time ever, he suffered a mild yet disturbing sense of claustrophobia. Beneath and around him, he could feel and hear the rush of water against the steel hull as the ship knifed through the sea. With the unmistakable sensation of entombment, he realized he was locked in, and he recalled his coffin comment. Now, in this sour, musty black pit, those words were uncomfortably significant.

Jenny finished her work in the galley after Kozlov and his thuggish crew had retired for the night. Ruckman and Alfred had turned in early, each to wait his turn for his scheduled four-hour watch. Gravendeel, given one of the better cabins, had retired to it, although bitterly grousing about its inadequacies. Tournaire and William remained topside to guide the ship's progress through the tranquil sea.

Jenny came out of the deckhouse and walked a few steps forward to a rail to see and, as always, to appreciate the beauty of the star-spangled sky and the moonlit ocean. The cooling wind had calmed to an occasional zephyr, and the ship was chugging slowly along on the diesel. She thought of Glenn locked below in his cramped, dark prison, and reasoned that he was undoubtedly unnerved by his near-death event. To be sure, he had to be totally confused by what he was experiencing.

"Ever a wondrous sight, is it not, *ma cher*?" Tournaire said as he came to stand beside her.

She nodded.

"Too bad about the young man," he consoled. "You rather liked him?"

"Not enough to particularly care," she replied brusquely.

"This business is very cruel, and so we must be" he said. "It requires that we do what we must. I'm pleased that you did not object. Kozlov would have not have accepted that."

"Speaking of cruel, who the hell are these thugs, Alain? Eastern Europeans? Russians?"

Tounaire nodded, his expression grave. "Very dangerous men. I must warn you about our *Bratva* guests, former members of the KGB. Gravendeel tells me that *M'sieur* Kozlov is a Spetsnas veteran, a member of a Soviet military unit that was known for a very nasty reputation." He paused. "I must also warn you, he seems to distrust women."

"Me?"

Again, Tournaire nodded. "He did not want you aboard."

"Should I be worried?"

"No more than the rest of us," he said, and then flashed a reassuring smile. "Perhaps, however, we are being unduly suspicious. After all, they're paying a very handsome price for us and the ship to get them to their destination and back again. We follow orders, we should be all right."

"They may need the ship, Alain, but, later on, they may not need us," she countered. "Don't underestimate these people."

He smiled again. "You worry too much. They think they control us, but *we* may be in control before this voyage is through."

"Do you know what they're after?"

"Only guesses," he said evasively. He turned halfway to leave. "Get some rest, *ma cher*. Tomorrow will be an interesting day." He touched the bill of his cap and walked away.

She waited for a minute more and then walked quickly to the deckhouse, went in, and re-entered the galley. She opened a hanging locker and moved aside a cluster of fruit and vegetable cans. She reached to the back and took out a 9mm Glock automatic. She slipped the gun into a hip pocket of her shorts, and then rearranged the cans before closing the cabinet door. She walked into the short passageway toward the salon and hurried down the steps of the central ladder to the cabin deck passageway.

She moved to the crew's quarters entrance, eased open the door a few inches and leaned in her head to stare into the dark, listening. She heard the sonorous sounds of the sleeping crewmen. She waited for a few seconds to make sure that their slumber was deep, not fitful. Satisfied, she quietly closed the door and moved to kneel on the carpeted floor to unfasten the cover locks of Glenn's hideout.

"S-s-s-h-h," she hissed as she laid back the cover plate, her finger at her lips. She peered into the inky space, startled to see no sign of Glenn.

There was a rustle of sound and Glenn slid his face into view, blinking even in the dim illumination of the companionway. "Didn't know it was you," he muttered. "I was curled up in a ball."

"Whisper," she cautioned, her words barely audible.

He took a few moments before he nodded, waiting for his eyes to adjust to light. "Can I get out of here?"

She shook her head and reached to her hip pocket for the automatic. "I brought you this. You know how to use it?

"Never had a need."

With an initial sigh, she began a hurried instruction. She showed him how to release the safety and trigger the weapon. "If you're discovered, do what you can. You've got twelve rounds. Use them if you have to."

"How will I know if it's you?"

"From now on, I'll tap twice with a long pause in between," she told him. She didn't wait for his response. She quickly replaced the cover plate and gave each of the four twist locks a half-turn. Satisfied, she rose and walked to the crew quarter's door and let herself in.

"What a fucking day," she said under her breath as she stripped out of her blouse and shorts and crawled into her bunk and drew a blanket over her. Her hand searched for and found the slit in the wall side of the mattress, slipped it in and grasped a second Glock, an identical handgun to the one she had given Glenn.

Comforted that it was still hidden there, she withdrew her hand and closed her eyes.

27

Being caged in total darkness had become a timeless, frightening, and maddening existence for Glenn. He could find no physical position of comfort in this under-deck crypt; it featured a hard surface to lie upon, and the cold of the ocean to suffer as it was transmitted through the steel hull plates into the space. He was without sight, but certainly not without sound. The incessant whooshing of water against the cleaving bow of the ship became a constant irritant to him. As well, there was no relief from the repeated pounding and battering of the waves against the prow.

Above him, the thumping footfalls of men in the companionway caused him to hold his breath, with a fear that those few who came directly over him would unscrew the cover and discover him. He gripped the automatic at each close instance, but laid it aside as soon as sounds diminished. Unfamiliar with guns, he worried that, in a panic or by chance, he might nudge the safety off and accidentally discharge it to maim or kill himself.

The hours drifted endlessly and, with no vision, only memory images would come and go in random flashes. Some of those recollections were pleasant, but many were not. He tried to trick his brain into constructive channels, even recalling long ago arithmetic and algebra problems to solve. However, without a lasting mind picture of a writing pad or a classroom board to figure upon, the numbers quickly disappeared unsolved.

Most of all, this black-hole isolation spawned a repetitive rage against the criminals who had tried to take his life. Their psychopathic enjoyment of his intended murder had awakened a nearly equal psychotic reaction in him. As time passed, he gripped the automatic, no longer afraid of it, considering it to be his instrument of a future revenge.

In spite of the ceaseless noise, the cold, and the discomfort, he often slept. Whether a short nap or a longer slumber, he invariably awoke in some distress, muscles cramped and sore, his very bones seemed aching as well.

Only once had a welcome two-rap signal brought him relief from this dark dungeon. When Jenny opened the cover, with her finger to her lips as before, he almost wept with relief.

"God, I've got to get out of here," he exclaimed in his whisper. "I've got to pee."

"Okay, use the fo'c'sle head," she said softly. "Everyone is asleep except those on deck. But, for God's sake, hurry."

Glenn lifted himself up and out, stretched and walked stiffly a few steps to the door of the head and went inside. He lowered his shorts and briefs and sat upon the stool. He emptied both his bladder and his bowels, then stood and pulled up his grimy shorts. He took a minute more to take off his shirt, hand washed his face and chest without soap, then rinsed in plain water before he donned the soiled shirt once again.

"Damn, you took your time," Jenny swore in a hushed voice as he returned.

"I can't go back down there," he told her, with a nod at the black hole. "It's a tomb."

"Where else can I put you?"

"Back in the aft locker?"

"No good," she whispered. "William was in there twice today, and Ruckman once. Get in!"

"Well, damn—"

"Glenn, there are murderers sleeping just a few feet away. Someone gets up and sees us, we're done for."

"It's night?"

"Yes, about midnight," she answered. "Get down there."

With a sigh of resignation, Glenn flexed his knees twice, and then stooped and eased himself back down into the dark compartment. "Can you get me a can? Something to pee in?"

She smiled. "Are you hungry?"

"Yeah, but if nothing goes in, nothing comes out," he told her. "How long do I have to stay in here?"

"Playing it by ear, Glenn," she whispered. "I think we're going to make landfall sometime tomorrow. Maybe while they're busy with whatever, I can sneak you off the ship."

"Where? Onto some desert island?"

"I'll call my people, and tell them where you are."

"What works out here? A cell phone?"

"Some do, some don't," she replied. "Mine's rather special."

"How far away are they?"

"Half-day, I'd guess," she told him.

"Maybe you should call them right now, and let's both get off on the next dry spot."

"My job isn't over," she said. "Now, duck down, I'm shutting you in."

"And shutting me up," he said and laid back. "Don't forget the can."

She closed the cover, and darkness prevailed again.

28

At mid-morning, Ruckman, at the ship's helm, throttled back the diesel and reversed the propeller to maneuver the ship close to the shore. It was an oblong desert island jutting up from the sea, an eighth of a mile in length, and no more than a ten-minute walk from side to side at its greatest width. Tropical palms crowded the narrow beaches that surrounded the atoll. Through the occasional gaps in the surrounding foliage, a barren, rocky interior could be seen. It was one of several small islets in area, none of them suitable for habitation.

"Deep water right over there," Kozlov said to Tournaire, pointing to a minor cove cut into the shoreline. "Head in."

"Come about and bring her in astern," Tournaire spoke sharply to countermand . "Slow and watch our depth."

"We will need lifeboats," the Russian leader said. "You have?"

"Five inflatable lifeboats on the deckhouse roof lockers, and a dive raft in a locker below," Tournaire informed him.

"Two lifeboats will do," Kozlov said brusquely.

"We'll inflate them as soon as we drop anchor," Tournaire said with a nod to William who stood nearby. "See to it."

The deckhand nodded and walked to obey.

Two of Kozlov's brawny minions were on deck, standing at the port rail, watching as the ship maneuvered toward the island, the bow now slowly swinging out toward the open ocean as the stern remained the pivot. These husky, bull-necked Slavic hulks were wearing shorts, although they also wore nylon jackets in spite of the tropical heat. Each of them held a short-shafted shovel.

Gravendeel emerged from the deckhouse and lumbered toward the small group, his eyes on the shovel holders. "Digging for buried treasure?" he asked in mock levity.

"You have it correct, fat man," Kozlov said sternly.

"Captain Kidd's?" Gravendeel asked in a feeble attempt to continue his banter.

Kozlov ignored him, waved a hand at the men with shovels, and spoke to Tournaire. "When we are ready, I will take two of my men ashore . . . and several of yours."

"Of mine?" Tournaire questioned in surprise. "What about more of your own?"

"They will have other duties," Kozlov replied and nodded toward his men who were coming around the deckhouse, each openly bearing a lethal weapon. Four of them were carrying machine pistols, two with high capacity handguns, and a man with a stubby, pistol-grip shotgun.

"Dear me," Gravendeel exclaimed.

At the port rail, the two men leaned their shovels and brought machine pistols from under their jackets.

"Dear me," Gravendeel said once again.

"What is going on?" Tournaire asked.

"We've noticed some of you have started carrying weapons," Kozlov said. "Carefully remove them and place them on the deck. We will collect them."

"This is not necessary," Tournaire protested. "We have given you no—"

"We intend you no harm, but we must insist," Kozlov interrupted. "Your weapons, please."

With every gun aimed at them, the captain, Ruckman, and William surrendered their revolvers and automatics.

"I'm not armed," Gravendeel protested to no avail as a tattooed thug searched through his voluminous white linen suit, finding nothing lethal.

"This was to ensure that you will not cause problems," the Russian leader said in a loud voice. "We intend you no harm, but we must be cautious. The sight of treasure, as your fat man has called it, might excite members of your crew to act foolishly."

"This is piracy . . . you can't take our guns," Tournaire complained bitterly.

"Once our business is completed, you will be able to purchase many more," Kozlov told him. He walked to the rail to watch as one of his men threw the collected weapons over the rail.

"And what will my people be doing ashore?" Tournaire asked.

"Earning their considerable pay," Kozlov said, and turned to one of his henchmen. "Sergei, bring the rest of the crew to the deck."

The man gave a curt nod and walked toward the deckhouse.

"Don't let us distract you," Kozlov said to Ruckman. "Make sure you do a good job of . . . how do you say? Dropping the anchor?"

Glenn had been puzzling about the movement of the ship for the past several minutes. It seemed that it had reached some sort of a destination as the schooner had slowed its forward progress, come about, and was now apparently slowly backing. The sound of quick footsteps coming directly overhead aroused anxiety, but the signal of a rap, a pause, and another rap reassured him. Seconds later, the cover was unfastened, but the cover was lifted only an inch to show a thin line of subdued light.

"Glenn," came Jenny's whisper. "They're taking the ship. They'll be after me, any moment. I'm leaving this unfastened so you can get out.'

"Did you call your people for help?"

"I didn't have time to . . . oh, shit, here they come."

The cover closed and he was in darkness once more. He heard Jenny's footsteps as she moved toward the crew's cabin, and then he heard the heavy tread of another's feet pounding down the companionway.

"Miss!" It was a sharp command with a thick foreign accent. "You have gun?"

"Where in this outfit would I put one?" came her tart retort.

"You come!" The man's voice ordered.

"Just let me get something from the cabin—"

"Come now or I shoot," the man's voice cut her off.

Glenn lay very still as he listened to Jenny's protests as she was apparently being led away. He heard them go up the nearby steps and, despite an urge to rush to her rescue, he waited.

A minute later, he pushed the cover up and peered out into the passageway.

All clear!

He pushed the cover to one side, then levered his way out of his hideout. Gripping the Glock in his right hand, he remained in a crouch as he re-closed the bilge compartment. He walked warily to the base of the forward ladder and went up, step by step, until he was eye level just above the lip of the hatch. With no one visible in the immediate area, he left the hatch, lay flat on his belly, and crawled across the deck to get a better view. The ship had been backed into a cove of a small island and was now lying at anchor twenty or more yards from a sand beach. On the distant aft deck, he could see a partial view of what appeared to be a threatening confrontation between his enemies. However, it was a one-sided altercation with the ship's crew under duress. The Russian gangsters were obviously in control with their formidable weaponry held ready to use. He could see that Tournaire was in animated argument with the Russian leader while Gravendeel was standing nearby showing dismay and distress. He could make out a few words, but only a few. All of the members of the crew, including Jenny, seemed cowed and downcast

Whatever was going on back there, Glenn felt a strong need to know. If wholesale murder had been the hoodlums' intent, he reasoned, it probably would have happened already.

Can't hear from here. Got to get closer.

He retreated to the forward hatch and went down the steps to the companionway where he paused, unsure of what next to do. Then, with just a vague notion, he walked the passageway to the aft ladder and, silently and cautiously, took two steps up and then stopped, reconsidering.

If I poke my head up there, they're sure to see me.

With a flash of inspiration, he stepped back down and moved to the aft storage room where he had spent so much time. He eased open the door, closed it behind him and turned on the overhead light. He stepped to the shelves where the diving equipment was stored and rummaged through snorkel masks and scuba gear until he found what he was seeking – a stretchable black dive hood that would cover his whole head and neck, leaving only an oval opening for his eyes, nose and mouth. He slipped it over his head and tugged the fabric of the gap to merely a slit for his eyes.

He left the locker, returned to the steps, and began a stealthy climb nearly to the top where he paused. Once in position to observe, camouflaged in the black hood and well back in the deepest shadow of the hatch entry, he imagined that he might not be noticed. However, he would have to keep his head absolutely motionless; the slightest movement, even in the dark, would give him away. Even to rise into position would present the same dilemma:

Chance I'll have to take.

Well back in the hatch cover's gloom, he inched his head higher and froze, his eyes just above the deck level. This vantage gave him a low angled partial view of the aft deck. and the activities of those in his sight.

Kozlov and another gangster, with their backs to hmi, were the only ones in motion, pacing restlessly in front of the stock-still ship's crew. Ruckman had taken a few steps away from the wheel to stand near Tournaire; both men with anger in their faces and postures.

Gravendeel stood in a dejected stoop behind them, his massive bulk sagging. His only movement was a nervous wringing of his hands that he clasped below his protruding waist. Far from the arrogance Glenn had seen in him before, the heavyset lawyer now exhibited the greatest show of fear.

The three crewmen, Thomas, William and Alfred, wore expressions of anxiety.

Jenny stood a few feet apart from the other captives and, although her demeanor was solemn, she held her head high, almost boldly.

No one saw me, Glenn exulted.

Jenny's eyes flicked to the hatch and away again.

She knows I'm here!! Good!

"As soon as the boats are ready," Kozlov was saying, "We will escort your crew members to a location on the island."

"To do what?" Tournaire demanded.

The Russian took a long while before answering. ""Come, come, you *do* know, don't you?"

"The Venezuelan gold?" Gravendeel asked as he raised his head, his voice close to reverence.

Kozlov nodded. "I wondered when you would guess. Well, you will see it soon enough. Two hundred ingots of the highest purity gold, each bar just over twenty-seven pounds of weight, a total of nearly three tons."

"Two hundred gold bars, worth millions," Gravendeel said, enraptured. "Millions!"

"And, now, you can see the reason for our precaution," Kozlov said with a gesture to his armed associates. "The very sight of such a fortune would be a temptation for, well, people such as yourselves. Greedy people."

"I don't understand. How did it get here on this island?" Tournaire asked.

"A story the fat man will undoubtedly tell you while we are gone," Kozlov informed him.

"Millions, you're talking about?" Ruckman voiced a high whining question. "Seems like we ain't gonna get what's right."

"Perhaps, we will be generous," Kozlov said with a surprising manner, although his statement was to Tournaire and Gravendeel rather than to the deckhand. "Perhaps there will be a brick of gold, in addition to your fee . . . that is, for your assurance that there will be no trouble now or later. We'd call it a reward for causing no trouble."

"A very great reward, that would be more than generous," Gravendeel said, his unctuous manner returning.

"Then, let us get started! Prepare the boats, and we go to the island!" Kozlov said, turning his gaze to Ruckman, William, Thomas and Jenny, and then waving them to follow him.

Just before Jenny walked out of sight, Glenn saw her clench her right hand into a fist at her side with her index finger pointing down.

A clear signal! Stay hidden!

Glenn quietly descended the steps to the lower aisle, took off the hood, and considered what next he could do.

Hide where? Back in the bilge compartment?

He shook his head.

Back to the aft storage locker was a better option; no one knows I'm alive and surely no one will be coming off the deck while all this was going on . . . I'll be safe.

He walked to the aft locker door, opened it, turned on the overhead light and stepped inside. Closing the door behind him, he took a full minute to look again at the varied objects of this large chamber, and wondered if there was anything else here that could be of use to him. He scanned the contents of the room, but the only thing of lethal worth was the automatic pistol he held in his hand.

Once again, visualizing his path through to the back of the storage space, he turned out the light and, in the darkness, made his way carefully through the large and small items. Reaching for and touching the far bulkhead, he leaned down to grasp the deflated raft and sat down, slipping under it.

Once more stashed away in a black and sightless void, he had only his imagination to occupy his mind while he waited.

A buried treasure, a treasure of gold, so that's what they're going after! Bloody latter-day pirates, these Balkan bastards!

A grim humor possessed him:

Shiver me timbers, but it'll be Jenny and me hanging from the yardarm 'less I think of some sort of derring-do . . . but what the hell might that be?

29

Jenny walked single-file behind Kozlov and Ruckman, with William and Alfred carrying the shovels in line behind her. Two of the burly Russian gunmen trailed the procession. Each carried a high-load capacity gun, while Kozlov held a high capacity pistol in his right hand.

The ground was rocky in places, spongy in others; vegetation ranging from thick to sparse. They had walked about a third of the length of the island when Kozlov halted the group as they entered a half-circle of palm trees. He gave nods to Ruckman and William, and then pointed to a clump of knee-high weeds in the center of the small copse. "Start there."

"How deep," Ruckman's squeaky question was surly.

"You'll know when you get there," Kozlov "Get started."

With Kozlov and the other armed thugs standing guard, Ruckman and William faced each other, four feet apart, and began to shovel away the weeds. They worked with strong, muscular thrusts, the shovel blades scooping away the top layer of loose soil, and then digging down into the compacted earth below.

Jenny and Alfred stepped into the minimal shade of the surrounding palms, to watch their shipmates at work.

"Enjoy your leisure while you can," Kozlov told them. "You'll do your share."

Ruckman and William shed their shirts after ten minutes of hard work, and continued to shovel for almost an hour. The sun was high, the rays drilling down, and their bodies glistened with sweat. Although standing in the shade, Jenny and Alfred were perspiring, and even the shirt backs and armpits of their idle guards were soon darkly stained.

"Your turn," Kozlov said to Jenny and her shipmate.

As Ruckman and William stepped up out of the foot-deep, rectangular hole, she and Alfred took over the shoveling. They labored steadily for another thirty minutes to deepen the excavation, both wringing wet with perspiration.

"Sure you've got the right place?" she asked as they paused at their work, each standing thigh deep in the pit.

"Keep at it," Kozlov said curtly.

Fifteen minutes later, Jenny's shovel hit a hard, unyielding substance. She used the side of the blade to scrape away the covering dirt to expose the fabric of a heavy, gray-green tarpaulin. "This is it?" she asked, looking up to Kozlov.

The Russian stepped to the edge of the hole to look, and then nodded. "This is it, indeed."

In another half-hour, Jenny and Alfred had cleared an area around the rope-bound canvas that lay in the center of the hole. Alfred slipped the ropes from around the short bundle and pulled back the edge of the tarpaulin.

"My God!" Ruckman exclaimed as he came to the lip of the hole and looked down.

In the blazing overhead sunlight, it appeared that they had unearthed a solid mass of gold, a glittering rectangular block.

The faces of the pair, waist-deep in the pit and of those gathered above, were bathed with a yellowish sheen.

"My God!" Ruckman repeated.

"Welcome to treasure island," Jenny said in awe.

A wisp of a cloud passed across the sun, and the solid slab illusion became a mass of side-by-side individual gold bars, each one closely the size of an ordinary building brick. Packed tightly, the bullion ingots were stacked in a four-layer column, a yard long and a couple of feet wide with eight additional bars piled horizontally at the foot of the rows.

"Now we take them to the beach," Kozlov instructed. "And then to the ship." Looking down at Jenny, he gave a nod to Ruckman and William. "Load them up." He pointed to Alfred. "Him, too."

As Alfred vaulted out of the pit, Jenny wiped her sweaty brow with her forearm and moved to the end of the gold column. She bent to pick up one of the bricks and handed it up to William, then reached for and lifted a second to him. As she lifted ingot by ingot to the lip of the cavity, Kozlov instructed Ruckman, Alfred, and William to pick up as many as each could carry. As the heavy-laden men walked toward the beach and the lifeboats, one of the Russians with an automatic weapon walked behind them.

"This is going to take a while," Jenny said as she looked up at Kozlov. "Any reason you can't watch us, and let your other guy help out?"

Kozlov ignored her and stepped back into the sparse shade of a close by palm.

Jenny returned her attention to the gold bars and, one by one, resumed lifting them to the top edge of the excavation.

■ ■ ■

Jenny placed the last two bars onto the pile of jumbled ingots at the water's edge, a few feet from the beached lifeboats.

"At least, he didn't make us fill in the hole," she said as she slumped down beside her three exhausted shipmates. Alfred, alone, gave her an appreciative smile.

The Russian leader, who had walked behind her to the beach, was now several feet away in conversation with his two henchmen.

"It was the captain's fault," Ruckman said in a low voice. "Letting 'em get the jump on us."

Jenny didn't argue.

Kozlov broke away from the two thugs and walked to stand over the four captives sitting in the sand. "Now to the ship," he said.

"Give us a fucking few minutes," Ruckman complained.

"You can rest when the job is finished," Kozlov said. "Load your boat."

Wearily, Jenny rose with the others, and they formed a relay line from the heaped gold bricks to the nearest lifeboat. William handed the first bar to Alfred who passed it to Jenny, then to Ruckman who placed it on the center floor of the boat.

"Only ten bars at a time," Kozlov instructed. "That's close to three-hundred pounds. We do not overload." He stepped closer to the captives and, with deliberation, fixed his intense gaze on each, one by one, as he spoke. "Two men in the boat, and the girl is to row. When you reach the ship, you will hand up each bar with the utmost care to your fellow crewman or even to your captain. If any one of you, in the boat or on the ship, should drop a bar into the ocean, he or she who dropped it will be shot." He stepped back. "Be very careful."

With ten bars in the lifeboat, Jenny took the center seat with her feet atop the first load of gold bricks. As William seated himself in the fore section, Ruckman pushed the boat into the sea and vaulted into the back of it. She grasped the handles of the oars and began to row to the ship. A few strokes later, she glanced back over her shoulder to see Kozlov and Alfred standing on the beach, the henchmen off to one side with their weapons now held at high port, no longer at their sides.

Looking ahead, on the ship, she saw two more of the Russians with their weapons aimed at them

Midway across the distance, she stopped rowing for a few seconds and leaned to speak softly to Ruckman. "You know they intend to kill us. There'll be no fee paid, no extra gold bar as a reward."

Ruckman, staring at the *Lady Ruth*, didn't turn his head. "When?"

"Soon," she replied, and began rowing again. "Damned soon."

"I ain't going down without a fight," Ruckman vowed.

Jenny didn't respond, a faint hope that Glenn, somehow, might help her survive. "Fat chance," she muttered to herself.

30

Glenn eased the door open a crack, and listened for any sounds of activity in the companionway. Hearing no activity nearby, he slipped on the black hood again, stepped out and closed the door, and made his way to the aft hatch once again. He went quietly up the steps and paused, as before, his eyes level just above the deck.

He watched for a considerable time as boatload after boatload of the treasure was delivered, and his astonishment continued to escalate as the gold bar stack grew higher near the center of the aft deck. At last, the transfer of all gold from the shore to the ship was completed, and the conscripted work crew of the *Lady Ruth* climbed aboard from their boat, immediately followed by Kozlov and his thugs.

Now that everyone was back on the ship, Glenn sensed that something had drastically changed. The daylong menace now seemed highly intensified. Dismay plagued him as he witnessed a quickening of excitement: the Russians' manners were becoming cocky, their foreign utterances overlapping one another in tones of bellicose banter. As he studied the cruel, smirking expressions on their faces, he was especially aware of their leader's arrogant behavior. He was not only permitting his minions' escalating malevolence, he seemed to be pumping it to an even greater level.

"*Ubey ikh seychas, Yuri*?" a hoodlum asked eagerly.

"*Skoro, Sergey, skoro*," Kozlov answered.

Glenn recognized that the malignant mood on the deck was becoming frighteningly similar to that which had prevailed in those dreadful moments of his ordeal; being bound, gagged and dragged for his drop into the sea.

They're going to kill them! Glenn realized with dreadful clarity. *Everyone including Jenny*!

He glanced at his Glock automatic. It had seemed an efficient handgun only moments ago, but it now appeared an inadequate tool against the overwhelming firepower of the Russians. As a novice shooter, he reckoned he would be lucky to hit even one man before the rest sprayed his location with a deadly hail of bullets.

I need to do something! Some sort of a diversion to give me an edge! What, for God's sake?

He turned his gaze from the tense scene where murder hovered, his thoughts racing. An absurd idea suddenly flickered, disappeared, and then returned back with inane clarity.

Oh, my God! Maybe! Just fucking maybe!

He hurried down the ladder, worried that the shooting of the captives could occur at any moment. He was frantic with the thought he would be too late to take action and, with only faint hope, that what he planned might work. He sprinted to the forecastle head and dashed inside. "This is fucking stupid," he scolded himself.

Nevertheless, he pulled back the shower curtain, turned the water on full, and then stepped under the spray.

A few seconds later, drenched and dripping, he returned to the companionway and scurried up the forward ladder. He dropped flat on his stomach and crawled across the foredeck to a position, behind the foremast base, where he could see, as before, a partial view of the gathering at the stern of the ship. Two Russians, backs to him, were visible, their weapons held high and ready for use, their tense bodies signaling impending action. Beyond them, he could see Thomas and William, heads bowed and cowed, while Ruckman stood behind them erect and defiant.

They're going to pull the triggers!

Glenn crabbed his way back to the three foredeck storage bins and, rising to his knees, undid the latch on the EMER-GENCY container and opened it. He reached in and pulled the large case of flares out and placed it on the deck. He opened it, took out two of the large, jar-sized float-flare canisters as well as one of the flare pistols. He loaded a cartridge in the pistol, rose to a crouch and, awkwardly carrying all, crept past the foremast base to the front of the deckhouse, moved to the corner and peered around it.

Can I kill?

It had been on his mind for minutes now, and he still didn't know. The rage he had nurtured toward these monsters should have been cause enough.

Was it still?

He pulled the small ripcord that ignited one of the float-flare canisters and shoved it out onto the ship's perimeter walkway. As it began to sputter, he pulled the ripcord on the second and pushed it past the first.

As geysers of orange smoke from each container rapidly plumed into a single, billowing, cloud, Glenn rose behind it and disengaged the safety on the Glock.

Although he could see nothing through the dense, henna-colored fog, on the other side of it, he could hear the first outcries of discovery, alarm and confusion shouted in both English and Russian.

Kill or be killed!

Glenn plastered his wet hair over his forehead and raked other strands down over his ears. He thought of the words Jack Nicholson's Joker character had spoken in a Batman movie, and quoted under his breath, "Wait 'til they get a load of me."

With the flare pistol in his left hand and the Glock in his right, he strode through the nucleus of the thick, orange cloud, appearing to materialize from the roiling mists - a sea-soaked avenging wraith returned from the deep! His passage through the mist drew luminous streamers of curling, wafting, flame-hued vapors that clung to and trailed after him, adding to the image of a demonic apparition.

A hellish specter, he strode toward the thunderstruck gathering of armed and disarmed villains, all of them motionless with mouths agape. Confusion and bafflement caused three of the Russians to actually cower at the sight of a drowned, dead man rushing for them.

"*Chto eto takoe?*" came a frightened voice.

"*Chert s ada!*" screamed another.

Glenn triggered the flare pistol at a group of the thugs, and the shell exploded among them in a great burst of reddish-orange flames. There were screams of pain and terror as the Russians scattered away from the ball of fire, two of them dropping their weapons as they beat at the flames on their clothes and scorching their bodies. One of the pair, fully ablaze, dashed to the edge of the deck and threw himself over the railing into the sea. The other, totally engulfed in fire, ran past Glenn, screaming in mortal pain as he collapsed and burned to death on the sidedeck walkway.

Glenn, feeling elation rather than remorse, began firing his Glock repeatedly as he marched toward the milling Russian gunmen, not bothering to aim. To his surprise, he saw one mobster clutch at his body and crumple, his weapon dropping from his hands to skitter across the deck.

As he had hoped, Jenny had been quick to comprehend this incomprehensible diversion and was the first to react. She dove for one of the machine pistols, grasped it, and rolled over to trigger a burst that took out another of the bewildered Russians who fell with a dying cry into a still heap.

Ruckman was the next to react. The brawny sailor launched himself across a three-foot space to attack an equally brutish mobster, pinning the man's arms to his side. Even so, the Russian's right hand finger triggered the machine pistol and sent shots in a spray across the deck.

Alfred groaned and dropped where he stood, and Glenn felt an instant burn from the graze that ripped across the short sleeve of his upper left arm. He threw himself to the deck near Jenny as the captors and captives began to recover their wits and fallen guns. With automatic weapons turning their way, Glenn and Jenny crawled to a scant protection behind a small, on-deck storage bin a few feet away from the aft hatch.

Three of the remaining Russians, now firing wildly, ran for cover around a corner of the deckhouse. The man named Sergei tried to hide his considerable bulk atop the deckhouse behind the lifeboat storage bins while Kozlov threw himself behind the on-deck bar.

Wisps of orange smoke continued to drift over the scene of confusion, giving the deck of the ship sort of a surreal, battlefield appearance. The gunfire was erratic; all of the gunfighters more involved in their frantic searches for better protective cover.

"How'd you like my entrance?" Glenn asked, hunkering down as he faced Jenny.

"Unbelievable!" she answered. "You are a mad man!"

"How many down?" he asked.

"Two guys on fire, one over the side, that's two. You got one, I got one, and Ruckman, he's still busy." She paused to fire a short burst. "Four down, and counting Kozlov, five to go."

"And our people?"

She looked aghast. "*Our* people?"

"Looks like Alfred's down," Glenn said as he took a peek. "Rest are okay."

Tournaire had recovered one of the machine pistols and, with bullets flying about him, crawled to lay flat behind the protection of the helm wheel console. He popped his head up from time to time to send a series of short firing bursts toward the Russians.

Thomas, also with an automatic weapon, had taken refuge and remained inside the thin protection of the al fresco dining facility.

William, lying flat on the deck and totally exposed, suddenly leapt to his feet and tried a desperate flight across the deck toward the aft hatch. He almost made it before a hail of bullets stitched across his torso, and flung him lifeless near its entrance.

Gravendeel, a huge target, was shuffling back and forth in frightened uncertainty on the aft deck, bullets pinging the metal surfaces all about him. With no place to hide, he fell to his knees and bent his head to the deck, his big white hands clasped atop his planter's hat.

Ruckman's physical struggle with a thug came to a sudden end as one of the man's comrades fired an errant shot into the wrestling Russian's back. Bullets continued to slam into the thick, dead body as Ruckman kept it propped up in front of him. He tore the dead man's machine pistol from his hand and hunkered down, continuing to use the cadaver as a shield, peeking around to fire an occasional shot.

"We're target practice here," Jenny declared. "From both sides."

Glenn looked around. True, the low storage bin could give a somewhat adequate protection for one person, but, with two, Glenn was partially exposed to gunfire from the Russians' deckhouse corner position. Even more disturbing, as he shifted his gaze, the entire port side of the ship presented an open field of fire. All any one of the Russians had to do was to come around the forward end of the deckhouse to the walkway, and Glenn would be totally uncovered.

Glenn aimed his automatic at the far corner of the deckhouse, a guess that proved to be a life-saving measure.

One of the Russians stepped around the distant end of the deckhouse with his deadly weapon rising to fire.

Glenn swore under his breath as he fired two shots and, on the third trigger pull, heard a click, but no report. He held his breath, but then drew a sigh of relief to see the Russian's semi-automatic weapon fly out of the man's hands and over the rail. The would-be killer grabbed at his bloodied shoulder and staggered back behind the deckhouse.

"You got him," Jenny exulted.

"Just a part of him," he corrected. He gestured to the open lane of probable fire. "I was lucky. I'm pretty vulnerable here."

"I can scoot around a little," she responded.

"Not room enough for both of us," he told her. "How are you on ammunition?"

"Seems to be quite a bit in this thing," she told him. "You?"

"I'm out."

"Glenn, there's another gun in my bunk, inside the wall side of the mattress. If I can make it to the hatch—"

"I'll go," he cut in. "I'm the one that needs it."

"Something else," she said. "I've got to get to the galley."

Glenn looked askance.

"I've got a portable transmitter in there. I can call for help."

"Tell me where it is, I'll get it."

"Look for a sack of flour in the lower right-side food storage locker," she instructed. "Dig deep. It's wrapped in a plastic bag."

"Where's help?"

"Pretty far away, I'm afraid."

"I'm on my way," he said as he rose and sprinted for the aft hatch, two bullets pinging the deck beneath him, and another on the metal lid of the hatch as he leaped through the opening

31

Glenn's plunge down the steps was saved from a tumble by his grab for the handrail near the bottom. With only a glance at the empty companionway, he broke into a run toward the distant door of the crew quarters. As he passed the recessed entry to the central spiral ladder, he could clearly hear the sound of footsteps coming down.

Shit! Someone's coming!

He didn't look back, but raced on. As he reached and opened the door, he dove into the cabin just as a bullet punched with a bang against the far metal wall, then ricocheted with a clang to another.

Rising to his feet in frenzied haste, he moved to Jenny's berth and yanked the blanket and the sheet away. He reached across the mattress, his fingers frantically searching for and finding a slit in its side. He thrust his hand into it and clawed out another Glock, a mate to his own firearm. Another shot boomed in the hallway, and a bullet caromed dangerously about the steel-walled room.

Handgun, Glenn reasoned. *Not a machine gun, thank God!*

Glenn's new advantage of having a loaded weapon was offset in that he was bottled up. Reaching across to close the door to block gunfire would be a dreadful risk and, even if he escaped being shot, he would simply trap himself in the cabin – useless. Whoever was in the companionway had the upper hand. His assailant could pepper the open doorway with shots, hoping for a glancing bullet to wound or kill. Or he could merely wait until Glenn showed himself in the door-frame.

Glenn considered the shooter's probable position and killing strategy:

He would likely be hiding in the recess of the central stair-way, lean out from behind the steel bulkhead to fire, and then duck back to cover. He would be concentrating his sight and aim only on the side of the doorframe where he had seen me dive inside. He would not know why I had headed for this cabin, but he would presume that I was armed. He would also assume that if I could return fire, I would have to expose at least a part of myself in order to aim and trigger my gun. And, he would most likely guess that I'd slide into his view any place from my normal height down to the level of the floor.

And he'd be ready!

But would he expect fire from the very top of the door-frame?

Glenn heaved himself up onto Ruckman's bunk and knelt on the pillow at the head end of the bed. He began to lean forward slowly and carefully, then jerked back as another shot boomed and a bullet sped into the room.

Random shooting, Glenn decided. *Couldn't have seen me. Just trying for a lucky kill.*

He released the safety and transferred the Glock to his left hand, then leaned forward again, his upper body well past the end of the bed, his right hand on the upper part of the wall to steady himself. Warily, he lowered his head to the upper corner of the doorframe, just barely far enough to position his left eye to view the companionway.

The corridor appeared empty, but as he studied it, he saw a shadow of a man's movement in the central stairwell; the shooter was exactly where Glenn had supposed. Very slowly, Glenn brought the Glock up and, even though it felt awkward in his left hand, he steadied it against the doorframe and aimed it at a point about five feet above the deck at the edge of the shooter's protective bulkhead.

And waited.

Almost a minute passed, and then a figure moved into view; the man's head and torso clearly seen. It was the hoodlum, Sergei, not Kozlov – and he was aiming his handgun at the lower part of the doorframe.

Glenn pulled the trigger on the Glock once and, as the bullet slammed into the Sergei's chest, he saw the Russian's body lurch violently out into the corridor, his handgun flying from his grasp.

Glenn swung down from the upper bunk and stepped cautiously out into the companionway. He approached the sprawled body warily, ready to trigger another shot to finish if needed.

A look into the fallen man's face showed that a second shot would not be necessary.

Glenn stepped over the body to retrieve the Russian's pistol. He examined it and quickly noted the slight differences between it and his Glock. He released the magazine to determine the remaining ammunition and, disappointed to find only a few rounds, replaced it into the gun. He stuck it into the back waistband of his shorts and, warily, mounted the central stairway to the salon. He paused, his head just above the upper floor level, eyes searching. Seeing no one, hearing only the occasional sound of gunfire out on the deck, he climbed the remaining few steps, the Glock held chest-high. He moved cautiously along the central aisle, looking for danger in both directions, as he walked quickly to the galley.

He moved to the food storage cabinets, knelt on one knee, and swung open the lower doors of one of them to reveal the large cans and sacks of food staples stored on the cabinet's middle shelf and bottom. He bent his head to look below the middle shelf and was pleased to see two white sacks, one that had been opened, behind a jumble of institutional-sized food cans.

He laid the Glock on the galley floor behind him, and started lifting the cans aside and out of the cabinet to open a space to reach inside.

""Don't move and don't reach for the gun," Kozlov said from behind him. "And I'll take this one as well."

Glenn felt the second gun pulled from the waistband of his shorts. From the corner of his eye, he saw the Russian's foot kick the Glock away.

"Both knees on the floor," Kozlov instructed.

Glenn complied and turned his head. "Why haven't you shot me?"

"I wanted to speak to a genuine resurrection," Kozlov said with mockery in his voice. "Now, I have seen, and I now believe."

"Go to hell!" Glenn replied angrily

"Today, you'll precede me," Kozlov responded. "I'm curious. How *did* you survive? The girl?"

Glenn didn't answer.

"Well, I'll get to her later," the Russian leader said, the sarcastic mirth no longer heard. "Once more, I bid you good-bye?"

The blast of the gunshot was thunderous and, instinctively, Glenn ducked away.

No pain!

He turned his head to look up.

Kozlov's body fell onto Glenn, the weight knocking him flat to the deck and pinning him there. Glenn twisted his head upward once more and found he was looking into a dead man's face, the eyes open and lifeless, a last cruel smile frozen on his mouth.

Glenn pushed the body back and squirmed out from under it as Jenny stepped into view from the companionway.

"That was my last shot," she told him.

"Damned glad it was a good one," Glenn said with a sigh of relief. He rose to his feet. "I thought I was gone."

"I saw him duck into the deckhouse so I made a beeline for the hatch, figuring you might be in trouble," she explained. "You get the guy down there at the bottom the salon steps?"

Glenn nodded and leaned over to retrieve the two guns Kozlov had dropped as he died. "By the way, that's your Glock from the mattress over there by the stove." He knelt once again and pulled the flour sack from the bottom shelf. "This it?"

She picked up the Glock, stepped over Kozlov's body, and knelt beside Glenn. She unfolded the top of the sack and reached inside, dug to the bottom and, amidst a scattering of flour, brought out a plastic-wrapped packet containing a small black object inside. She rose quickly, moved to another drawer and took out a large plastic bag, and sealed the packet inside.

"Aren't you going to unwrap it and call for help?" Glenn's question was a near reproach.

"Later, not here," she said. She spun the top of the plastic bag into a tightly coiled cord, looped it around her belt and tied it. "We're getting off the ship. The Russians or the ship's crew, both sides want us dead."

"Off the ship? Where? You mean to the island?"

"Better chance staying alive there than staying aboard," she said.

Glenn took a few moments before he said, "Before we go, I've got three questions."

She looked at him.

"First, is there any fresh water on the island?"

"I didn't see any," she replied.

"Anything to eat?"

She shook her head.

"Any ships that might be passing by, say, in a day or two?"

"This is pretty well off the sea lanes," she answered.

Glenn sighed deeply before speaking, "Maybe we should take our chances here, and forget about jumping ship?"

"Look," she said. "You, especially, should understand that we've used up all of our luck. Next bullet that comes your way or mine, it won't miss." She shook her head. "We stay on board, whoever wins, we lose."

"Speaking of bullets coming our way, don't you think we're easy targets out in the water," he complained.

"Chance we've got to take," she countered. "We need a better place to hide while we wait for help." She stepped over the dead man once again and into the passageway. "Let's go!"

"Who's going to help, and where are they?" Glenn asked as he followed. "And when can they get here?"

"Once we're on the island, I'll ask them," she said, walking swiftly, bending to stay out of sight beneath the deckhouse portholes as she headed for the wheelhouse.

From the sounds of gunfire on the aft deck, it was apparent that the battle was still going on, but the shots seemed much more sporadic. There were long silences between an occasional single shot or a brief burst from a rapid-fire weapon.

"How many do you think are still there?" he asked.

"Last I saw, about the same," she replied. "With Karzov gone, and that fellow you did down below, I think there's two Russkies left."

"You counting the guy I only wounded, coming around the deckhouse?"

"I guess that makes two and a half," she said. "And then, there's our shipmates. Alain, Bobby, and Thomas were still alive, last I saw."

"Gravendeel?"

"Still moving, but, big a target as he is, I doubt he will be much longer."

"Any chance they'll finish each other off?"

She shrugged. "The ship's bunch is probably running out of ammunition. If the KGB boys have reloads, they'll have the edge."

"Speaking of ammo, what have we got?" he asked, releasing the magazine from Sergei's handgun. "Four left in this one." He checked Kozlov's gun. "Five in this one.

"Eleven," she told him, snapping the magazine back into her Glock.

She entered the wheelhouse and crept to the port side door. She opened it just enough to look outside. "All clear, let's go," she whispered.

"You go first, I'll cover," he replied.

With her gun in her right hand, she eased out of the port side door. With quick glances left and right, she moved across the outside passageway and swung over the handrail, crouching with the toes of her feet on the edge of the deck as she looked for Glenn to exit the wheelhouse.

Glenn started to open the door, and then paused. He stepped back inside to the ship's control console, his eyes sweeping over it. To his delight, the master key was in its slot. He turned it on, and then touched the ignition button. He, listened to the electronic hum of the starter, and smiled as the diesel stuttered and then rumbled into a steady drone. He shifted the drive from neutral into reverse and a very slight tremor ran through the frame of the ship as power surged to the propeller and it began to turn.

Gun in hand, Glenn slammed through the wheelhouse door and across the walkway to Jenny. With a summoning bob of his head, he slapped his left hand to the top of the rail and vaulted over to plunge into the sea.

With a swear word silently uttered, Jenny rammed the Glock into a pocket of her shorts, then released her handhold on a rail stanchion and dropped over the side to splash in the water beside him.

"Swim for it, goddamn it!" she sputtered as she rose to the surface, and began swimming toward the open ocean. "What the hell did you just do?"

"I thought you'd already gone," he answered, his arms stroking as he followed her, one of his guns still in his hand. "Why are we heading out to sea?"

"To get out of range," she replied angrily. "We'll circle back to the island when it's safe." She continued to churn her way through the sea swells, glancing back to the ship. "What the hell have you done?" she asked again.

Glenn looked over his shoulder as he continued to swim beside her, a smile on his face. The *Lady Ruth* was in motion, the propeller set in reverse and the magnificent sailing ship was slowly backing toward the island.

"Think I was going to let them run off with my ship? And all that gold?" He stopped swimming and turned about, treading water. "I'm beaching her."

"Running her aground?" Jenny was aghast. "Why, you damned fool?"

"When your people show up, they won't have to chase her all over the Caribbean," he answered. He turned to her. "Think we're out of range?"

Jenny turned, paddling in place, not looking at Glenn, but her eyes fixed on the ship. "Now you've done it."

Glenn followed her gaze as the schooner slowly traveled backwards, not in a straight line into the cove, but angling now, the now taut anchor line and the tide swinging it toward the nearest shore. Suddenly, there was a grating, grinding sound that carried across the surface of the sea and an abrupt secession of the diesel sounds as the *Lady* Ruth tilted sharply and stopped, the two masts now swaying and, after a minute or more, steadied at an eighty degree slant.

"I hope I didn't tear the bottom out," Glenn said in anguished awe.

"That's the least of our worries," Jenny said bitterly. "There was a good chance they'd sail away and leave us alone. By beaching the ship, you've stranded the whole murderous bunch ashore with us." She shook her head and started swimming with powerful, angry strokes.

Glenn paddled for a moment, and then kicked his feet and swept his arms into a crawl and followed the young woman toward the only dry land in sight.

32

Glenn waded ashore and sat on the beach to rest, his right hand carefully raised to keep the handgun away from the sand. Jenny was standing a few feet away, intent on unwrapping her black transmitter

"Did it get wet?" he asked.

"Supposed to be submersible, but I was taking no chances," she answered brusquely. She switched it on and tapped in a number. She walked away from Glenn and the surf sounds of the lapping ocean waves.

Although, occasionally, he could hear her voice, he could not determine exactly what she was saying or get an inkling of her reactions. After a few minutes, he saw her conclude the conversation and end the transmission.

"What did they say?" he asked as she returned to join him.

"Gave them our location," she replied, a frown on her face. "Coming as soon as they can."

"How long is that?"

"Four, maybe five hours," she told him.

"They're that far away?"

She gave no response.

"I haven't been hearing any shooting," he said. "Not that I'm rooting for either one bunch or the other, but I sure don't like those Russians."

"Think our shipmates will be any better?"

He shrugged. "At least they're not from the KGB."

"Don't forget about Bobby," she said. "He's ever bit as bad or worse." She shook her head. "Our best hope is that they all kill each other off. Whoever survives, they won't leave us here alive."

Glenn didn't comment for a while, and then asked, "What's our next move?"

"Assuming one bunch or the other wins out, we've got to find some place where they can't find us," she said. "And hope we can last 'til help arrives." She started walking, heading away from the beach, and into the nearby tropical thicket. "Stay off the sand. Footprints will lead 'em right to us."

■ ■ ■

"Fortune smiles," Gravendeel said, his gaze shifting from the stacked gold to the remaining Russian who stood with hands raised before Tournaire's machine pistol. "However it works out, we owe a debt to our young apparition who returned from the deep in the nick of time." He nodded to the Russian who, like he and Tournaire, was trying to stand straight on the slanting deck. "These animals were moments away from killing us all."

Tournaire flicked an angry glance at the fat man. "That might give him a merciful death when we find him, but that is all he gets." He paused. "And for Jenny who must have saved him and betrayed us."

"As we thought," Gravendeel said with a nod to Ruckman and Thomas as the deckhands emerged from the aft hatch. "It appears that neither of them is still aboard."

"Couldn't find 'em, Captain," Ruckman said as he approached. "Kozlov is dead. The bitch or the kid likely done him. Another Russkie is stone cold below deck."

"You looked everywhere?" Tournaire questioned.

"They ain't aboard, Captain. Nowhere's," Ruckman assured him.

"How can we be sure?" Tournaire asked. "Hathaway seemed to have been on the ship for all the time, while we thought him at the bottom of the ocean."

"I guess he fucking fooled us," Ruckman said. "Hate his guts, but gotta hand it to him . . . that was a neat trick he pulled, coming at them Russkies and we'uns like a ghost outta hell."

"Leaving us bodies all over," Gravendeel said with a gesture at the several dead men sprawled on the aft deck. He turned to Alfred. "Speaking of bodies, we thought you were dead"

"Play like dead, *mon*," the deckhand said, smiling broadly. "Good idea, hey?"

"We have other concerns," Tournaire said impatiently. "We might be able to get the ship afloat again. As near as I can tell, it's mostly sand beneath us, and we're not severely aground." He turned to Thomas. "Dive under and, see what you can see."

Thomas gave a half-salute and walked to the aft hatch and descended out of sight.

"About this fellow," Gravendeel said to Tournaire, and gestured to the Russian standing forlornly nearby. "Could you understand what he's been trying to say?"

"As near as I can make out," Tournaire replied. "He saw 'em go off the bow while they were running the ship aground."

"Good for us that they beached her," Ruckman broke in. "Them Russkies was so flummoxed, they broke cover, and that was all she wrote for 'em."

Tournaire nodded, and held his free hand up into the steady breeze. "We'll use a couple of our lifeboats and pull from the bow. And we can raise the sails full with the wind behind us and, between all, we might set her free."

"Pulling loose, damage the hull?" Gravendeel asked.

"I doubt it," the captain said. "It is a sturdy ship."

"We give 'er a try now, while we still got sun?" Ruckman asked. He glanced at the sky. "Three or four hours 'fore dark."

"What about him?" Gravendeel said with a nod to the Russian.

"A problem easily solved," Tournaire said, and pulled the trigger of his weapon.

■ ■ ■

"Still shooting," Glenn said, pausing in mid-stride at the distant sound of a gunshot. "First I've heard in a while."

Jenny didn't comment and continued to lead the way through the wide swath of vegetation that ringed the island. They were walking the length of the small atoll, putting as much distance from the ship and its dangers as this bit of land could provide.

"Ought to be dark soon," Glenn ventured, "and make us harder to find."

"Plenty of daylight left if they take the time to look," she countered.

"What else would they be doing?"

"If it's our crew still alive, they'll be trying to get the ship off the beach."

"Think that's possible?"

She nodded. "Underwater, it looks like that's a steep, drop-away sandy beach. It should slide off pretty easy. If it's a rocky bottom, maybe not."

She spied a fallen tree trunk and seated herself on it. "Sit down, we've got to think."

Glenn took a seat beside her, glancing back uneasily. "Shouldn't we keep going?"

"Where? To the end of the island, and then start swimming once they track us there?"

"Then . . . what?"

She cocked her head to indicate the foliage around them. "Hide somewhere, under a bush, behind a tree; wherever."

"I didn't see many trees or bushes that would hide much of me," Glenn observed skeptically. "How will they come?"

"If there's two or more, they'll come up each side, zigzagging in and out of the undergrowth."

"Can we zig when they zag?"

She smiled. "Likely zig right into them." Significantly, she raised her handgun. "If they do find us, we're in for another firefight."

Glenn nodded, and then asked, "Before anything else dreadful happens, can you tell me what the hell this is all about? People are trying to kill us and I'm trying to shoot them. There's Russians, bars of gold, crooked lawyers, and bad shipmates all over the place and . . . what's going on?"

Jenny took her time to answer, "Okay, you remember seeing anything in the news a couple of years ago about a cargo plane disappearing over the Caribbean?"

"Vaguely."

"Here's the story," she went on. "For some time now, Venezuela has been spending billions buying military weaponry from various places in Russia, some above-board suppliers, some purchases from certain rogue factions left over from the Soviet Union."

She waited until Glenn nodded.

"Intelligence sources from our country, as well as several others, have told us that that an airplane, a Russian Tupolev, was carrying a large amount of gold ingots, a payment commodity preferred by many underground arms suppliers."

"Gold like what's piled on our ship," Glenn interjected, then asked, "What kind of arms?"

"The usual lethal kind," she told him. "Assault rifles, cruise missiles, anti-aircraft systems. While it's a fortune, as far as this gold shipment goes, it's pretty small potatoes. It's more than enough for small arms and missile purchases, but not enough for a lot of tanks or high-priced combat aircraft." She paused, her mind shifting elsewhere, eyes warily sweeping their surroundings.

"Go on," Glenn urged.

She nodded. "People thought it extremely suspect that a plane carrying gold would just disappear. Floating wreckage was found, and it was pretty well confirmed that a bomb had been the cause. If there was gold aboard, it would have been scattered in one of the deepest areas of this ocean."

"If?"

"There were immediate speculations that the gold had never been loaded," she told him. "There were rumors that, somehow, a switch had been made and the gold stolen. There were stories that the plane's crew had been involved, only to be double-crossed and blown out the sky." She paused. "Throughout the Caribbean, there was an intense scrutiny, agencies of every country looking for any plane, any vessel, any sign of the supposedly stolen gold."

"So why did they bring it and leave it here?" Glenn asked.

She shrugged. "Our hunch is that this island might have been as far as they could take it. My guess is that searchers were closing in, so they buried the gold here as an eleventh-hour resort to avoid discovery. As time went on, we didn't see any signs that the gold had surfaced anywhere, so we figured it might be hidden somewhere in the Caribbean

"And Kozlov and his crew were the ones that stole it?

"Well, they knew where it was buried."

"And they've waited two years to recover it?"

Again, she nodded. "They were waiting for the surveil-lance to cool down. Venezuela and other countries have been watching commercial ships, even planes and helicop-ters. With that extreme surveillance in these waters, those we call the Russian Mafia apparently thought a vacation char-ter ship like the *Lady Ruth*, roaming willy-nilly around these islands, might have a good chance to bring it out without look-ing suspicious."

"How did you people put all of this together?"

"As I told you, originally, we were just keeping an eye on Gravendeel and Tournaire and their drug trafficking operation. When Kozlov contacted Gravendeel, it captured our interest and, suddenly, we thought he was worth looking at."

"You knew he was after the gold?" Glenn asked.

"Suspected, not knew," she corrected. "And we had no idea *if* they had it, or *where* they had it. My bosses thought I should play along and see what might happen."

"Have you told Venezuela what you suspected?" he asked.

A wry smile came to her lips, accompanied by a chuckle. "Why should we do that outfit any favors?" She rose to her feet. "We need to find a hiding place."

"If things work out, are we going to return the gold" Glenn persisted as he followed her into the brush.

She didn't answer.

33

With Thomas in one lifeboat and Alfred in another, they were simultaneously gunning their outboard engines to zenith power, each small propeller furiously churning the sea. Lines from the boats, tied to cleats on the bow deck, were taut, while the unfurled sails of both the main and foremast were puffing out with the intermittent strong gusts of the late afternoon breeze.

Suddenly, the ship lurched away from the shore and rocked from side to side. The lifeboats immediately throttled back their power, and the lines grew slack and drooped.

"She's free!" Ruckman shouted gleefully. "By God, we done pulled 'er loose!"

"The boats helped," Tournaire amended, 'but that last gust of wind did the job."

"Thank heaven," Gravendeel exclaimed as he swayed back and forth, trying to retain his balance as the vessel righted itself. "Now, are we able to make it to our destination?"

"The answer is yes," Tournaire told him., "Under sail if need be, but we may have power." He turned to Ruckman. "As soon as they come around, tell them to leave the boats afloat, and one of them check the propeller and the shaft again while there is still light."

Ruckman gave a curt nod and hurried away. .

"We're leaving this evening?" Gravendeel asked.

"Perhaps," Tournaire replied, his eyes on the low sun. "We have two hours, maybe a little more."

"You're leaving the boats afloat . . . you intend to go after the young man and young woman?" Gravendeel asked.

Tournaire nodded. "There is a chance that they will not die on the island . . . not unless we help. There is a very slim possibility that another ship might come by to rescue them. Jenny is no fool, and we don't know what she's been up to." He nodded to the stack of gold bars. "In any case, it would not do to leave them alive . . ., especially her . . . to tell of our new fortune."

"You are right, of course," the lawyer agreed. "Rather a shame . . . I had always rather liked Miss Jennifer."

Tournaire shrugged. "She betrayed us, and we don't know why."

"She puzzles me," Gravendeel mused. "She had riches to gain, so why this turnaround with the young man? She was that smitten with him?"

"Maybe she is not what she seemed to be," Tournaire said."

"Meaning what?"

"What do we really know about her?" Tournaire continued. "Could she be working with law enforcement of some sort? Perhaps, something more to do with our drug trafficking rather than, say, some amorous feelings for Hathaway?"

"Maybe Kozlov was right about her all the time," Tournaire said. "We should have listened."

Their speculation was interrupted as Ruckman returned, accompanied by Thomas, the latter soaked and dripping wet as he marched toward Tournaire with a wide grin on his face.

"Ship's okay," he said cheerfully. "No bent blades, shaft straight, no crooked."

"Good news," Tournaire broke into a smile. "As soon as we finish with our runaways, we can weigh anchor."

"Perhaps we should sail right away," Gravendeel said. "If the young woman is involved with the law, she may have already contacted them.'

"Even more reason to find them quickly," Tournaire said in sharp command. "It is a small island. We will find them and be back, ready to sail before nightfall. Only an hour or two, likely less."

"Let's hope so," Gravendeel opined. "Some things have gone well for us, but others, not well at all. No, sir, not well at all."

■ ■ ■

"If they're coming, it ought to be soon," Glenn said, his eyes on the late evening sky. "Be dark soon."

"You really do have weird ideas," Jenny said sarcastically.

"You said yourself that they'd search every inch of the island," he reminded her. "So?"

"This isn't going to work!"

"Then, I guess, we're dead in the water."

"You've got a sick mind!" she said crossly, but then gave voice to a chuckle.

Glenn, resting on his elbows to hold his head just above water, was lying in the shallows of a tidal pool, the rest of his body beneath the surface, lying on the sandy, sea grass bottom. A few feet away, on his left, Jenny was also similarly submerged.

241

Two-thirds along the length of the island, Glenn had made a discovery. He had spotted a section of the beach where an underlying rocky reef caught the incoming swells and gentled the small tidal pool in which they were now immersed. Sheltered from the onslaught of crashing waves, some plant life had grown in and above the surface of the eddying pond. There were also small sea creatures that inhabited the pool beneath them; a crab had scuttled away at Glenn's entry into the water although tiny curious fish continued to hover.

It was his suggestion, surely, but he had acknowledged to Jenny that this brainchild rightfully belonged to someone in Hollywood, the creator of a movie where a desperate fugitive, fleeing from lawmen and their bloodhounds, had taken to the swamp and hid under water.

"What if they've seen that movie," Jenny said in a scornful reaction. "Besides, I think they caught the underwater guy."

Undeterred, Glenn had examined the pool's floral out-growth and found a few wild plants with hollow stems; nature's snorkel tubes.

Reluctantly, she had agreed to his absurd measure, and they had used their hands and forearms to brush away their footprints from the sand as they backed their way from the island foliage, across the narrow beach, and into the tidal pool.

■ ■ ■

Tournaire stepped from the front end of the lifeboat, and strode several yards along the beach while Ruckman, Alfred, and Thomas pulled the inflatable boat further ashore. His head turned slowly, from left to right, and then back again as he scanned the gathering gloom of the island's forested areas.

"Hurry!" he commanded. "The shadows are already long! Night will be to their advantage!"

Dutifully, the three sailors hurried to join him, both now carrying the semi-automatic weapons of their deposed and departed enemies. Tournaire carried the multiple-load shotgun he had retrieved from the deck where a dead Russian had dropped it.

"It ain't like they ain't armed," Ruckman said uneasily, his eyes fastened on the dark wooded section before them. "Why not just set sail and let them die here, no water no food."

"We leave no witnesses," Tournaire said brusquely

"I know's there's four of us a'gin them two," Ruckman complained. "But luck they's been having, I still don't like them odds."

"Just a girl, and a nervous young novice!" Tournaire said impatiently as he strode forward. "We sweep right to left, left to right, the entire island!"

"Miss Jenny and Mista Glenn," Thomas whispered to Ruckman as they followed their leader. "No matter what captain say, they done good, mebbe better'n us."

Ruckman nodded. "Keep your eyes peeled."

"Getting night," Thomas said. "Not so easy, come the dark."

34

It was dusk when they heard Tournaire's voice, and Glenn's first instinct was to duck beneath the water. However, interest in the shouted words overcame his caution, and he kept his head up.

"Jenneeeeee!" came the next not-so-distant call. "No need to be afraid! It's over! We wish you no harm!"

"Doesn't say the same about me," Glenn whispered.

"Shut up!" Jenny whispered in return, her head also above the pool surface.

"They can't hear us," Glenn countered.

"They can't if you'd just keep quiet!"

"Jenneeeeee! Master Glenn! The Russians are dead, all of them!"

"That's good to know," Jenny whispered, breaking her own counsel for silence.

"Come out!" Tournaire shouted, his voice now nearer. "There is gold enough for all to share! We don't wish to hurt you! You both can be rich beyond all your dreams! We will put all this aside! The ship is free and we can sail! You can be our shipmates once again! We will hold no grudges! You have my word on it!"

"Bullshit," Glenn whispered. He gripped tight the automatic he held in his hand. "These guns still work after being in the water?"

"Of course," she whispered. "Be ready to use yours. They're coming this way, through the woods".

Without another word between them, both placed the long tubular plant stems in their mouths, and lowered their heads beneath the surface. Completely submerged, they took careful, miniscule breaths through the stems, trying not to excessively exhale and create bubbles.

A few minutes later, although the surrounding water somewhat muted sounds, Glenn heard the approach of feet scrabbling through the edges of the nearby underbrush and even the scuffing of sand as one or more walked out upon the narrow beach. With the barest amount of air in his labored lungs, he still held his breath, not daring to inhale or exhale as footsteps came as close as a half-dozen feet away.

He prayed that Jenny was doing the same.

Even submerged, he could hear Tournaire's water-distorted question. "Anything?"

The man was near, very near!

"Nothing, sah," replied Thomas's garbled voice. "Where you reckon they is?"

"Heading for the far end of the island," Tournaire exulted. "Nowhere else to run!"

Hardly daring to breathe, even to risk the tiniest inhale through the tubular stem, he was elated to hear the welcome sound of the homicidal searchers moving away, shuffling ahead into the wooded areas. Even then, he did not take a miniscule breath until his body forced him to.

A full five minutes later, he eased his head above the surface and looked right and left, seeking the hunters.

No one in sight!

Jenny's head came up, water dripping from her plastered hair, and she turned to Glenn, a smile on her face as she whispered. "Gotta hand it to you."

Glenn nodded his thanks. "They're moving up toward the tip of the island."

"That was interesting," she mused aloud. "What Alain said about the Russians being all dead, and the ship being able to sail."

"Interesting how?" Glenn asked.

"I was just thinking," she spoke softly. "Now, we're behind them, with Alain and what's left of the crew prowling the island ahead of us, maybe we could double back and take the ship.'"

"How do you know there isn't someone guarding it?" Glenn asked pointedly.

"I don't," she countered, "But I'll betcha Alain's got every trigger-happy cutthroat searching the bushes, ready to blow us away."

"Then, who would that leave?"

They looked at each other, and then spoke in unison: "Gravendeel!"

She laughed softly. "If that evil tub of lard did survive, and is guarding the ship, we'll take him prisoner, weigh anchor, and pull far enough from shore that it will be Alain and the others stuck on the island."

Glenn grinned and said, "Let's do it."

They rose from the pool, each of them still crouching warily, looking for any silhouette of one of their enemies coming back through the gloomy wooded area. They moved into the shelter of the overhanging trees and made sure to travel through the scratching underbrush, both realizing that to take a faster and easier path along the beach would expose them to gunfire should one or more of their pursuers return sooner than expected.

■ ■ ■

The last pale radiance of sunset had dimmed to a dark gray illumination by the time they came to a lifeboat on the beach. As Glenn started out of the concealing woods towards it, Jenny quickly reached for his arm and pulled him back. "Leave the boat alone. If he's there, Gravendeel might be watching," she warned. "Probably looking right there, expecting the others."

"What do you want to do?"

"We got off swimming," she replied. "That's the safest way to go back."

"I thought you said Gravendeel was no threat?"

"A fat man can still shoot a gun," she told him.

"Okay," he agreed, and pointed ahead where the tropical growth came close to the water's edge. "How about up there?"

She nodded. "Good!"

They continued their stealthy progress through the undergrowth and, at their targeted area, turned to creep toward the ocean.

"Wait!" Jenny hissed as she flattened herself amidst a cluster of broadleaf plants a few feet from the water. "There he is!"

Glenn lay down beside her and looked.

Sure enough, the dark, bulky figure of Gravendeel appeared silhouetted on the aft deck, the lawyer apparently keeping an anxious watch on both the beached lifeboat and the nearby forested area. Outlined against the night sky, he stood for a few minutes, and then walked away and disappeared from sight.

"Come on," Jenny whispered, "and stay under water as much as you can." She pulled off her shoes, crept across the sand, and moved almost silently into the sea

Glenn tucked his gun into the side pocket of his shorts, and followed her into the ocean. With a great gulp of air, he angled beneath the surface, his arms moving in a restricted breaststroke to minimize any sign of swimmer turbulence as he moved toward the ship. Just ahead, Jenny was doing the same as she swam toward the under curve of the ship's hull.

As she, and then Glenn, touched the hull, they rose silently to the surface only a few feet away from the utility ladder that hung over the port side from the amidships gangway. Jenny lifted a finger to her lips. With her hands propelling her toward the ladder, she came to it and reached to grasp the lower rung with both hands. Showing great care not to ripple the water, she lifted herself slowly and silently. She reached again for the next rung, and then the next, hoisting herself to make room for Glenn. Bent low, her head just below the edge of the deck, she took the Glock from a hip pocket of her shorts and held it in her right hand with her left grasping the next to top ladder rung.

Glenn reached for the lower rung and eased himself up to hang just below Jenny.

Footsteps on the deck signaled the return of the ponderous Gravendeel as he walked toward the gangway opening, the sound indicating he was no more than a half-yard away from the edge, so very close that it seemed impossible that he would neither sense nor hear something that would reveal their presence. Another step forward and he would see them.

"Tournaire, what the hell's keeping you?" Gravendeel questioned aloud.

Then, he turned and walked away, pacing in his anxiety.

With nimble agility, Jenny leaped up and onto the deck, landing softly on her bare feet, her Glock trained on the lawyer's huge backside. Gravendeel, uncertain of what he had just heard, turned slowly to face her, his eyes widening and his mouth agape.

"You!" he exclaimed.

"And me!" Glenn announced as he clambered onto the deck. "Surprise!"

"Where . . . I don't . . . what ?" Gravendeel stammered. "Where did you come from?"

"We're here, and your friends are not," Jenny said brusquely. She turned to Glenn. "Search him."

"I have no weapon," Gravendeel protested. "I don't like guns."

"Search him, anyhow," Jenny instructed.

Glenn walked behind the corpulent lawyer and ran his hands over his voluminous jacket and baggy trousers, even between his legs and down to his ankles. "He's clean."

"Can you yank up the anchor?"

Glenn nodded.

"Let's move the ship a bit further out to sea," she commanded. She waved him toward the helm. "Fire up the diesel, and let's put some distance between us and our friends on shore."

"Yes, ma'am," Glenn answered with a mock salute. He hurried to the aft deck console, flipped the switch for the anchor winch, and heard the distant metallic-chatter sound of the anchor chain being reeled into the howsehole at the ship's bow.

Jenny waved her Glock, signaling Gravendeel to precede her as they walked to join Glenn on the aft deck. Walking heavily, Gravendeel was flustered and speechless, obviously dismayed. Consternation played on his face as he walked past and looked longingly at the stack of gold, now appearing a dark mass on the deck in the early night gloom. Finally, with smarmy urgency, he began to speak to Jenny, voicing an unctuous plea: "My dear, there is still time to be rich; you, the young man, and me. We could sail away, just the three of us and—"

"Enough, fat man," she cut in. "Game's over, you lost."

"But . . . I never intended violence," Gravendeel protested. "That was all Captain Tournaire and the others. I didn't want to kill anybody! Surely, you cannot hold me in the same—"

"Shut up!" she cut him off once again. "Glenn, how're you coming with the anchor?"

"About there," he told her, his words immediately followed by the faint clunk of the anchor entering the anchor well and the abrupt silence of the hoist reel.

"Don't dawdle," she said calmly with a nod of her head toward the beach. "They're coming back." She peered intently, than added, "There's Alfred! I thought he was dead."

Glenn looked to island. Coming slowly along the beach, Tournaire was leading the way, his head turning from time to time to look back at the forested areas. Ruckman and the others were walking backward, their eyes still searching the gloom for any sign of their intended prey.

Glenn turned back to the console, touched the start button and, a few moments later, the diesel coughed into life, and then pulsed into a steady murmur. Slowly, the great schooner began to move away from the island. From the shore, there was an unintelligible shout from Tournaire, joined immediately by the voices of Ruckman, Alfred, and Thomas. A burst of automatic weapon fire coincided with the sound of the bullets striking the hull of the *Lady Ruth*, the whistle of still others that cut through the air a few feet above the helm.

Glenn, at the wheel, ducked instinctively although the angle of gunfire at this distance did not present him as a target. Jenny and Gravendeel, as well, crouched down, even though there was no danger other than the unlikely occurrence of a stray ricochet.

As they moved further out to sea where the field of fire flattened, they moved out of the range of the guns on the shore.

Glenn throttled back the engine and looked to the island. From this distance, the men had diminished in size to agitated tiny black figures scuttling about on the white sand beach. Finally safe, he walked to the very end of the aft deck and watched the frantic antics of their stranded foes with some great satisfaction. Out of the corner of this eye, he saw Gravendeel being herded to the stern rail at gunpoint by Jenny.

"They've still got the lifeboat," Gravendeel said with faint hope.

"They know better than to try for the ship," Jenny said. "They're easy targets any way they come." She paused. "And with no place near to go, Alain isn't a fool to take it to sea."

"Now, what?" the lawyer asked, perplexed.

"We wait," she told him.

"Wait?" Gravendeel asked. "Wait for what?"

"For the Coast Guard cutter that's on its way," she answered. "I don't think those on shore will make a fight of it when they arrive with what they call, an overwhelming force."

35

The Island Class cutter arrived and rendezvoused with the *Lady Ruth* a couple of hours before midnight. A tender was lowered and a Coast Guard officer, a senior DEA agent, and a contingent of eight armed seamen boarded the schooner. Gravendeel was immediately placed under guard and taken to the salon for interrogation, and then to await transfer to the cutter. Glenn and Jenny remained on deck where they were extensively interviewed.

"We can offer accommodations on our ship," Lieutenant Ralph Donavan said, "or would you prefer to remain aboard your own?" A trim man in his middle forties, with a still handsome face despite the weathering of years at sea, he acted and spoke with a no-nonsense authority.

"Stay aboard," Glenn responded as Jenny nodded her agreement.

Donavan, DEA agent Robert Slade, Jenny, and Glenn were seated in the on-deck dining facility, bright moonlight giving faint illumination to their faces. Throughout the discussion, the drug enforcement agent, a slim balding man in his late thirties, had asked few questions and made even fewer comments, leaving the bulk of conversation to the Coast Guard officer.

"Commander Clifford and I have decided that we hold off until the morning before we move onto the island," Donavan told them. "Although, as you've pointed out, the four men are armed and present a threat, they will soon realize they have no options other than surrender."

"And if they don't?" Glenn asked.

"We will use deadly force to resolve the situation," the officer said bluntly.

"And what happens after that?" Jenny wanted to know.

"We see no need to risk transferring the gold over open water to our ship," Donavan said. "We shall temporarily commandeer your ship and, with our cutter as an escort, take it to a secure United States port. There, the gold will be handed over to the appropriate federal authorities. The State Department will determine the disposition of the assets."

"They'll return it to Venezuela?" Glenn asked.

"Not without making them beg a bit," Donavan said, sharing a grin with the usually taciturn DEA operative.

Just then, a Coast Guard seaman, with his side arm in his right hand, emerged from the deckhouse and was followed by a slow-moving Johan Gravendeel. Behind him, a second guard stepped onto the deck and, with his companion, started their captive toward the starboard gangway.

A vain man, the corpulent lawyer was a mess; his clothing in disarray, his gray hair uncombed with tufts springing from the scalp. As he passed the seated group, he did not glance in their direction, his face wan and indicative of anxious introspection. Two additional guards, waiting below in the cutter's launch, watched the stout Dutchman labor his way down the straight ladder and into the transfer craft. A minute later, the outboard roared, and the boat sped across the ocean span to the Coast Guard ship.

"He'll spend the night in the brig," Donavan told them. "And he'll have companions some time tomorrow."

"A comeuppance, long overdue," Jenny said.

"We're about done here," Donavan said. "Think you can catch a little shuteye?"

Glenn and Jenny exchanged glances, the latter shaking her head.

"Too revved up," she admitted.

"Me, too," Glenn added.

"Better reconsider," the officer suggested. "It's going to be a busy day, tomorrow." He walked away.

"Coming?" Glenn said to Jenny, rising from his chair.

"In a minute," she responded, turning her attention to the slender quiet man, and began a soft-spoken conversation.

Glenn gave a goodbye nod, and walked forward along the starboard side of the ship. He paused at the rail near the chained gangway, looking across to the long sleek lines of the Coast Guard cutter, a formidable white ship at guard on the moon-sparkling sea between the Lady Ruth and the island.

A rescue vessel bringing life to me and Jenny. Conversely, to those on the shore, it would appear a grim dreadnaught bringing capture, prison or even execution.

"Think they'll give up?" Jenny asked, coming to his side.

Glenn shrugged. "Even without today's body count, there will be murder charges." He paused, and then added, "My aunt and her husband."

"In cold blood," she said in agreement. "Possibly not so bad a sentence for Alfred or Thomas, but for Alain, Gravendeel, and Bobby, it'll be the max."

"It's been a hell of a day," Glenn said, turning his back to the night sea. "That Coast Guard guy might be right. Maybe laying down for a little while might be a good idea."

"What about the owner's cabin?" she asked. "You might want to get used to it."

36

Glenn, showered, shaved, and dressed in fresh clothes for the first time in days, had a bounce in his step when he emerged after sunup to the aft deck, Remembering that Kozlov had slept in the owner's suite, Glenn had snoozed, instead, for a couple of hours in one of the unoccupied cabins.

"Just in time," Jenny said, breaking away from the lieutenant and her DEA confederate to join him. She, too, had apparently showered and changed her clothing. "We've been invited over to the Coast Guard ship to have breakfast with the commander."

"And to get a better view of what happens on the island?"

"Absolutely. Don't you think we're entitled?"

The escalating sound of the tender's engine signaled the imminent arrival of the cutter's launch and, as it came alongside with the outboard idling, Jenny descended the ladder while Glenn looked askance to the lieutenant.

"I'll be staying aboard with the guards, securing your ship," Donavan told him. "We have a few of our sailors with sailing ship experience. While we're moving to a secure port, they'll be aboard to help and relieve you and the young lady."

"That would be a great help," Glenn said. "Much appreciated."

With a touch of his right hand fingers to his brow in an awkward salute, he clambered down the ladder to join Jenny and the seaman at the tiller. As Glenn seated himself, facing her, the sailor revved the engine and turned the boat toward the Coast Guard ship.

A few minutes later, they were on the deck of the cutter, shaking hands with the craft's skipper.

"Commander Carl Clifford," he introduced himself. He was a slender young man with an athletic build, appearing to be in his mid-thirties, Despite his impressive uniform and captain's cap, his wide smile made him seem boyish. "Welcome aboard."

"Thank you, sir," Glenn responded. "The sight of you, your ship and your men was one hell of a welcome one."

"I appreciate what you've been through," the officer said. "How's it go? All's well that ends well?"

"Not until my outlaw shipmates are rounded up," Jenny said.

"As soon as the day brightens a bit more," Clifford assured her, but then a frown appeared. "We maintained night-vision surveillance during the night . . . and we saw two men moving their lifeboat."

"Moving it? Where?" Glenn asked.

"Into the woods," Clifford replied. "We presume they were carrying it across the island to the opposite shore."

"Alain is not that big a fool," Jenny declared.

The commander stroked his chin as he nodded. "If they hoped to escape, there's nothing around here to escape to."

"Any chance they could hail a passing ship?" Glenn asked.

"Maybe," Clifford replied. "Caribbean is busy with all sorts of traffic, but, in this area, there's little to bring a vessel this way. Hell of a chance to take without food or water for, Lord knows, how many days to be at sea in an open boat."

"They might think it better than life in a cell," Glenn countered.

"Speaking of food," Jenny interjected. "I'm tired of my cooking."

"Right this way," Clifford said with a sweeping gesture to show the way. "Exquisite cuisine provided for your dining pleasure by the United States Coast Guard."

■ ■ ■

Three hours later, the first boatload of searchers, including Lieutenant Donavan, returned to the cutter with two captives aboard; Alfred and Tournaire. The deckhand was the first to board the cutter, his head bowed, his manner cowed. His downward gaze was directed straight ahead, not making eye contact with anyone as he was escorted to a hatch where he would be led to the brig.

By contrast, a disheveled and somewhat bruised Tournaire was only slightly subdued and, as he walked toward Glenn and Jenny, a flash of defiance straightened his spine and brought a sardonic smile.

"*Bonjour!*" he said sarcastically, pausing in mid-stride. "Here to gloat?"

Behind him, a pair of guards frowned and stepped close, ready to push him on. Jenny raised her hand, a signal to let him continue. The seamen, with a glance at Lieutenant Donavan, stepped back at their leader's permissive nod.

"A dangerous game, Alain," Jenny said evenly. "You had the advantages, we had none."

259

"You had much luck," Tournaire said.

"Sometimes, that's what it takes," Glenn interjected.

Lieutenant Donavan gave another nod, and the sailors steered their prisoner out of sight.

"What about the others?" Glenn asked.

"One more, dead body coming in the next boat," Donavan told them. "Native fellow, name is Thomas I understand."

"Dead?" Jenny questioned, showing some surprise. "He put up a fight?"

"Not with us," the officer said. "Captain Tournaire told us he followed while that man, Ruckman, had this Thomas fellow help him carry the lifeboat over to the far shore. By way of thanks, he just up and shot the poor guy, and then shoved off by himself in the boat."

There was a period of silence before Glenn spoke, "What was Tournaire doing all this time?"

"Ducking for cover, I guess," Donavan told them. "He tells us that the Ruckman guy tried to shoot him, too." He paused. "I'll give your captain this: He came to the shore without his gun and gave himself up without any fuss as soon as we landed."

"I said he had more sense than to use that boat," Jenny said. "And I'm not surprised about Bobby. He's not only stupid, he's mean and stupid."

"We'll swing around the other side of the island and likely find him," Donavan assured her. "We'll catch him."

"No food, no water, no land for miles and miles," Jenny said. "But what if you don't?"

The officer shrugged. "He'll be all the worse if we don't pick him up."

For the remainder of the day, the Coast Guard skipper dispatched two boats to speed around all sides of the island,

and then widening their search to a greater range in the surrounding sea. With the thought that Ruckman might have doubled back to hide on the island, a searching sweep was conducted, but found no sign of him. Late in the afternoon, the boats returned to the cutter.

"No sign of him," Commander Clifford said with a sigh. "For a guy with an outboard and a paddle, he must have covered some distance."

"That's a worry," Glenn said.

Clifford nodded. "A loose end, to be sure. However, we've posted a warning to all ships and craft in the area to watch for him, and to call in to authorities if he is spotted."

"You're not continuing the search?" Jenny asked.

"Command decision that we escort you, your ship and the gold immediately to a safe port," Clifford said. "Ruckman's chances of survival are slim to none, and it isn't considered worth the expenditure to conduct an extensive search."

"I hope that isn't a bad decision," Jenny said.

"Whatever it is, it is the decision," Clifford said, showing a wide smile to offset the finality of his words. "Let's think about weighing anchor on both our ships and get everything and everybody to safe harbor."

37

For the next few days, with the cutter slowed to match the *Lady Ruth's* diesel-powered speed, the two ships traveled side-by-side to a port at Puerto Rico. There, Tournaire, Alfred, and Gravendeel were jailed, awaiting the procedures necessary to return them to the Netherlands Antilles for trial and punishment. Robert Ruckman's fate remained an unknown with no reports of his capture, death, or survival. He was eventually presumed lost at sea.

The bars of gold were secured by the Coast Guard and, later, turned over to the U. S. State Department. With some elaborate foot-dragging, that department contacted the government of Venezuela to inform it of the gold's recovery. Stormy phone calls and heated conferences were held and, finally, the issue was settled with the transfer of the precious metal to that nation. However, a part of the settlement was that a sizable reward was to be paid to the man responsible for the gold recovery, Glenn Hathaway, owner of the charter ship, the *Lady Ruth*.

Jennifer Warren of the Drug Enforcement Agency, an undercover operative with a carefully manufactured criminal past, was privately credited by her peers; a few words of agency praise, and no reward was to be tendered. Along with

Glenn, she participated in extensive interrogative sessions to explain the events prior to and leading onto the horrific events that took place on the *Lady Ruth*. Both she and Glenn agreed to appear as witnesses at the Willemstad trials of Alfred, Alain Tournaire, and Johan Gravendeel.

■ ■ ■

"Ready to weigh anchor?" Jenny asked as she walked him to the port side gangway.

"I suppose," Glenn said. "Odd as it may sound, it will be very strange without you and our regular—"

"Cutthroats?" she broke in with a wry smile.

"Hope these fellows are better natured," Glenn responded with a nod to a sailor preceding them up the gangplank.

"You've hired a good skipper who knows these waters," she assured him. "He'll steer a sure course back to Willemstad."

With a temporary crew of four deckhands under the command of a seasoned, licensed captain, all of whom vouched-for by local and reliable sources, the *Lady Ruth* was ready for a voyage to its home port.

"And what's next for you?" he asked as they came to a halt at the top of the gangplank.

"Nothing right away, I expect," she answered. "A time for me to get some rest here in Puerto Rico, coast a while after what we've been through." She tilted her head, a questioning look in her eyes. "What about you? Still want to be a sailor?

"Still trying to talk me out of it?"

She laughed. "I was pretty horrid, and you were pretty stubborn."

"Pretty stupid says it better."

"Well, there were times," she said with a smile, and then her expression sobered. "How are you dealing with all that happened?"

Glenn didn't answer immediately.

"Sleeping okay?" she prompted.

"Nightmares you mean?" He shook his head. "No, my flashbacks come in the daylight when I'm wide awake. I'm mad as hell when I think of them trying to drown me, furious when I think of Bobby trying to drop me from the top of the mast . . . " He shrugged. "Hey, I lived through it and so did you. It's over and, to voice a cliché, I figure it's going to be smooth sailing here on."

"Just don't fall overboard while I'm not there to keep an eye on you," she merrily warned him. She leaned close and kissed him on the cheek. "Do take care."

"Will you be coming back to Willemstad?" he asked.

"Perhaps, one day. I go wherever they send me." She raised her hand in a small wave of goodbye, turned and started down the gangplank.

Glenn watched as she descended to the wharf and began to weave her way through the bustling activities of the port; dodging the onrush of a pallet-laden forklift, and sidestepping the rolling approach of a loaded cargo cart. At a corner, she turned away from the waterfront and walked along a truck-busy avenue, lined with warehouses on both sides. Never looking back, her quick stride seemed indicative of putting the schooner and all that had happened behind.

Glenn wondered if he, too, was being left behind.

38

Three weeks later, Glenn traversed the length of the ship from bow to stern, down one side and up the other. He nodded his satisfaction to the supervising foreman whose ship-refitting crew had painstakingly restored the ship to a pristine appearance. Glass in the wheelhouse had been replaced, gunshot holes inside and elsewhere had been ingeniously repaired, surfaces had been repainted, the diesel engine checked and okayed, the propeller and shaft examined and deemed in good condition.

"Nice job," Glenn said to the foreman.

"Start chartering again?" the foreman asked.

"Not quite yet," Glenn said, a slight frown on his face. "I don't have a permanent crew and I need a new captain."

"You're not a captain?"

Glenn shook his head. "Maybe someday, but I'm far from ready right now."

"Check for crew here in Willemstad?"

"Not sure about that, either," Glenn admitted. "I just might move the ship to Puerto Rico or the Virgin Islands. I haven't yet decided."

"Hate to see you go," the foreman said. "Well, we're finished now. You happy with our work?"

"Absolutely," Glenn responded. "Total it all up, and send me the bill. You'll get your pay right away."

They shook hands, and Glenn watched as the foreman and three of his workers went down the gangplank and walked the jetty to land. As they entered a truck and drove away, he walked to the on-deck dining area and noted, with satisfaction, the new seats and tables that took the place of the bullet-riddled, plastic fixtures. These replacements were of plastic as well, although made of sturdier stuff. Each chair and bench was outfitted with waterproofed back and seat cushions that would wear well, and hold shapes and colors for some time before needing to be replaced.

Glenn sat down in one of the chairs and looked toward the low sun that was casting a glittering, golden shaft of light on the harbor ripples. He watched as it painted the clouds with a fusion of both rich full colors and pastel hues.

He turned at the sound of approaching footsteps.

"Evening, Mr. Hathaway. Beautiful sight, isn't it?" The voice belonged to a husky, blond-haired young man who wore brown shorts and a matching brown short-sleeved shirt with epaulets and bore a round insignia above the breast pocket that identified him as a security guard. "Staying on the ship tonight?"

Glenn rose and turned to greet him. "Evening, Peter. No, I'm still on shore, at least for a few days more." He waved to indicate the ship. "Repairs all done, so maybe I'll move back in at the end of this week or so."

"We'll take good care of her," the night guard assured him. "See you in the morning."

"Goodnight," Glenn said, and walked to the gangway where he bid a goodnight to the second guard, and descended to the long pier.

The ship's motorbike had been retrieved and, on occasion, Glenn used it for movement around the city, but, usually, he left it parked at the guard station. However, it was a beautiful evening for a walk, and the small hotel he had found was only a few blocks away. It was an older building with a clientele of mature men and women, a little reminiscent of the rooming house in Kansas City.

Heading to it, he passed through the outer belt of ocean front hotels, restaurants, touristy gathering places, and then into localities of quieter back street buildings. He walked past a street of closed and closing commercial establishments that housed supplies, equipment and services for the sea-going trade - snorkel and scuba stores, swimsuit and tropical beach clothing establishments.

With three more blocks to reach the door of the modest hotel, Glenn entered a darker residential section of the island city. Many years ago, it had been a neighborhood of stately homes built by affluent residents who desired short and easy access to the beach. Most houses remained in good condition, repaired and maintained by occupant families that had lived in the vicinity for years. A few, however, were showing signs of neglect; the neighborhood somewhat diminished by the commercial encroachment.

It amused Glenn to reflect that he was still a bit of a cheapskate, choosing this out-of-the-way, inexpensive hotel. However, it still made sense not to spend lavishly for a place to sleep. What he had said to the guard was true; he would likely be back on the ship for his full time residence and, this time, perhaps even in the owner's luxurious quarters.

At a cross-street junction, a block from his destination, Glenn saw a dark figure emerge from the shadows

Immediately, Glenn knew who it was.

Even in silhouette, he recognized the brawny outline of Bobby Ruckman, slowly approaching. In the darkness of nightfall, with no one else about to help, Glenn knew the oncoming danger was apt to be lethal. He could turn and take off, his best option, but there was no guarantee he could outrun a bullet if Ruckman was armed with a gun.

And, despite the danger, the thought of running rankled.

Bravely, foolishly, he stood his ground as Ruckman came near and stopped, a dozen feet away.

"I'm carrying, Bobby."

"No, you're not," Ruckman countered, his high-pitched taunt chilling. "Sissy sailor boy thinks we're all dead, no need to carry no more."

In the pale nocturnal light, Glenn saw the long-bladed combat knife in Ruckman's right hand.

Despite the gloom, Ruckman had noted where Glenn's gaze had gone, and he raised the knife to shimmer in the faint light of the stars. "Yes, you see, I *am* carrying, Master Glenn," he said. "Better'n a gunshot, cut you up, you feeling every slice going 'long your skin. Gonna be a hurt like you ain't never felt hurt a'fore. You ain't gonna be no pretty guy laying in your casket." He moved two steps forward, and stopped once more. "Run for it, pretty boy. Maybe you can get away."

Glenn turned his left side to the assailant, his arms shoulder-high to ward off the impending assault. He expected Ruckman's first thrust would be to his body, but he also suspected that would be a feint before going for a slash at his face. From Ruckman's words promising facial disfigurement; that would be his target.

Ruckman took another step and hunched down into a crouch, his eyes darting up and down Glenn's body, a sly maneuver to make Glenn drop his arms down to guard his torso.

The thrust came and Glenn was ready for it, leaping back as the huge sharp blade slashed a few inches from his face. He backed away, with Ruckman moving toward him with the knife in his hand slashing back and forth.

Suddenly, there was a sound of shared laughter approaching; voices of women a half-block behind Glenn. He dared not turn; he kept his eyes focused on the deadly antagonist before him.

Ruckman sprang forward, his knife hand thrusting the blade toward Glenn's lower body, then arcing up toward his chin.

Glenn leapt away, the point of the knife nicking his left bicep and ripping through the sleeve of his polo shirt.

Behind him, the chattering of two women was louder, the pair coming closer.

"Get out of here!" Glenn shouted, not taking his eyes from Ruckman who was moving from side to side, ready to lunge again. "Get the hell out of here!" Glenn yelled again. "You women! Man with a knife!"

The laughter ceased immediately, but he didn't hear the sounds of the womens' panic or the pounding of their feet running away.

Footsteps running toward us!

To his surprise, Ruckman rose from his crouch and moved back.

"Hi, Bobby!" came a familiar female voice. "Brought a knife to a gunfight?"

Glenn looked to his right to see Jenny coming to his side and, to his left, another familiar face; Vicky, his curvaceous abductor. Both were aiming handguns at Ruckman.

"Drop it, Bobby, be nice now," Jenny spoke again. Ruckman made no move to drop his weapon; instead, he glanced at each of the two women, murderous intent still showing in his face and in the tense pose of his body.

"I'll shoot you if I must, but that's up to you," Jenny said.

"Me, too," Vicky said, a phone at her ear. "So, why don't we all just take it easy. I'm calling for backup that'll be here right away."

Ruckman dropped the knife, his mouth twisted in an ugly scowl. With glances at both Vicky and Jenny, he fixed a glare at Glenn. "Pretty boy had to have a couple of fucking women to save his ass."

A few minutes later, a Willemstad police car, running silent and without flashing lights, rounded a corner and sped toward them. As it pulled to curb, Ruckman clasped both hands behind his neck as two policemen emerged from the car and moved swiftly and efficiently to physically manhandle and cuff the thug. Then, with the prisoner in the caged back seat, the policemen signaled their goodbyes, entered their car and drove away.

"Where did you two come from?" Glenn asked.

"Been keeping an eye on you," Vicky said, acknowledging a confirming nod from Jenny. "A few days ago, a small sloop turned up on the other side of this island, no sign of the people who owned it. Husband and wife supposed to be aboard, but no one there,"

"They were last reported sailing down near our 'treasure island'," Jenny told him.

"And they picked up Ruckman?" Glenn was incredulous.

Vicky nodded. "We considered it a possibility. When Jenny heard about the missing couple and their sailing course, she called and told us to put a tail on you, just in case our hunch proved out."

Glenn touched the tip of his finger to the cut on his arm to staunch the blood seepage. "Been nice if you could've tailed me a bit closer," he said, and then added, "Still, thanks for getting here soon as you did."

"The fact that the sloop turned up here in Willemstad was the key to our thinking," Jenny said. "I flew in this morning to take a look."

"And?" Glenn asked.

"We found blood in places," Jenny said. "Those Good Samaritans rescued a murdering sonofabitch."

"No bodies found?" Glenn questioned.

"Davy's locker, I'd guess," Jenny told him and changed the subject. "We need to get you someplace to patch up your arm?"

Glenn shook his head. "Just a scratch. I'm sure the hotel can round up a Band-Aid." He looked to Vicky, and then turned back to Jenny. "What now?"

"We'll walk you home," Jenny said, tucking her arm under his right arm.

"Get you there safe and sound," Vicky said, careful to place her hand under the injured one.

"It's only a block, what else could happen?" he protested.

"With you, we never know," Jenny said as, all together, the threesome stepped out along their way.

Epilogue

"I won't have her in here, I just won't," Jenny hissed.

"You're upset," Glenn whispered, trying to soothe her. "I'm sorry, I didn't think you'd care. After all, she's—"

"Taking over," Jenny cut in. "The minute I turn my back, you go and—"

"Hush," Glenn interrupted. "She'll hear you."

"I don't care, I want her out!"

"Okay, okay," Glenn said with a sigh. "I'll break it up."

He walked from the wheelhouse, past the navigation and communications facility, and into the galley. "Mom Daly, the folks on deck are asking for you. You'd best come along now."

The two women at the ship's stove turned at the intrusion: Mom Daly in innocent surprise, the heavy-set native chef, Gretchen, scowling and rolling her eyes.

"Why, I'll be there in just a bit, Glenn," Mom Daly said. "You go ahead. I'm showing Miss Gretchen here how to pan fry this here bass fish—"

"It's a *sea* bass, not a *lake* one, ma'am," Gretchen broke in, appealing to Glenn. "And I don't have any of them bread crumbs like she wants."

"She's talking about broiling it, and then going to stuff it, Glenn," Mom Daly complained.

"We hire Gretchen to do the cooking," Glenn said. "You don't want to waste your vacation down here in the galley.

We're getting ready to make sail, and you'll miss seeing all that."

"Well," his former landlady said with uncertainty, reluctantly moving away from the stove. "I just wanted to help out where I can."

"This is your vacation," Glenn reminded her, again. "You should be on deck, not in here."

"Everybody else already out there?" Mom Daly questioned.

"Waiting for you," he said, nodding to the door. "You go on, I'll be right behind you."

Mom Daly cast a longing look back to the galley and, with a sigh of resignation, walked down the companionway on her way to the aft dining area.

Glenn gave a sigh of relief as Jenny hurried into the galley, giving him a sharp, irritated glance as she moved to console Gretchen.

"I'll swear, Miz Jenny, that woman was driving me crazy," the Gretchen complained. "Lordy, if she's gonna be here some of the time, I surely ain't gonna!"

"That's all right, Gretchen," Jenny said, her hand on the woman's arm. "Just this one time, and that's the last you'll ever see of her." She gave Glenn a look that challenged dissent.

Glenn turned away, adjusted his yacht cap to a jaunty angle, and hurried after Mom Daly. Stepping out of the deckhouse, and striding toward the aft deck, he saw that his former landlady was just arriving at the al fresco dining facility.

"Sit here, Mom Daly!" Ben Mosser called to her. "Put Glenn right next to you. It'll be just like back at home."

Mom Daly wedged herself at the head of the table, assuming the same position of authority she'd occupied in the rooming house. Glenn sat down across from Ben and looked around at the assembled group. Indeed, the roomers from the boardinghouse were sitting at one of the tables, just in the same arrangement as always.

"All back together," Betty Lundgren said in a gushing euphoria. "We're sitting on a real yacht in the Ca-*rib*-be-an."

"That's pronounced, C*ara-bee*-an, like the natives say it," Rose Armstrong put in. "Isn't that right, Pete?"

"Heard it both ways," Pete Wilson, her same-age companion, said. He turned his head to look toward the deckhouse. "Supper 'bout ready?"

"Don't expect too much," Mom Daly warned. "Hope that funny-talking woman in there don't go and ruin it all."

"This is really wonderful of you, Glenn," Jean Hurth said pleasantly. Her agreeable attitude was a surprising change from this usually blunt-spoken woman. "Taking us all on a cruise at no charge."

"We had to pay for the airplane tickets," Betty put in.

"Shut up, dear," Jean said, flicking a glance at Betty, and reverting to type. She returned her steady, interrogative gaze to Glenn. "That floozy blonde there in the kitchen, what's she do on the boat?"

"Just about everything," Glenn informed her. "She pretty well runs the entire cruise. She gave up a full time job to sign on again with me." He nodded to the open sea beyond the harbor. "You all are going to have the time of your lives."

"You and that dame . . . something going on between you?" Jean persisted.

"Damn right," Glenn agreed. "Something between us."

"Hey, Glenn," Ben spoke from across the table. "Whatcha been up to?"

The End